SAANVRI

the story of a concubine

VINOD PANDE

NIYOGI
BOOKS

Published by

NIYOGI BOOKS
D-78, Okhla Industrial Area, Phase-I
New Delhi-110 020, INDIA
Tel: 91-11-26816301, 49327000
Fax: 91-11-26810483, 26813830
email: niyogibooks@gmail.com
website: www.niyogibooksindia.com

Editor: Jayalakshmi Sengupta
Layout Design: Ganga Rai
Cover Design: Misha Oberoi

ISBN: 978-93-85285-45-5

Publication: 2016
First Reprint 2017

This is a work of fiction. The names, characters and incidents portrayed in it are the work of the author's imagination. Any resemblance to actual persons, living or dead, events or localities, is entirely coincidental.

Printed at: Niyogi Offset Pvt. Ltd., New Delhi, India

Dedication

Journey of life…a book in itself!
To my elder daughter, Rachna, who quietly slipped her fingers into mine again; my younger daughter; Pimmi, who never left my hand; my partner; Preeti, who kept the doors open, and my former colleague Bobby, who prevailed upon me for a second innings with the pen.

Prologue

The rain was unrelenting. In the headlights of the SUV, it looked like a shimmering dancing sheet of sheer muslin, sometimes slanting sideways, sometimes straight down, sometimes oscillating from side to side. The large windshield wipers furiously fought the fearsome pounding from the skies, which had opened up unapologetically. Suddenly, the vehicle leapt through the space like a roaring beast and came crashing down on a long stretch of watery surface, which looked like a lake under attack from the piercing onslaught of raining lances.

"*Madarchod,*" screamed the moustachioed middle-aged man, seated next to the driver on the front seat, "You want to kill us, or what?" In a grip of anger, he put his gun to the driver's temple, while barking, "*Saale*, I'll kill you before that."

"What can I do, Chauhan-sahab? Can you see any potholes in this lake of a road?" muttered the hapless driver.

"But *bhaiya*, this way you'll only take our dead bodies back home; there's no way that we can make it alive," said the saree-clad woman seated next to another man at the rear seat.

"Then, don't ask me again and again to hurry…Okay *ji*?" The driver expressed his frustration curtly.

"Okay, okay…you drive the way you want," said the man from the back seat, in a conciliatory tone. The vehicle jumped once again, even as he spoke.

Just about then, in a small bedroom of an ordinary middle-class house, an attractive woman in her mid-thirties, dressed in a simple housecoat, tended to a bedridden girl of about seven years of age. The girl appeared quite ill. The woman took out the thermometer from the young girl's mouth and read it in the light of the overhead bulb. With deepening anxiety on her face she deposited it back in its case and turned to her husband, a man in his late thirties.

"It's a hundred and two…I won't go!"

"But they must be on the way." The man looked quite apologetic.

"And what about my daughter? Isn't she ailing, too?" She reacted curtly.

The man lowered his head, saying nothing. The woman spoke again, a little gently this time: "Let's pray that they don't come, that they manage to find somebody else."

Precariously negotiating the heavily potholed surface of the flooded road, the SUV reached the end of the sparsely populated lane. Still in motion, its headlights passed along the outer walls of the houses, suddenly illuminating the face of a young boy of fifteen or sixteen, seated close to a window on the upper floor of one of them. Emerging from a small ditch-like pothole, the vehicle stopped with a thud, very close to the outside yard of the house. The driver didn't kill the headlights. Their sharp beams shone through the continuous string of rain, falling obliquely on the house, in a bit of an eerie spectre.

The teenaged boy, who had been immersed in his studies in the small room upstairs, switched off the table lamp and craning his neck over the table peered down the adjacent window to watch the vehicle come to a halt. He immediately bolted down the steps and hurriedly entered the room where his parents were tending to his younger sister. His other teenaged sister slept close by.

"Mummy, a motor has just come; there are two or three men and a woman also." The boy spoke hastily.

His parents exchanged a meaningful look before the man told

the boy, "You go and open the door. I'm coming in a minute."

Just as the boy exited, he appealed to his wife, "It'd be nicer if you also came. At least meet them, explain to them the situation. It'd be more convincing."

The woman gave a long, hard look to her husband, who lowered his eyes as if in surrender before raising them again in an expression of plea. The woman seemed to relent.

"Okay, you go. I'll just come." She scowled disapprovingly.

He nodded and moved off.

While the driver and the passenger at the front seat remained seated in the vehicle, the mid-fortyish man and the woman, seated at the back, made a dash for the front door of the house, struggling under their umbrella in the face of the wind and rain. They had hardly banged at the metal door-beater when it was opened by the young boy. Ushered in by him, they entered the small *baithak* or sitting area and stood uncertainly in the middle. Their eyes went to a cot by the wall on which someone lay asleep, fully covered with a sheet. The person, an old woman, stirred and pulled down the sheet from over her head. Her hand went to pick up her glasses, kept in an alcove in the wall. Just as she put them on, the man of the house entered. The male visitor looked at him with a mysterious, questioning expression; the householder nodded equally furtively. None of it went unnoticed by the old woman.

Just then, the woman of the house entered hurriedly and addressed the visitors apologetically: "Sorry *ji*, it's absolutely impossible for me to come. My daughter is very ill. She is running a temperature of 102 degrees."

The faces of the visitors turned gloomy. They exchanged a dismayed look before the visiting woman suddenly broke down and made a go at the feet of the lady of the house, pleading: "Don't do this to us, madam, our amma will die. She's losing her breathing as it is. Please save her." She clung to her feet, howling.

Her companion also bent down and pleaded with folded hands: "You just check her once, madam. We'll bring you back straight away, Saanvri-ji...in the same vehicle, we promise." Noticing Saanvri's non-committal expression, he bent down further on his knees and continued, "We had gone to the dispensary also...but there was nobody there. Doctor-ji has gone on leave, Saanvri-ji."

Saanvri, the lady of the house, looked searchingly into the eyes of both the visitors. The woman began howling even more. Saanvri exchanged a look with her husband and said to the visitors, "All right, but please, you must definitely bring me back straight away."

"Yes, yes *ji*...absolutely," the man said quickly and reassuringly; his voice cracking up. "Have faith in us, madam."

"Please sit," Saanvri said, pointing to the sofa chairs, "I will come with you in a minute."

After she exited, the male visitor exchanged a knowing look with Saanvri's husband. Then slowly he reached out into the inner pocket of his khadi waistcoat and withdrew a small bundle, which he surreptitiously extended towards him. They again exchanged a meaningful look as a wad of five-hundred-rupee notes swapped hands; this again did not go unnoticed by the old lady, who had donned her glasses by now.

Meanwhile, in the other room, Saanvri lovingly caressed her younger daughter's forehead. "Sonu-beta, I have to go out for a little while...a patient is very ill. I'll be back in no time. You shouldn't worry while I am away," she said reassuringly, before pointing at her husband and the old lady who had entered the room. "Papa and Dadi are also here...They'll be with you," she continued.

Sonu slowly opened her eyes and nodded slightly. Saanvri bent down to kiss her forehead.

A while later, seated at the back seat of the SUV, between the man and the woman, a morose looking Saanvri was lost in her thoughts, oblivious to the bone shattering bumps of the pathetic road. She remained anxious about her daughter's condition as the vehicle sped through the narrow lanes between the closed shops of a dark and sleepy village, braving the unending onslaught of rain and spray of muddy water and negotiating crater-like potholes.

The rain had turned into a light drizzle when nearly an hour later the SUV pulled in front of an haveli at the outskirts of a small town. Though old from its outward appearances, the building smacked of new money. Latest models of half a dozen luxury cars stood in the front courtyard, and priceless murals adorned the walls of the corridor adjoining the main entrance.

Saanvri was led into a well-decorated modern bedroom at the back of the house by the man and the woman with whom she had come. A couple of anxious looking men were tending to the patient—an old woman in her mid-fifties who was lying in the large bed under an expensive sheet. The atmosphere seemed tense and melancholic.

Saanvri took a cursory look at her and checked her pulse. Then she bent down to open her bag and took out a stethoscope and a blood-pressure monitor. As she readied it and proceeded to tie the cuff around the arm of the patient, she found that the old woman had sat up on the bed with a grin playing on her lips. Shocked and startled, Saanvri got up and turned around to face the couple who had brought her. She froze in her place. There was horror written in her eyes as she came face to face with a person, she had least expected to see.

The person was a regal looking woman in her mid-fifties, dressed in an expensive nightgown. Before Saanvri could utter anything, she was subjected to a stinging slap across her face by the older woman.

"*Saali, bhenchod*,"she screamed.

Saanvri crashed on the floor with the force of that savage slap.

ONE

It was a huge congregation. The Maharana Pratap ground, with a capacity of nearly a lakh, was almost full to the brim with people. Many had come from villages and hamlets afar, as was evident from their bullock carts, tractors, motorbikes, jeeps and in some cases even cars, all parked at the periphery of the ground. Except for some in the front, who were seated on their haunches on the durries and large jute mats, most squatted on the ground on the sheets they had carried with them.

Relishing the comforting warmth of a January morning sun, the crowd exulted at each word of the highly charged rhetoric of the speaker at the rostrum—a miniscule figure for the ones who were right at the back.

"*Ma-ki* (mother's)...*bahen-ki* (sister's)...*betti-ki* (daugher's)..." The man took a practiced pause after punctuating each word poignantly and then to arouse the desired emotional charge, he thundered..."*Ijjat* (honour) is above all else. People are forever ready to sacrifice their lives for their *ijjat*,," sending the crowd to a roaring applause.

He was a short, slim man in his early sixties, with an ordinary disposition. He was attired in a khadi kurta and dhoti and a Nehru waistcoat, but due to the large, colourful pagri donning his head, he looked imposing and powerful as he continued his grandiloquence:

"In our country, especially in our Rajasthan, the status of a woman is that of a devi—a goddess. There is no such example anywhere else in the world."

The crowd again applauded with a huge round of clapping as he continued, "I ask you—what are some of the most important things we need in this life?"

The bustling crowd went quiet instantly, waiting for him to solve the tease, which soon followed:

"*Rupiya-paisa* (money), *buddhi* (intellect) and *taqat yani shakti* (strength meaning power). Right?"

He had hooked them again and they gawked at him; but he teased again:

"Now who is the god for *dhan* (wealth)?" People looked nonplussed. After a playful pause he obliged, "Lakshmi Mata!"

A collective sigh of happiness rose through the huge congregation. He knew that now the audience was all his. He went on, "Who is the god for *gyan* (knowledge)?" He answered it himself, "Saraswati Mata!"

"And the god for *shakti* (strength, power)?" Pumping his clenched fist through the air, he exclaimed aloud, "Durga Mata!" Responding to the beaming faces of the crowd, he thundered, "*Arre*, for us the earth is also our mother and Ganga (river Ganges) is so, too."

Just as the crowd went rapturous, he suddenly raised his hand high, gesturing from his open palm for all of them to be quiet and listen. All went silent.

"What do we address our *des* (country) as?"

He took a well-calculated pregnant pause while looking at the vast crowd with searching eyes. All around, the people stared at him blankly. Even the distinguished guests seated on chairs behind him were mesmerised, though grudgingly, for he was truly in his element. He smiled benevolently before speaking in a commanding voice: "Bharat?"

And now the crowd responded equally spiritedly, in a collective roar: "*Mata*!"

Assured that the crowd was now completely in his grip, like the composer of a grand orchestra he beckoned with his outstretched arms: "So now tell me, whether it is our duty or not to give respect to and provide protection to each and every woman of our country?"

The crowd went berserk, screaming: "It is; absolutely it is."

Now the man switched gear. In an impulsive action, he grabbed the stem of the microphone in front of him, as though it was the neck of an adversary he was wringing, and shaking it back and forth he thundered with an avenging gleam in his eyes: "Anyone who doesn't give respect to a woman, considers her a slipper on his foot, is not a human being. He is a beast, a beast."

Almost like a well-rehearsed movement, he stopped rocking the microphone—though his hand still remained on its stem—but his fingers clenched more tightly around the stem as he said in a venomous whisper, "Such beasts deserve no forgiveness, they deserve the wrath of justice."

All of a sudden he let go of the microphone, which with a rumbling sound rocked on its heavy base, searching for stability. Slowly, like a hunter with a fiendish expression, moving his face from one side to another, he looked at the stunned faces of the people all around him. Once again, like a virtuoso performer his eyes spewed fire. He clenched his teeth and then screamed: "Look at their dare. After indulging themselves in such filthy and despicable acts, they have the evil audacity to put the blame on somebody else." He took a calculated pause of a second or two and then barked scornfully, "They have the temerity to make a fake DVD and circulate it."

After a pregnant pause of a couple of seconds, he slowly turned his face from one side to another with the look of a wounded animal, and sized up his stunned audience. Then all of a sudden, clenching his fist and pumping it in the air, he screamed at the top of his voice with emphasis on each word.

"Punishment! They...Will...Get...The...Punishment; we'll see to it!" He stopped abruptly.

The crowd started howling and clapping heartily; some started shouting in chorus, "Punishment—Punishment—Punishment!"

Empowered by their reaction, with clenched fists he bellowed, "And the punishment would be such that never again would one think of doing such bad deeds with any woman, ever."

Suddenly a youth from the front rows, leapt into the air and raising his hands high, shouted like a sloganeer: "Yashpal Singh Sarena..."

The crowd roared approvingly: "Zindabad (long live)..."

Another youth jumped in front of the rostrum and shouted: "The country needs a leader like ?"

"Yashpal Singh Sarena!" roared back the crowd.

Yet another man shouted with all his strength: "Move forward, Yashpal Singh Sarena..."

"We'll follow you," thundered the crowd.

A while later, a convoy of three vehicles came onto the tarred, narrow road, negotiating the *kutcha* path, about a quarter of a kilometre away from the Maharana Pratap ground. Ensconced between the two jeeps—the first one full of police personnel and the rear one with armed commandos—seated inside the white Ambassador car with the national flag fluttering on the top, Yashpal Singh Sarena looked quite pleased with himself. The response he had received from his listeners—"his people, his children" as he often called them—had been overwhelming. Seated alongside him in the back seat was a man in his late forties dressed in a pale kurta and white pyjamas. A uniformed security man with an AK47 on his lap was seated at the front seat, alongside the driver.

Visible through the back window, a cloud of pale dust billowed behind them as the car picked up speed. Many in the crowd got up and moved about in a state of disarray.

The man seated beside Yashpal leaned over and said slightly conspiratorially, "Yes Bado-hukum, he is still there; trying to have the FIR filed in the thana."

Yashpal turned his face to the man and with the piercing gaze, asked, "Your information is completely reliable?"

"Yes, hukum!"

A sinister look glimmered in his eyes as Yashpal straightened and stared ahead of him over the shoulders of the driver and the security man seated in the front. He turned to his companion and, drilling his eyes into him, ordered, "I want a minute-to-minute report Ramlal; you understand?"

"Absolutely, malik; I'll give you the full report, malik…I have put highly reliable people on the job, hukum." Ramlal responded.

Something engaged his mind at that point and Yashpal peered out of the window thoughtfully, before turning back and taking out his cell phone. He punched the contact list and searched through it. He was about to punch a name when he stopped, mumbling to himself, "No, not from mine."

Ramlal quickly took out his cell phone and said, "Use mine, malik."

Yashpal gave him a chastising look and mumbled again, "*Abbe*; how can I use yours, either?" Then tapping at the shoulder of the security man seated at the front seat, he addressed him, "*Arre*, give me your cell, will you."

The security man responded meekly, "*Ji* hukum." He quickly took out his cell phone from his pocket and wiped it against his shirt before handing it over to Yashpal, saying subserviently, "Hukum…"

Yashpal punched a number and, on hearing the voice at the other end, he spoke secretively.

"This is me. Everything is under control, right?" His forehead wrinkled into deep furrows as he listened intently to the voice on the other side before mumbling grimly, "Yes, go ahead; and listen, this is how it should remain," and he hung up.

Right then, in the local thana in the neighbouring town of Saanvri's small settlement, the sub-inspector on duty was snubbing her husband, who was seated across the table.

"Listen Khoobchand, I told you three days ago also—first, search among friends and acquaintances, then, go for the report. Otherwise, unnecessarily it'll spread all kinds of evil gossiping in the community."

"Hukum, I have searched all over...asked all the people I know. Couldn't get any information," said a teary eyed Khoobchand before pleading, "It'll get too late, hukum...take down the FIR, sahab."

At this point a jeep pulled up outside the door in the courtyard. The Station House Officer (SHO), a mid-fortyish, slim man, jumped out and entered the room. He crossed the large room that had a few more tables with uniformed staff behind them, to get to his own chamber. On noticing Khoobchand, he suddenly stopped halfway and turned to the SI and asked, "What is it, Tyagi? What is going on?"

SI Tyagi immediately got up and explained in a rather offhand manner, "Sir, his wife has run away some five days ago...I am trying to explain to him that first he should search for her privately among friends and relatives, and then only go for the report. Otherwise, it will unnecessarily spread a bad word all around, but he doesn't try to understand."

The SHO looked at Khoobchand with penetrating eyes and then slowly walked over to the SI's desk. He looked conspiratorially at him and said almost in a whisper, "Write down the FIR." He nodded meaningfully and continued, "I've had a talk..."

"*Ji* huzoor," acceded the SI, bowing his head.

Two

The slanting pinkish rays of early morning sunshine fell across the front courtyard of the palatial old haveli. It was a huge space tucked away behind the enormous outer gate. High walls encompassed the paved compound, like that of an old fortress. Inside a covered garage—one among six—a middle-aged chauffer, attired in a white uniform and an orange pagri, touched his curled-up moustache, admiring himself in a small mirror hung up on a side wall.

He then boarded the imposing white Mercedes car and turned the key. A smug smile appeared on his face as the engine responded in an almost noiseless purr. He slid the gear of the car to move out majestically, from the garage, savouring the feeling of power. He gently steered it towards the main entrance of the mansion and positioned it right in front of it.

In a corner, under a lone neem tree that had a circular cemented platform around it, a camel was tied to a *khoonta* (a short iron stake). Its keeper, a frail, grey haired man in his sixties, was feeding lumps of grass to it from a loose bundle lying close by. There were a couple of other men tending to other cars—one was washing a red Honda and another had his head buried under the open bonnet of an SUV. A jeep and a couple of bicycles were parked by the outer wall of the courtyard.

The chauffer of the Mercedes got out of the car unhurriedly and walked around it quietly, inspecting it for any blemish or speck of dust on its gleaming body. Here and there, with caring strokes of his fingers, he brushed off unwarranted particles of dust, though hardly noticeable.

Inside the haveli, many idols of different sizes of various Hindu gods, in both gold and silver, and several paintings in expensive frames, adorned one side of a large puja room. A trinity of long cotton wicks, their length submerged in pure melted ghee, contained in a big silver *deepak* (lamp), burnt at the altar on which the idols were placed. A powerful aroma spread from a cluster of incense sticks burning in brass holders.

Rana Suraj Bhan Singh, a handsome man in his mid-fifties, clad only in a crisp white dhoti, sat cross-legged on a *patra*—an engraved wooden plank—in front of the altar, which had a group of idols of various Hindu gods placed upon it. He chanted hymns as he went about his activity of performing prayers with an air of complete solemnity. In the process, in an act of symbolically purifying it, he dipped the fingers of his right hand into the water in a small copper pitcher, a couple of times, and ran it along the length of the white *janeu* across his bare chest.

His eyes betrayed a sense of cold aloofness while he mechanically chanted the shlokas in obeisance to the different gods of the Hindu pantheon. His invocations had a distinct edge of vainness in them as he mumbled the hymns, partly to himself and partly to the deities:

"Ya devi sarvabhuteshu vishnu-mayeti sadbita

Namas tasyai, namas tasyai, namas tasyai namo namah..."

Suddenly, his cell phone started ringing. He picked it up and answered it, seamlessly, in between his recitation: "Yes...yes, I...yes, yes...I am coming...yes, leaving in a short while," he said snappily ending the call and continuing with his recitation:

"Ya devi sarvabhuteshu Shakti-rupena samsthita

Namas tasyai, namas tasyai, namas tasyai namo namah..."

Just then a side door opened, bathing the room in early morning sunlight, which fell on him and the puja paraphernalia across the corridor. His wife, nearly his age, and attired in a designer saree, entered through the ornate door and addressed him, "The driver is here…the parcel has been put in the car." She had an air of authority about her and spoke with the nuanced poise of a royalty.

Rana nodded slightly without turning around to look at her and went back to the chores of his puja. His wife acknowledged his gesture with a silent nod and left.

Some fifteen minutes later, the uniformed *dwarpal*, tending to the main door of the mansion, opened it with great alacrity and bowed in deference to Rana, who emerged breezily from the inner quarters. Now dressed in a designer kurta and churidar, he looked very dapper as he walked straight to the Mercedes; its rear door already held open by his chauffer to usher him in.

All other staff—drivers, minders and cleaners—sprung up in attention, after a quick movement of their hands in *adab*, as a mark of obeisance to him. With an indifferent wave of his hand at them, he proceeded to sit in the car, but then he suddenly remembered the camel and quickly walked to it.

Even in his hurried steps, he had a majestic elegance about him. With a benign smile he took the small bundle of grass, held in readiness by the camel-minder, and fed it to the animal. He patted its neck softly and lovingly and then walked back to the car and boarded it.

The chauffer softly shut the door and walked around the car to reach his door. His aide-cum-guard, also dressed in a *dwarpal* outfit, quickly slipped in beside the driver on the front seat. Within seconds the car sped out of the huge outer *phatak*, the doors of which were already held open by a couple of other *dwarpals*.

The smile on Rana's lips broadened to a grin of self-satisfaction as he slid down to sink deeper into the plush leather seat of the car. He took out his Blackberry and punched the keys to convey to his resident personal assistant in Jaipur that he was on his way; and the traffic remaining agreeable he should be in time for the meeting. Almost instantly he received a reply that it would be confirmed to the CM's Secretariat. Rana now reached out for the pile of the day's newspapers that had been left stacked beside him in the rear seat. He opened an English newspaper and became engrossed in it.

The Secretariat was housed in an imposing building. The entire campus—the architecture, the driveways, the lawns, the manicured bushes, the eclectically coloured flower beds—had the aura of the days of the Raj; the days of *adab* and protocol, maintaining the impregnability of the space between the 'ruler' and the 'ruled'.

Rana involuntarily straightened in his seat as his car entered the huge gate after the mandatory security check. A tiny, albeit smug, smile appeared on his lips. He felt a surge of self-satisfaction at the thought of how his life was about to change from that day. He, too, was going to be the occupant of one of the office suites of the ruling elite in that building; his car would also be entering the compound without being stopped for security checks and always amidst a convoy of two other vehicles from now, never singly.

On reaching the destination, his aide swiftly got out of the car in the large portico and held the rear door open for Rana. He unhurriedly stepped out and then stretched himself languidly to ease his muscles. It had been a long, four-hour, non-stop journey.

Catching his sight from the entrance, Rakesh Pareek, his resident PA, emerged from the guest registration cubicle with the visitors slip, and ran towards him, down the steps. Rana was adjusting his dark glasses when Rakesh reached him huffing and greeted him:

"Pranam sir. You made it quite fast, sir? Didn't you have a break at Ajmer, hukum?"

Rana nodded smilingly and acknowledged Rakesh's ingratiating bow with folded hands. Then climbing the steps with a slight spring in his feet, he said, "No; it was an auspicious journey, so I didn't want to take a break. Besides, I had chosen to observe a fast too, today."

"Fine hukum, absolutely fine hukum; after all it's a very important day for all of us, hukum," he said, beaming ear to ear, while keeping pace with Rana.

Waiting for the lift, Rana looked across the huge high-ceilinged lobby that appeared like a small railway station. It was largely crowded with MLAs, moving about and coming in and out of the lifts. Barring one or two, who perfunctorily nodded in a gesture of greeting, nobody seemed to take much notice of him. Perhaps they did not even recognise him. Some probably feigned ignorance.

As the elevator travelled up, Rana reassured himself: *Never mind, it will all change after today—after only a short while.* He mumbled to Rakesh: "Press conference…what is the score on it?"

"Under control, hukum…I've kept it on standby. As soon as we have a word from you, it shall be organised within an hour's notice," he too whispered back, careful not to be overheard.

Rana nodded back in acknowledgement with the hint of a smug smile on his lips. Sure enough, if the warmth and the enthusiasm he encountered at the chamber of the Principal Private Secretary (PPS) to the CM, a little later, was anything to go by, he couldn't be faulted for letting his dreams take wings to an extent. Whether it was the normal reception to all members of the legislature or visitors, he couldn't be sure, not at least today—his antennae were either dulled or on a flight of their own. As soon as he appeared in the doorway, the PPS to the CM—a smart, suit-clad man in his late forties sprung up from his chair and moved towards him briskly, saying: "Good afternoon Rana-sahab…Come, come sir…You are looking absolutely dashing sir, if I may say so." He clasped Rana's extended hand between his, in a gesture of a very warm handshake.

"You look no less, Sinha-sahab; how is the family?" Mused Rana, good-humouredly and with a touch of counter flattery.

"All is well, hukum…All is well."

"Good!" Rana took a long patronising look while withdrawing his hand. Turning around to address his aide, who had been following him close behind holding a large decorated parcel of approximately four feet in height, he said, "Yes, come in; bring it in."

Rana turned back to Sinha, saying, "I had brought something small for Mananiya Mukhya Mantri-ji (Honourable Chief Minister). Can you arrange to send it to his residence, please?"

"It certainly does not look all that small Rana-sahab." Sinha looked astounded and asked, "What is it, hukum?"

"It's just a painting of the 16th century…I know madam has a taste for period paintings."

"Oh yes, yes. That's true; that's very true, sir," Sinha concurred, flatteringly, and then pointing at an empty table he addressed the aide, "Keep it here, keep it here, *bhai*; put it here."

Now he again looked at Rana, and said courteously, "You go in sir, you go in…CM-sahab is waiting for you." With this, he quickly moved to the connecting door to the CM's chamber and softly tapped it twice before half opening it for Rana to enter. Rana nodded at Rakesh and his aide and went in through the door held open by Mr Sinha.

Rana was amused to see the chief minister, Ghanshyam Das, a portly man in his mid-sixties, immersed in watering plants in small pots placed on the window sills of his large chamber. With a watering can in his hand, he was attending to cute little plants with the concentration of a surgeon. His thick glasses, slung from loosely hanging chains on two sides, was perched on the bridge of his parrot-like nose. With his slightly stooping back and unseemly paunch hanging out, like a large football underneath his kurta, he presented a pathetic sight. Since he appeared to be completely lost in himself, Rana hesitated and stopped at the door. However, Sinha, who was still there right behind him, understood his predicament and helped him by clearing his throat to attract the CM's attention:

"Sir; Honourable Rana-sahab is here."

As if distracted from caring for an infant, an absent-minded looking Ghanshyam Das turned around slowly and peered over the frame of his glasses across the huge space of the room. Sinha retracted his steps and exited, closing the door behind Rana. Ghanshyam Das's eyes widened and became bright. He quickly placed the can on the window sill, removed his glasses from his nose to let them hang on his chest and exclaimed heartily:

"Your Highness!" He walked enthusiastically to greet Rana. He pumped Rana's hands in an energetic handshake. Pulling out a chair, he beckoned him to sit.

"*Baithen* Rana-sahab; please sit."

Taking a seat, Rana tried to flatter him with a candid comment, "You tend to the plants just like a parent would to a child, Ghanshyam Das-ji."

"*Khandani* habit Rana-sahab; it doesn't go away easily." He laughed throatily. He walked around his large desk in great spirits, put down his glasses and sank into his chair. Leaning back, he said in a sudden formal tone, "Tell me Rana-sahab. What can I do for you?"

Taken aback, Rana leaned forward on his chair and putting his elbows on the edge of the desk, said, "I thought it was you who was going to tell me what to do."

Ghanshyam Das did not speak for a few seconds. He looked at him silently, with a contemplating stare. Then, he leaned forward and said softly, "Sorry Rana-sahab, I have no news to give."

"What do you mean?" Rana was surprised. His voice rose, "What are you trying to say?"

"They didn't agree."

"Didn't agree to what—the ministry I wanted?"

"No sir, not just that...not to anything at all. They don't want to take you in, not yet," he said with a shifting glance.

For a moment Rana stared at the CM, dumbfounded. Then with a start he pushed back his chair and stood up angrily. Visibly shocked, he roared in protest, "What is it you are trying to say? You had told me yourself that everything has been finalised this time...that either Urban Development or Youth Welfare is definitely coming to me."

"Everything had happened. I myself got your name finalised. But at the nth hour," he stopped abruptly. Putting on a deferential gesture he continued, "Your Highness..."

"Scrap all this drama," Rana cut him out abruptly. In a loud reprimanding tone said, "And stop addressing me as 'highness-venness' and all that..."

"What are you saying, hukum?" The CM pretended to be hurt and then with a flourish said, "At least privately, it is our right to address you as such."

Rana stared at him for a moment, struck by his wiliness.

Ghanshyam Das continued, "Sir, what is in my hand? I am merely a servant, looking after your state—your kingdom so to say—to keep it in shipshape; just as a gardener keeps a garden. But in the real sense it is yours. It is not mine!" He spoke with all the alluring slyness of a master politician.

Rana fumed at the man's duplicitous character, "To hell with the kingdom and all that...Right now I have been simply brought down to begging on bended knees in front of the political machinations."

All of a sudden he slapped his palms together and trying to lower himself on his knees, he screamed, "How much more would you like me to go down, Ghanshyam Das-ji? Should I prostrate myself in front of you?"

The CM got up and walked around his desk to come up to Rana. Touching his elbows with both his hands, he persuasively nudged him back to the chair, "Come; sit Your Highness...Please sit, *na*."

Rana abided. Now the CM also went back to his chair and sat down. After a brief silence, he addressed Rana in a slightly injured tone:

"Why are you saying such things, Your Highness? See, there was no deficiency in the effort from my side at all. If this Saanvri matter had not gotten out of hand suddenly—you were there—the decision had already been taken to anoint you as a minister."

"Stop playing this 'if' and 'but' nonsense," Rana retorted. "I've done so much for you, for the party...This is how you repay me? Promises were made to me by all of you, but look who is enjoying the rewards of a ministership for last four years—Yashpal Singh Sarena! Huh."

"Just look at the volume of votes he brings from his caste, hukum," the CM protested. "The government would have collapsed, if we hadn't made him the minister..."

Rana reacted with a quizzical look. The CM continued conspiratorially: "This is the problem with politics—even a person you would detest having to share a hookah with, you have to accommodate as a minister." He continued bitterly, "Now see his audacity—despite the fact that the entire media has gone to town with this case, he is claiming in full public gathering—in front of huge masses of people—that the CD is fake. And they are lapping it up...singing encomiums for him."

"But you are also holding him in your lap as if he were the cutest child you had," Rana cut him off angrily. "The bastard doesn't deserve to be even a *santri* (guard) and you've made him a *mantri* (minister)."

"It's only because of you that my hands are tied, hukum," The CM murmured with a touch of helplessness.

Rana looked confused. CM continued with a mysterious, yet questioning look on his face, "I believe at the reception of your daughter's wedding, a woman created a huge scene after having consumed a lot of booze."

Rana was dumbfounded, neither able to rebut nor utter anything. After a meaningful exchange of silent looks between them, the CM said patronisingly, to the completely vanquished challenger, "You don't bring into your house, the leftovers from outside, Rana Suraj Bhan Singh-ji...Its filthy odour doesn't let anybody stay in peace, thereafter."

Rana was speechless. His throat went completely dry as he struggled to swallow the spit in his mouth; utterly deflated and helpless. The CM said, "Now see, everything had been fixed—your name had already been passed—but this news made its way to the High Command." He looked at Rana accusingly.

"They returned the file," he nodded sympathetically to Rana, who looked on quizzically. Then pausing before completing his sentence with a gesture of resignation, he said, "...with a cross." Rana looked pathetic as he collapsed on his chair. It was a daze after that.

Rakesh immediately sensed that something had not gone quite right in the brief meeting, when he saw Rana emerging from the CM's room with a defeated smile on his face. His hawk-like eyes had processed every tiny nuance when Rana and the CM shook hands in a perfunctory goodbye at the door held open by the latter. It did not need to be told that, what he and his master had expected had gone awfully wrong, for some reason.

They remained silent as they went down and boarded the car for Rana's office in the capital. Rana's mind was still reeling with all the information Ghanshyam Das had filled him with about how things had gone at the Working Committee meeting. He locked himself into a cocoon of silence, contemplating the consequences of the events. Having gauged the situation, Rakesh had quietly mumbled instructions on his mobile to cancel all the standby arrangements for the press conference.

Rana broke the silence, all of a sudden: "Rakesh, today there is an afternoon flight for Jodhpur; isn't there?"

"Yes hukum, Jet has one."

"We have time for it, right?"

"Yes, just about," he said, consulting his watch.

"Let's get to the airport. You can fix the booking and all that, can't you?"

"I'm sure I should be able to handle that, hukum." He started punching some numbers on his cell and instructed the driver: "Take that second lane for the airport—the one after this one; quickly, we are pushed for time."

"Ramvilas, I'll take the flight. You and Dharam follow by road, later on," Rana instructed the driver and his aide sitting at the front.

An hour later, when Rana landed at the Jodhpur airport, both his aide and the SUV driver, who had come to receive him, were quite baffled. He was not expected back for another two days.

"Rani-sa, home?" Rana shot the question to his aide, as if suddenly waking up from a slumber. No words had been exchanged between them until then, except for customary salutes and acknowledgements.

"No hukum, I believe Rani-sa is gone to the *badi* haveli for the evening," answered the aide deferentially.

In the rush to catch the flight at the last moment, he had not informed her about his sudden change of plans. Now speaking almost in a whisper, he asked her to return home early and also to ensure that Khoobchand, her driver, did not leave without meeting him when he dropped her.

•◆•

Rana chose the roof terrace for the meeting. The descending sun behind the Chamunda hills reflected a reddish gleam to the glistening dome of the Chamunda Mata temple. The terrace-nursery at the middle of the huge empty roof of the haveli presented a haunted calmness—quite unlike the upbeat brightness and accompanying hot air from the Thar Desert that bathed the dwellings, giving the city its epithet: the Sun City.

Clad in a black kurta-pajama, Rana looked like a mysterious sentinel as he stood with one of his arms resting on a column, staring at the enveloping redness of the sun, setting in the bosom of the hills, far away. He stood very still; only his kurta fluttered loudly in the breeze. There was no other sound except the whistling echo of wind, creating a melancholic atmosphere.

The redness of the setting sun reflected on his face. His eyes looked empty and stony as he peered into the enveloping blackness, which further accentuated the darkness he felt inside. Something moved in the far distance behind him, not immediately discernible because of the fast diminishing light. But even the soft footsteps of the approaching figure were enough to alert Rana, despite the occasional howling of the wind. His jaw stiffened a bit as he greeted his guest, who was clearly expected.

"Through with the day's duty, Khoobchand?" He asked sombrely without turning around from his position, just as the figure stopped three or four feet behind him.

"Yes, hukum." Khoobchand said reverently and then asked equally sombrely, "You asked for me, huzoor?"

Rana turned around slowly and stood still. He looked at Khoobchand, sizing him up for a few seconds. Feeling uneasy under his penetrating stare, Khoobchand lowered his eyes. Rana relaxed and took a step forward. He put his hand on his shoulder and asked gently, "How are you, Khoobchand?"

"You know very well, malik." Khoobchand said hesitatingly before slowly raising his eyes and continuing, "You understand everything."

"Been to the thana? Got the report filed?"

"*Ji*!" He nodded.

Without letting go of Khoobchand's shoulder, Rana turned him round and motioned him to walk with him up to the parapet, some distance away.

"Life is an eccentric entity; it plays strange games," Rana said with a long, cold exhale while continuing to walk. "We both share almost an identical story," he laughed and asked, "Don't you think?"

By now they had reached the parapet. Khoobchand stopped and said, "I didn't quite understand, sarkar."

Rana made him sit down alongside him on the parapet. After a pause and yet another long exhale, he said philosophically, "*Arre bhai*, you know very well that, after all, I too shared a bond with her, *na?*"

"*Ji*." He sounded non-committal.

They receded into a long silence. Though acutely conscious of the gravity of the moment, neither was able to speak. Then slowly, Rana turned his face to look pointedly at Khoobchand.

"I had to make a request..."

Besieged by apprehension, Khoobchand slowly turned his face to meet Rana's eyes.

"Tell me, sir…"

Rana searched his eyes. Then a strange gleam appeared in his eyes. Was it a plea?

"It is about Sonu; it can have a devastating effect on my family. It can disintegrate us all completely…You are following what I am saying?"

Khoobchand nodded agreeably. Rana continued, "There will be pressure on you for her DNA tests. If that happens, it can bring forth so much destruction; so many things can get ruined, so completely." There was an element of fear in his voice and then it changed to resignation as well as vengefulness, "And when someone's family begins to break down, a person can go to any extent…even the innocents get burnt sometimes, right?"

"Yes, sir," Khoobchand nodded, "I've understood, sir."

Standing up Rana put both his hands on Khoobchand's shoulders and said, "That's all."

Khoobchand also stood up slowly and said with folded hands, "*Ji*… Shall I take your leave now, sarkar?"

"Just a minute, Khoobchand…" Withdrawing a wad of notes from the pocket of his kurta, Rana shoved it in Khoobchand's breast pocket. "Keep this. It's for your children. You'll get more, from time to time…"

Khoobchand again nodded silently. Rana steered him back towards the column where he had been standing earlier. As they reached it, Rana bent down to pick up a box containing an expensive imported whiskey and offered it to Khoobchand.

"I had brought it when I had gone to London, last time. Keep it."

"There is no need for this, sarkar. Such an expensive bottle!"

"Keep it."

"Whatever you say, sarkar."

Even after Khoobchand left, Rana paced across the full length of the deserted roof-top terrace immersed in conflicting thoughts—thoughts about his ambition being so unexpectedly and so rudely denied, thoughts about self-preservation in the eye of the storm, which could brew up unforgivingly.

Moments later, he walked down in a stupor, still besieged by the unrelenting currents of fury and fear lashing at him with full force. The stony steps and the stony walls of the narrow stairway of the haveli, unwittingly created a sequestered and restrictive feel of an unwelcome place—a kind of jail.

At the bottom of the stairway, as he emerged into the corridor, his eyes strayed to his wife, who stood across, in the open doorway to her private chambers. There were questions in her eyes, lined with beseeching tension and lurking inquisitiveness. His were non-committal as he gazed at her for a while. Then he mumbled with an edge of irony in his tone, "She was a *golee*, after all. He is a *gola*, likewise. One has to take care of things…"Saying this, he abruptly turned and walked away.

She watched him move further away from her, along the long corridor with shafts of light falling on him. Then, she too turned and went inside her chambers.

•◆•

It was semi-dark around the deserted lake, even though it was only the early hours of the night. The atmosphere was gloomy with a foreboding silence pervading it. An insignificant amount of pale light fell around the only two working lamp-posts at the promenade, circuiting the lake—others had been robbed of their bulbs. This accentuated the dreariness of the surrounding.

The oppressive silence was suddenly punctured by the noise of an empty bottle being flung across the placid surface of the water with great force. The bottle zipped over the watery surface and crashed on a rock on the opposite side with a splintering sound.

"*Saali, bhenchod*," a man's booming voice, cursing obscenely, penetrated through the deep stillness of the night.

The man, who now staggered out from the shadows of a tree, was a heavily drunk Khoobchand, swaying on his unsteady feet and continuing to look in the direction of the bottle, which he had just flung. He swore aloud at himself: "*Abbe*, fuck the country liquor you've been drinking so far. Now you have been presented with a bottle of foreign liquor, in bribe. Rana-ji brought it from the airport, when he had gone abroad—that's what he has given you as gift; that's what you should drink now, you *bhadwe*!" Then he screamed aloud in disdain and self-pity, "Drink *that*, you *bhosdi-ke* Khoobchand."

He nearly fell on the ground, fiercely working his fingers over the cap of the bottle Rana had given him. He took a large gulp as soon as he opened it. Gripped by a dark and self-deprecating mood, he let his hand stray across to some salty peeled onion, placed on a piece of old newspaper, lying nearby. He picked a handful and unsteadily flung them into his mouth before guzzling a little more, swearing further: "*Dee-en-nae*..." He laughed obscenely and in abandon. Then he stopped in the middle of the laughter and turned serious. After a pause of a couple of seconds, he slowly leaned forward and spoke softly, almost in a whisper, as if to caution an invisible entity.

"*Bhaiya* Khoobchand, don't let them do the *dee-en-nae*—no, too dangerous!" He put his unsteady index finger on his lips and continued. "A whole lot of secrets can come out tumbling, Khoobchand! No; no *dee-en-nae*."

A film of sadness descended in his eyes. Overtaken by an unknown fear, he whispered secretively, "People will get to know all the secrets..."

Again, he took a large swig from the bottle and said beseechingly, as though to some other person, "My wife—no longer mine; my young daughter—not really mine." Tears flashed in his eyes as he continued bitterly, "Everything will be exposed; all the secrets will tumble out..." He became quite emotional now.

He took another swig, spilling a bit of whiskey from the corner of his mouth, his eyes becoming redder and his mood fouler. He snarled in a reprimanding tone, as if someone was seated across him:

"*Saale bhadwe*...sole of your wife's shoe, *saale*...No, no, not even that...You're not even your wife's shoe...Your wife's sandal also has a price...What is your price? Is there any price for you, tell me? You are worthless...*saala* Khoobchand...*gandu*...that's what you are, *saala gandu*!" He took even a bigger gulp from the bottle this time and shouted mockingly, "*Dee-en-nae*."

All of a sudden he turned sombre and solemn. Without uttering any word, he continued to drink his whiskey in slow and small swigs, in complete silence. The only sound interrupting was the splash of the whiskey inside the bottle, each time he took a swig. His mind seemed to have strayed to a distant thought. His eyes began to moisten as if with nostalgic recollection. Slowly and involuntarily he dropped himself on his back; his eyes now filling with tears. Feeling remorseful he mumbled, almost in a whisper, "You were mine...mine, I thought..." And the tears rolled out of his eyes, silently...

THREE

It was hardly a road; more like a dusty lane reaching out to a forsaken hamlet. As the weather-beaten jeep lurched over a small rock jutting out of the uneven earth, the assistant sub-inspector (ASI), seated at the front alongside the driver, cursed loudly, "*Abbe teri ma-ki.* Is it a road or a bone crusher?"

"We are nearly there, hukum," said one of the uniformed constables seated at the back.

"We better be…" The ASI readjusted his glares on his eyes. He turned around and tapped at the constable's pagri with his cane and said threateningly, "We better be, Chattar Singh, otherwise this umbrella of yours is definitely going to be turned into a football under my feet…Do you understand?"

"Hukum," said Chattar Singh uncomfortably.

Amid bare mud walls on three sides and two mud-walled rooms on the fourth side, the small *aangan* (porch) of the impoverished house was abuzz with activity. A marriage ceremony was in progress. An old sheet had been spread over four banana stems stuck into the holes dug in the ground like columns, to create a temporary canopy for solemnising the wedding. In the midst of a small crowd of mainly women, three youths—one of them being a very young Khoobchand—were seated cross-legged in a row on an old *durrie* (mat). Facing them were three girls, also seated cross-legged in a row, on the same large *durrie*.

Although the faces of the three girls were partly covered by *ghunghat* (veil) up to their noses—one of them was clearly very young, hardly more than twelve years or so. A middle-aged priest with a long beard sat cross-legged between the two rows, performing the ecclesiastical rituals. He was being helped by a haggard looking woman in her late forties, seated opposite him.

The three brides held *malas* (floral garlands) that they put around the necks of their respective grooms when nudged by the priest, along with appropriate invocation of hymns. In the background, a bunch of women sang a marriage song in a low chorus. Most of the men-folk, squatted on the bare earthen floor or on the cots, had a passive presence, wearing blank expressions on their faces.

Just as the *malas* were being put around the necks of the grooms, the old wooden door flung open with a powerful kick by someone from outside. Before anyone could react, a posse of policemen barged into the compound. Their senior, the same fellow riding in the jeep earlier, thundered, "*Aye*; stop all this." Then he ordered his fellows, "Arrest all of them bastards...*bhenchod, saale*...forcing an underage into marriage. Come on, put handcuffs on this priest also...*saala*."

Suddenly, it was all commotion. The priest sprung up from his place and tried to scramble his things together and run; so did other male members in the congregation, including the grooms—trying to slip away. The women attempted to stand up but remained frozen in their places, stricken with fear. Likewise, the three brides did not move from their places; they remained seated where they were, confused and fearful of making any move. In no time, the constables had hauled up everybody: all were shaken out of their wits. An old man tried to reason with the ASI: "What are you saying, malik? Someone has given you wrong information."

The ASI turned to him angrily and grinding him with a threatening gaze, he hit him with his cane and shouted out obscenities:

"Get out of the way, *saala*...Trying to teach me, *madarchod*."

He then darted towards the three brides, who had stood up by then. One by one, he lifted up their veils with the tip of his cane. He let go of the two girls who looked old enough, but when he came to the third girl, he stopped in his tracks. Turning to the old man, he barked, "Now tell me old man, *saale buddhe*, what is this? What is her age? Tell me, *saale*? Why are you tongue-tied now? Trying to pass on a ten-year-old girl as a grown up? *Saale*."

At this, the haggard looking woman who was participating in the rituals, walked up to the ASI with folded hands and pleaded, "Sarkar, she is not ten years old...She is more than twelve...I am the mother of this girl...I am telling you the truth, sarkar."

At first the ASI glared at her, apparently at her audacity to speak up despite being a woman. Then a smirk spread across his face. Without letting go of his piercing gaze that dug into her eyes, he sauntered up to her. Feeling threatened, the woman shifted in her place. He spoke calmly as though he understood her plea.

"Oh, ho. She is twelve years old, is she?" Suddenly turning to address all the people in the *aangan*, he said mockingly, "Come on people, look what this *budhia* is saying—her daughter is twelve years of age."

He then turned around to face the old woman. Slowly and theatrically folding his hands, he asked her with feigned deference, "Now, you tell me, dear mother, if your daughter is twelve years of age, how is it that she is not a minor?"

The old woman was dumbfounded; so were all the others. An ominous silence followed as all the participants gaped at each other with fear writ on their faces. The ASI thundered at his constables.

"Arrest this *budhia*, and take these six brides and grooms too, along with the *pandat* and that old man, to the thana."

With menacing eyes, he looked around him and said threateningly, "Who else is family or a relative? All have to come to the thana. Who are the parents of the three grooms?"

At this point, another old man approached the ASI diffidently with folded hands and whispered in his ears, "Sarkar...please, for a moment come inside, let's talk it over. It'll take only two minutes."

Even as the ASI glared at him, the old man transmitted a suggestive signal through his eyes while mumbling, "Just two minutes, sarkar."

The ASI stared into the old man's eyes searchingly before nodding and saying, "Alright, I might as well hear what you have to say." With this he moved to the door to the room inside, led by the old man. He instructed his subordinates to wait till he came back.

While he followed the old man into the room, the people congregated in the courtyard turned to each other, murmuring fearfully their concerns and apprehensions.

But, the scene inside was hardly cordial. The old man had barely proffered some notes to the ASI, when he snatched them from his folded hands, threw them at his face and exploded: "Thousand rupees? *Abbe*, you think I am a *bhadwa*, a pimp or something?" Tapping his forehead with the tip of his cane, he said threateningly, "PREVENTION OF CHILD MARRIAGE ACT—Section 9, section 10 and section 13... two years hard labour and one lakh rupees as fine...each one of you... do you understand, *tau*?"

He shifted his fiendish look to each one in the small group comprising the parents of the brides, a couple of other old men, the young grooms and the child-brides. All, except a small girl, stood with folded hands in front of him.

"*Saale*, committing a crime and then having the gumption of showing just ten notes of a hundred rupees each."

Everybody was tongue-tied. They gaped at the ASI fearfully before another old man made a move. He picked up the notes thrown on the ground and ventured, "Don't take it wrong, sarkar. Everybody is in a very bad state here." He took a small pause and then, pointing at the girl, tried to reason, "Besides, sarkar, only this small one is underage, the rest of them are all, already adults in age, malik."

Noticing a moment's uncertainty in the ASI's eyes, he quickly reached into his pocket to withdraw some more notes and said, "Malik, here are another two thousand rupees. We are all very poor people and have nothing more with us now." Proffering the notes through his folded hands, he pleaded, "Please be merciful and handle it somehow, sarkar."

Before the ASI could respond, the old man who had first tried to solicit his cooperation, cut in again with folded hands, "Then sarkar, this is only the half-marriage...*gauna* is still to take place. Real marriage is solemnised only after the *gauna*, which won't take place for another six years, malik."

"*Abbe*, are you trying to teach me things? You think I am a stupid fool?"

"I am speaking the truth, huzoor. I am the father of the groom, malik," the old man said tearfully.

The ASI took a long, hard look at both the men before snatching the notes out of the younger one's hands. He shoved them into his pocket and then turning he took a step up to the mother of the bride, who stood with folded hands on one side.

"*Oye budhia*...this girl should not go with these people for another six years, I am warning you, failing which not only will they go inside, you will go inside too. Do you understand?" He said threateningly.

The woman, who wore a very frightened look, nodded readily and spoke appeasingly to the ASI. "Yes sahab, yes sahab. I had thought that along with my two older daughters, I would, in one go, let off the burden of this younger one too, but if you insist that I should not do that, then so be it. I won't send her with her groom just yet—will send her only after the *gauna, sahab*."

While the old woman reeled off her spiel to soften the ASI, Saanvri, the little girl who had just been spoken of so derisively, stood quietly in one corner of the room, feeling rejected, away from all the elders who were engaged in making pacts about her future. The emptiness of her eyes gave way to loneliness and pain. Perhaps, even at that tender age, she was not wholly un-impressionable to the compromises and capitulations the adults made to get on in life, and to the feelings of loss and denial that paved the path of an ordinary being. On a day when celebration and merrymaking should have been the theme of the event, the child-bride had matured to an important realisation—to determine the steps she would take while encountering the rigours of her life in the future. But she was yet to mature to the cruel onslaughts of the 'real' world, supposedly governed by 'civility', 'morality' and 'legality'.

The book of life had just opened up for her. Even its early pages were not immune to the lurking threats from the predators of evolved society.

•◆•

About a year and a half after Saanvri's mother had been chastised by ASI, Mangal Singh Chauhan against child marriage, both mother and the daughter were once again face to face with him, hauled into the thana this time.

It all started when the duo were at the gates of a local junior school, performing. To the beats of her mother's *dholak*, Saanvri was showing her tricks on the rope, tied between two poles. Being the midday recess, children were enjoying the show and were clustered in a good number around the amazing child performer. As usual there were two or three between them who were indulging in lumpen dalliance.

During one of her rounds, just as Saanvri had taken the first step on the rope, a long, thin straw of a jungle weed slipped slyly under her lehenga. Saanvri immediately tripped and would have had a nasty fall had it not been for the balancing bamboo in her hands, which enabled her to bounce off to safety. But she still suffered some bruises on her arms, legs and some on her face. A furious Saanvri sprung at the naughty boy and slapped him hard across his face, sending him rolling to the ground. Now the friends of the boy were at her. Before the matter could take a nasty turn, they were hauled up by a policeman who was passing.

Even before ASI Mangal Singh could hear what Saanvri or her mother had to say, his pocket had been taken care of by the errant boy's father, who on hearing about the incident had rushed to the station to placate the police.

Saanvri and her mother were in for a surprise. Mangal Singh had recognised them and he now had a new dimension of wickedness to offer.

"Put the *budhia* in the lock-up," he ordered his assistant sternly.

"What, what are you doing, sahab? It is that boy who was at mischief, sahab. He poked my daughter in a dirty manner, making her fall down. Look, she is bruised all over," Saanvri's mother protested.

"Why did you make her work in the first place? She is a minor. Don't you know it is illegal to make children work for a living? Shall I spell out how many laws apply against this offence?" He took a small pause and then demanded threateningly, "Since when have you been making her walk on the rope, tell me?"

Saanvri's mother was nonplussed for a moment, unable to think what to say. Then she attempted a defence: "But it is only a *khela,* sahab. Everybody performs a *khela*; even ordinary children play such games."

"Hold your tongue *budhia,*" Mangal Singh sprang up to his feet and snapped, hitting the table angrily with his cane. Everyone around froze in fear.

"*Saali,* trying to teach me things." He turned to his assistant, "Take her to the lock-up and all of you vacate the room. I shall investigate this myself. I will talk to the *chhori* alone."

Saanvri's mother was pushed out of the room. A few others, reluctant to move, lingered on, wanting to know what punishment awaited the girl. Leaning over his hands on his desk, Mangal Singh now barked at the small congregation of people, "Vacate the room; I don't want anybody inside while I talk to the *chhori* here."

Slowly everybody moved out. He went up to the door and shut the latch. Saanvri watched him with fearful eyes as he returned to his desk and sank in his chair behind it.

"Tell me what had happened?" He said lightly without even looking at her.

She did not say anything; her eyes remained pinned to the floor. He tried again, this time more persuasively.

"Don't fear, tell me what had happened."

He pulled open the drawer of his desk and withdrew a paper wrapped toffee. He extended it towards her.

"Take this. It's nice, you will feel good." Noticing her hesitation he insisted again, "Take it, take it."

Scared of annoying him, she moved up to him and took the toffee. But before she could get back to her place, he swiftly grabbed her arm and pulled her close.

"You have suffered scratches, is it? Show me where you have been bruised, I'll fix that rascal then," he said slyly.

She tried to free herself but he quickly locked her in his arms from behind her. His hand had already made its way on her thigh underneath her lehenga. He touched her inappropriately, inserting his fingers through the lining of her homemade underwear

"Did he scratch you here with his *khapachchi*, did he?" He asked with an amused grin.

With a lot of effort, she pulled his hand out, with both her hands. Her voice cracked as she spoke. "Not here," she protested. Her eyes brimmed with tears, the resentment on her face was vivid.

Realising her state, he eased his hand out but did not let her go yet. Instead, he slowly turned her around and said a little bit conciliatorily, "Okay, have the toffee."

She did not make any move.

"*Arre*, eat it, it's good, quite sweet."

She still did not make any move. He pressed on.

"Okay, let me open it for you." He extended his leg to confine her in the little space between the table and himself. He then took the toffee from her hands, threw away the wrapper and offered it again: "Here, take it."

She shook her head slowly to decline it. He persisted, little sternly this time: "Eat it, I'm asking you to."

Too frightened to annoy him, she accepted this time. He watched her as she chewed it, unhurriedly. Then slowly he began to spell out the scene graphically, as if to ascertain the facts from her for the official report.

"So, you had just taken a couple of steps on the rope high in the air, balancing yourself with the bamboo held in both your hands, when this boy slyly sent up the *khapachchi* under your ghaghra and scratched you, which made you lose your balance and made you fall down." He paused for a moment to acknowledge her nod and continued, "You got scratches on your hands, leg, thigh and even your face…that's what your mother alleged, right?"

She nodded again, seeming to be relaxed a bit. He continued, putting on an air of reassurance.

"Now, I can see the bruise on your forehead here, also on this arm of yours," he said holding the arm in his hand as though a doctor would and then quickly went down on his knees, saying, "Let me check your leg and the thigh, too."

Before Saanvri could do anything, he had quickly lifted up her lehenga again and found the scratches on both her legs and inner thigh. He caressed the one on the thigh softly even as she squirmed and tried to free herself.

"Hurts, does it?" He pretended to be concerned.

She nodded again while stiffening her leg to pull away. He let the fold of the lehenga down and stood up. He moved his fingers on her face tenderly and said,

"I'll punish the rascal, don't you worry."

She said nothing except raise her head to look at him searchingly just once, and then looked down again.

He once again sank into his chair before saying casually, "You need to put medicine on that. *Hilte-ka arak* would do the trick." His eyes had a mysterious gleam as he considered her before asking again, "Have you heard of the *hilte-ka arak*?"

She looked confused and shook her head. He waited for a moment and then in a deft movement he slyly undid his fly and oblivious to her he brought out his penis, keeping it covered under the already pulled-out shirt. Now he slowly extended his other arm to take hold of her hand. Uncertain and apprehensive, she let him.

He pulled her close and without letting go of her hand, with his other hand he removed the fold of the shirt to reveal his organ, saying, "This is what produces *hilte-ka arak*. You shake it and the juice, the *arak* comes out, which you can apply." He said with a wicked smile.

Shocked, she tried to back off, but he was too quick for her. Tightening his grip on her hand he forcefully pulled her closer, and with the help of his other hand he pushed his enlarging penis in her hand, ordering at the same time, "Shake it, play with it."

Tears flashed in Saanvri's eyes as she tried to struggle herself free. Suddenly. his eyes spewed fire, and he slapped her across the face and forcing her down he shouted, "Bring your mouth down, suck it, quick."

In no time, his large organ had been pushed inside her mouth and she was held firmly in one place to perform a forced fellatio. Soon, with his pelvis rapidly going up and down, his thrusts getting fiercer, he groaned loudly as though in pain. She, on the other hand, was almost choking with the severe pounding and the repulsive act of having to take in the awful shaft in her mouth.

As he screamed and shuddered with his release, it was not just the jet of his semen but also the reflexive fountain of her vomit, which suddenly flooded her mouth. Tears spewed out of her eyes at the inescapable punishment. After the unbearable spasms of the two simultaneous acts, he had hardly pulled out his shrivelled organ that her mouth burst into a torrent of spray all over—a mixture of his semen and her vomit.

"You bitch, you *saali bhosdi ki*...What is this you have done?" He slapped her with full force as he looked at the mess on his uniform.

She was reeling on the ground and barely got herself together that he kicked her in the stomach, shouting more obscenities. "*Bhenchod*, haven't you sucked it before? All my clothes are spoilt. Now what will I do?"

She doubled up with the impact of the slap and went slightly blue in the face due to the sudden breathlessness. Even he looked frightened as he watched her gasp for air and her eyes glazed with trauma. It took good three seconds before she regained her breathing followed by an unstoppable deluge of coughing. He pounced on the earthen pitcher held on a stand nearby and filled a glass with water. He quickly brought it to her looking panic-stricken.

"Drink, drink the water."

Ironically, in the grave helplessness of the situation, her reluctant hand had to go out to the very tormentor for assistance, who had put her in a life threatening condition in the first place.

Some ten minutes later, when Mangal Singh unlatched the door and bellowed, summoning his assistants inside, they were amused to find him engaged in a peculiar exercise. Held high in his hands, he was desperately trying to dry his wet shirt under the fan while stupidly trying to hide the front of his wet trousers, underneath his vest.

Standing near his desk the little girl sobbed incessantly; her smeared dress and crumpled hair presenting her pathetic story. Mangal roared pointing at her, "Throw the bitch out…*Saali* vomited on me, dirtied my entire shirt."

As one of them began to push Saanvri out, Mangal thundered at the other one, "*Oye* Jumme, listen, let her mother go for now…I'll fix her the next time."

What was to hurt Saanvri even more was the way her mother chided her in front of people, as she helped clean her dress under a public tap, outside the thana.

"Ever since this *chhori* has been born, there has been trouble after trouble for me. What was the need to hit that boy?" She screamed and muttered to herself, "*Put it in my mouth...*" She suddenly blew her top again, "*Arre*, he only put it in the mouth. He didn't strangulate you, did he?"

Saanvri was crestfallen with the crudity, cruelty and the savage indifference of the comment. The solitary moment was enough to mature her by eons. She had learnt instantly as to where she stood with her mother.

But more was in store for the young Saanvri.

Ten months later, after much argument one morning, she had been sent to the *bawdi* (stepwell) by her mother to wash the clothes that had accumulated in a large pile. None of her friends had come that day with their washing. All the other women had left after collecting their wash, leaving her alone. Having arrived late, some of her clothing was still spread around for drying on the small boulders at the bank of the *bawdi*. She thought of having a little swim. As usual she took to the fresh, inviting water, like a fish.

Lost in her exhilaration, she swam with long strokes on the surface of the water as well as beneath and then like a plank floated idly on her back. In the process, she did not notice that a jeep had passed by on the dirt road, high at the top of the hillock, and had slowly reversed. Ending her frolicking as she emerged joyously from the surface of the water, she suddenly noticed the jeep.

Her smile deserted her instantly for she recognised that it was a police jeep. In a quick reflex she looked around for human presence. She found none. Panic gripped her. Swiftly and silently, as if worried that somebody might catch her, she got out of the water and tiptoed to gather all her washing in a pile. Then she zipped across into a deserted ruin, close by.

She began peeling off her wet clothes in a hurry to change into the dry ones. She had already taken off her top and was busy unfastening the strings of her half-cup Rajasthani *choli*, when she felt someone's presence behind her. She froze for a moment and then in a jolt, turned around. Her mouth fell open in a shock. Mangal stood in the broken doorway with a leering grin on his face.

"*Arre*, you look so irresistible in this state...look at your two *narangiyaan* (oranges), god, they are too..." he licked his upper lip inadvertently and said, "Go on, free them." His eyes dilated with sudden passion and he extended his arm almost in an involuntary action, "*Na, na*...Let me free them."

He grabbed the hem of the *choli* and snatched it away from her grip. Before she could do anything, he was all over her. Like an unleashed animal he pounced at her and pushed her to a broken wall behind her, roughly fondling her small breasts with his paw-like hands. He licked at them, suckled them roughly and even bit them like a hungry dog.

With all her might she tried to push him away from her but he was unrelenting. In a desperate attempt to free herself, she bit at his hand, sending him into a rage.

In a reflex he pulled away his face from her breasts and then cursing her he administered a stinging slap on her. She staggered sideways on her feet and then collapsed on the ground. Blood trickled from a cut at the side of her mouth and tears flashed in her eyes.

Quickly turning around and hunching over her hands and knees, she began to back down slowly while pleading, "Spare me, hukum... Forgive me for the mistake. Please spare me."

He too bent down to his knees now, very close to her and grabbed her jaw in a claw-like grip before saying in a reassuring, yet menacing tone: "Don't worry...I won't put it in your mouth today."

Not bothered about her reaction, he buried his mouth forcibly on her half-opened mouth, sending his tongue on a serpent-like exploration. Then, all of a sudden he pulled back and stood up. Quickly he unbuckled his belt and unzipped his trouser while ordering in a guttural voice, overlaid with unadulterated passion.

"*Chal, palat ja*... Turn over...there," he said pointing at the cluster of clothes.

When she regained consciousness, she found herself in some other world. She found her body hanging by a skewer over a stove of burning coal in a meat-seller's shop. Her body seemed to be slipping down a slab of ice among many other bodies somewhere. Gradually, as she regained consciousness, she was immediately gripped with panic. But there was no sound and no movement anywhere. There was only stillness around her, a death-like stillness. As she stirred a little, a numbing pain shot through her and she fell unconscious again.

Much later, in the afternoon, when Saanvri's mother Ghumri returned from her errands, she found her slumped in a state of disarray on the floor of the inside room, amid the washing, which lay scattered. Then she noticed stains of blood on some of the clothes. She was unable to make out anything from the scene and sat down befuddled by the wall. In a moment, she noticed Saanvri open her eyes as if from a dream. She seemed disorientated and stared at her strangely. A gleam of hope surfaced in Saanvri's eyes for a moment and then slowly it withdrew behind stoniness. An impenetrable silence returned.

Ghumri instinctively knew that something dreadful had happened. But she also knew that considering the mood Saanvri seemed to be in, there was no way any information was likely to be volunteered by her. She thought of checking with the neighbours who surely would have noticed something. Being a small hamlet, houses were neither too clustered together nor arranged in any sort of order. There were only two houses close to hers. The occupants of one were not home at the time, but Dulli, the woman in the other, was not only forthcoming, she had her own observations to offer:

"She lay like this...like this...on the donkey's back," Dulli tried to demonstrate by action, "Just like a corpse, hanging from both sides. Dholu had to hold her carefully throughout...Poor fellow."

"Where did Dholu find her, did he tell you?"

"Near the *bawdi*, where else? All her washing was with her too. That's how he brought her somehow. Mounted on top of the pile of clothes, otherwise how would she have made it on the back of his donkey in that state?"

Sixty year old Dholu seemed equally unaffected by the whole episode. When asked, he calmly narrated the whole story—how he had the donkey loose to graze around and how it had strayed over to the patch of green, near the old broken down structure at the bank of the village *bawdi*. After his little snooze under the tree, when he went over to get it back, he had spotted Saanvri. She was staggering like a drunkard with arms loosely around the pile of clothes, trying to make her way up the slope. She hardly moved a few steps before she collapsed with her washing beside her. Then, with a lot of effort she struggled to get up again but fell instantly. Dholu noticed all of this and also the patches of blood on her clothes and knew something was amiss. He sprung up to help her and she let him. There was no scope for making inquiries. He took her to Dulli immediately. With no questions asked and no explanations offered, they brought her home to safety.

Later, Ghumri found Saanvri in their little washing space in the room, struggling to apply oil to her anus. She watched silently and noticed stains of blood on her daughter's hand as she went about it. Ghumri understood everything. Without saying anything she went to the cooking area and made some turmeric lotion. After warming it a little, she returned to Saanvri, who had by then lied down on the bed. Without asking anything and disregarding her mild resistance, she turned Saanvri over and lifted up her lehenga.

"Who did it?" Ghumri asked grimly as she applied the lotion.

Saanvri winced in pain

"Who was he, I asked you…" She was stern this time.

"What will you do?" Saanvri replied with a mocking tinge to her tone.

"*Khoon pee jaoongi saale ka*…I will cut him into pieces. Tell me the name," her eyes blazed.

Saanvri gave her an equally piercing look. A tiny smirk appeared on her lips. "It was the ASI Mangal Singh. Now tell me, what will you do?"

Ghumri's hand stopped abruptly and she froze in her place, like a statue. The angry gleam in her eyes faded away in face of the challenging gleam in Saanvri's eyes. Ghumri seemed to melt down to the ground, like a puddle of water. Slowly, resignation replaced the smirk on Saanvri's face as she closed her eyes. She did not even hear the footsteps of her mother retreating away to the other room.

Four

Mangal Singh was an animal and he had tasted blood. Though like one or two of his subordinates who were equally sexually exploitative, he too was not indiscriminate in pouncing upon anything that looked remotely like a woman; he had kept himself on the leash as far as minors were concerned. But the encounter with Saanvri had emboldened him.

One afternoon after some months, he went again, looking for her at the *bawdi*. It was deserted. He had chosen nearly the same time as before, yet there was no one there. He waited and drank whiskey from a bottle he had confiscated that morning. Within half an hour the alcohol had set his loins on fire. He then decided to go to the girl's house.

Saanvri had just sat down to have her meal in their little kitchen, when she heard a mild roar of a vehicle. Not a thoroughfare, it was seldom that any motor passed their house. Hence out of curiosity she got up from the mat to go to the window to have a look. Even through the billowing cloud of dust engulfing it, she could see the police jeep lurching over the potholes and turning at the corner to head towards their house. Fear gripped her instantly and she tiptoed towards the door.

Ghumri, who had dozed off on the *khatia* got up with a start as the door of the courtyard flung open and a staggering Mangal walked in. Saanvri laid her ear to the narrow gap between the two planks of the door to listen in.

With the bottle still in his hand, Mangal swayed on his feet as he addressed Ghumri with a loutish laughter, "*Arre*, what is it? Didn't you recognise me, *budhia*? I, the *thanedar*, who saved you from the jail, twice."

"What happened, sahab?" Ghumri stood up and folded her trembling hands.

"*Arre* sit, sit down *Mai*. There's nothing to worry." He lurched forward and lowered himself on the cot.

"Then, what do you want, sahab?" Ghumri mustered courage to ask.

Mangal took a small swig from the half-full bottle, then narrowing his eyes he considered her for a couple of seconds before saying nonchalantly, "Why? Can't I visit you? We have known each other in the past, haven't we? Tell me."

Ghumri was flummoxed for a moment. She struggled for a response: "But..."

"*Arre*, I was passing through here. Saw your house, so I thought *bhai, jaan-pehchaan hai hamari, toh*, why not meet. Did I do anything wrong?"

"No...*nahin*, sahab," she tried to appear composed.

He took another little swig before asking casually, "So what's the news about your daughter, what's the name...yes, Saanvri. How is she?"

"She is fine, sahab." A shadow of darkness swam across her eyes. Then she spoke further hurriedly, "She is not here, sahab."

"Who are you kidding, *Mai*?" He said with a penetrating gaze, "I noticed her in the window as I was turning the corner."

"Oh, is that so?" Ghumri was flabbergasted for a moment and quickly tried to explain, "I had dozed off...she might have returned without my knowing."

Unable to withstand his mocking gaze, she dropped her eyes. Scrambling to get up, he said perkily, "Fine, why don't I meet her, too?"

Ghumri swiftly tried to block his way.

"Don't do this, sahab, it's not right."

"What are you trying to say? What is not right?" He said sternly as he stood up erect.

"It'll create problems, malik. Last time she bled so much," she pleaded with folded hands.

He stood still and tense for a moment. Their eyes arrested in each other's, both understood what it implied. He slowly relaxed and reached into his pocket.

"There won't be any problem. I'll go from the front this time... Last time I didn't have *this*." He grinned and withdrawing the packet of contraceptives, he dangled it in front of her face, "I have brought it with me today."

"She is only a child, malik. Don't do it," Ghumri tried to go for his feet.

"*Arre na, na.*" He stopped her promptly and said lightly, "She is not that young either. She is getting filled up pretty well. Now if she won't come of use for people of *jaan-pehchaan* then who else, you tell me?" His grin expanded ear to ear while he tried to move to the door.

"Don't do this, sahab," Ghumri pleaded weekly.

"*Arre haat.*" He angrily pushed her aside and said, "Clinging on for nothing."

Ghumri fell to the ground while Mangal flung open the door to the inner room and barged inside. Ghumri quickly scrambled up and followed him.

But Saanvri was nowhere to be found. It was a very small house with two very ordinary rooms and a small alcove used for cooking; hence within seconds he had scanned the whole place. Ghumri was also baffled about Saanvri's disappearance as she could see that her thali, on the floor, had food on it. She could sense him getting steadily angrier as she saw Mangal go back and forth, stomping his booted feet. Returning to the kitchen space he fumed.

"Where has she disappeared? *Saali bhosdi ki.*"

"I told you malik, she is not here."

"Who are you kidding *budhia*, can't I see that the food is all laid in the thali, ready to be eaten? Do you think I am a *chutia?*" he snapped, "Didn't I tell you that I saw her at the window. Now how could she have moved out in such a short time from right under my nose? Did she turn into some kind of wind that I didn't notice her leaving. Now tell me?"

Ghumri lowered her eyes to the ground meekly. Suddenly his eyes went to the little window.

"Not unless..." he uttered speculatively to himself and his mouth fell open in bemusement.

Ghumri also raised her eyes and followed his look but there was disbelief in her eyes. She knew that Saanvri wouldn't have fled through that window because there were brambles right outside, which the girl very well knew, but Mangal may have not noticed so much.

She heard him curse, '*Saali, bhenchod*'. He turned in rage and all of a sudden flung his hand in a stinging slap across her face.

"Tell me *bhenchod*, where has she gone?"

Ghumri went off balance and staggered and fell at the doorway. Tears filled her eyes as she tried to plead with folded hands while taking small steps backwards.

"I don't know malik, how can I know? I have been here in front of you all the time."

He caught her by the neck while pushing her further back, threatening: "*Saali*, I won't spare you till you tell me."

He pushed her right across the room till her body hit the wall and tightened his fingers on her neck. Her eyes bulged out as she choked and struggled to get free. In the scuffle, as the hook snapped off, her large breasts burst of her *choli*.

"Tell me, tell me *randi* where has she gone to?" he continued to thunder.

"I...I really...*m-a-a-l-i-k*," she struggled and choked as she spoke.

Suddenly, he eased his grip. The blazing redness of his eyes melted into a lusty darkness. He stared into the valley between her heaving breasts. He let go of her throat and roughly pawed one of them. While retaining his grip on her hands, he pinned them to the wall above her head. He then twisted one of the defiantly protruding black nipples between his unkind fingers before pinching it hard, sending a shiver of pain through her body. Not bothered about her mild shriek, he did the same with the other breast.

"*Arre taubah…saali, tere thaan toh*, bloody solid, aren't they." He put his mouth on one of her breasts.

"Sahab, sahab…*thamo* sahab," Ghumri squealed in protest, but she seemed to surrender a bit.

He let go of her hands and with both his hands and mouth, slobbered over her huge, firm breasts—sucking, biting, licking and squashing with ravenous fury—moving from one to another. Her freed hands, which at first weakly attempted to push his head away, had in no time become the willing accomplices in the furious sexual onslaught unleashed by him.

Suddenly, he lifted his head and stood perplexed for a second or so. And then, even as a stupid and lusty grin overtook his face, in a desperate urgency of their own, his hands began struggling with the zip of his trousers. This had a contagious effect, as her hands too, almost at their own will, hurriedly went searching for the string, which had held her lehenga in place.

She was shorn of her skirt in a quick sweep to reveal the mysterious mass of black fur at the summit of her ample and not so shapely thighs. As Mangal tore out of his trousers, his inner-wear exposed his raging weapon. In a furious motion he lifted her up by her trunk and thighs and flung her on the cot. Forthwith, he also jumped on and tore off the front of her *choli*, freeing her large inviting breasts while shouting in an intimidating growl.

"*Le bhosdi ki, le*…you'll also remember that you were given some fucking in your old age…*le*."

He was afire and so was she. It was a brutal assault, which was as much desired as feared by her. He was unsparing as he rammed into her with the ferocity of a demon. The rough walls of her rapturous cave, which perhaps had not experienced moisture in a long while, were torn by million knives at first, but were soon secreting juices invitingly to each of his punishing thrust. The barrage of obscenities and abuses he showered with his unrelenting pounding, sent her on an unbounded vulgarity of her own. Baying like a wild boar gone berserk as he collapsed on her sweaty breasts, she too let out a maddening scream like an animal pierced in the gullet by a flying spear.

As both trembled from the after-spasms of a 'duel of lust', her watery eyes noticed something over his shoulder, which was to explain the mystery behind Saanvri's disappearance. In the ventilator, higher in the wall facing her, one of the horizontal iron bars was missing to make enough room for a slender person to slide through. Also visible was the rope, knotted to one of the bars. An enigmatic smile appeared on her lips.

•◆•

Standing behind the partially open door to the inside room, when Saanvri heard Mangal tell her mother that he had noticed her standing at the window while turning the corner, she had been seized by a sudden fear. For a moment, she hadn't been able to think what to do. But then in a flash, she had picked up some of her clothes, hanging on a string, and shoved them and her footwear in a plastic bag. Next, she picked up a rope, which they used for walking between the poles, flung open her mother's personal trunk and stolen a few banknotes and stuffed them into the cups of her *choli*.

Stepping on the planks of a built-in shelf, she had hurriedly climbed the wall to reach the ventilator. With some effort she had been able to dislodge one of its bars that she knew was loose. She had thrown the iron bar out and then quickly tied the rope to the other, firmer horizontal, bar and squeezed through the space, along with her bag. With the aid of the long rope, she had climbed down to the other side, safely.

Her toes had barely felt the earth when she heard the sound of Mangal barging in shouting obscenities. Energised with extraordinary clarity of mind, she acted with great speed. She picked up the iron bar, for she felt it could come handy. She then slung the cloth bag on her shoulder and made a dash for the jungle, some fifty feet away.

As soon as she got into the undergrowth, high enough to hide her, the first thing she did was to put on her footwear. The soles of her feet burnt badly from the heat of the burning earth. Crouching low she started running through the wild and thorny shrubs, which easily reached up to her height to offer reasonable cover. Even when she was completely out of breath and her feet ached badly, she rested only a few minutes on her haunches before running again. In the vast vista, there were no trees or shade to offer her any respite

Soon, pangs of hunger and thirst had taken over and sent her reeling. Her throat dried up and her feet felt weighed down under her own body. She slowed down gradually and then stopped to take a breather. A whiff of the scorching wind sent a strange wintry shiver, rather than a burning sensation. Breathing through her mouth, she gaped at the inhospitable span of burning earth and wild shrubs spread afar, in front of her. Her pupils dilated with increasing brightness; she seemed to spot water, some distance away. Perhaps there was a *bawdi* somewhere. Her mouth widened in a smile, and with renewed hope she moved on, even managing to run, limply.

But there was no water. She had mistaken. Just as she turned her face around in disappointment, she noticed it again, on the other side. Perhaps, she had misjudged the direction. Her eyes brightened again and breathing even more heavily through her open mouth, she ran again, now in the other direction, a little faster this time. Again there was no water. Her breath turned to laboured gasps now, and she mumbled curses while looking around in despair.

Her sand-crusted eyes were clearly playing tricks. Now she was seeing two *bawdis*—one upon the other. With a good bit of effort, she once again lifted her leaden legs and took to heels. But neither was there any *bawdi* nor any water in sight. All she could see was a massive stretch of scorched earth. And before she knew, she had started to fall down.

Her head had not even touched the ground when she heard bleating goats. They seemed to be frolicking in the water. The sun shone directly into her eyes. Surely there was water around; there were handfuls of it being sprinkled on her face, as if to tease her.

Five

Saanvri woke up to a weather-beaten face staring at her. Was it that of a woman or a man? She could not tell. The person leaned over her and threw some more water on her face from a small tumbler. She opened her eyes wide now. The man smiled. A benign smile.

"*Jag ja, jag ja.*" He twiddled his fingers encouragingly.

"Where…" She was caught in a bout of cough as she tried to get up. "Where am I?" She asked.

"At my house." The smile widened on his face.

She found herself in a hut. The man looked like a nomad with long hair. Furrow-like creases ran from the sides of his eyes, all the way down to his chin, with wide curves around the ends of his ever-smiling mouth. His eyes seemed to narrow into light-emitting slits with an infectious smile reflected in them. He held out the tumbler for her to drink some water. She snatched it and went at it with a maddening urgency, spilling, choking, coughing, yet not giving up till she was quenched. She reclined at the low wall of the hut to regain her bearings while breathing heavily through her mouth

He went into a corner where something was boiling on the small *angeethee*—a portable earthen stove. He poured some of the broth into an old aluminium *katori* (bowl) and brought it to her.

"*Kha*. Have it." Happiness danced in his eyes as he blew at it from his mouth to cool it and then offered it to her.

She grabbed the *katori* and went at it ravenously.

"Slowly, slowly," he tried to caution.

She looked up in his eyes for a moment and then quickly attempted to blow at her food to cool it down. But impatience had the better of her. She took another quick swig and reflexively pulled back as it burnt the tip of her tongue. She blew again and got down to drinking it, not bothered about the man's mild laughter at her predicament.

The man sat down in front of her, resting his back on the wooden pole at the centre of the impoverished hut, staring at her benevolently as she ate. She felt shy but hunger made her go on eating, nevertheless.

"Jhumma!" he said tapping his chest with the finger and asked, "You?"

She stopped for a moment. A frightened look appeared in her eyes. He understood and nodded reassuringly.

"Sa...Sa-a-nvri," she mumbled.

He regarded her kindly as she went back to eating the broth. He attempted his next question.

"Where were you headed?"

She stopped eating and looked up at him guiltily. Her eyes began to moisten and a trace of fear emerged in them. Then, all of a sudden she burst out crying. A startled Jhumma asked no further questions. He intuitively let her empty herself of her tears. It was only when she went into hiccups of after-sobs that he cautiously leaned forward and put his hand on her hair. He patted it softly, a couple of times. There was reassurance in his touch. Without any exchange of words, a bond was formed; tenuous perhaps, but a bond it was.

Saanvri learned that Jhumma was a nomad. He did not stay at one place for too long. In fact, he did not remain attached to any particular group of nomads for more than a month or two. He was essentially a loner and tread alone, with no fixed work or fixed routine. He was at the moment looking after someone else's goats till the owner got back from the Haj pilgrimage.

It was while he was minding the goats that he had noticed Saanvri, some distance away, running erratically like a kite cut off from its string, disorientated, and finally collapsing like an uprooted tree. With great difficulty, he had lifted her on his back and managed to bring her to his hut.

The sun had already descended on the western horizon, leaving a deep red hue outside the hut. A wave of high tension and deep anxiety spread through Saanvri at first, but she let it pass. Despite the inherent distrust that she had developed about the male species in general because of so many revolting instances witnessed from early childhood, she felt intuitively secure with Jhumma, the weird *banjara* (nomad).

She tentatively shared her story over a meal of boiled wild turnips and crabs that Jhumma had dug out for her from the banks of the *bawdi*. She could see his eyes sparkle with a kind of parental emotion, reflecting both anger and admiration, which made her feel even more safe with this strange old man. But she had no answers to the question where she was headed to, yet. The uncertainty or ignorance about it triggered a fresh burst of tears in her. He suggested that she rest for the night and in the morning they take a call on that. She nodded in grateful acceptance and lay down to sleep.

But the night was not completely uneventful. Affected by the rigours of the day, she had fallen asleep as soon as she lay on the charpoy. Soon nightmares started haunting her. ASI Mangal Singh at his fearsome worst, transmuted from one species to another—roaring beasts to slithering reptiles.

She screamed and got up with a start when she felt something sliding up her leg. A dark human figure quickly removed his hand and flung aside whatever it held in its grip, and immediately bludgeoned it to death with a rod. She jumped out of the charpoy to reach for the small oil lamp close by and raised the wick. She turned to find an unruffled Jhumma facing her with a weird grin, more pronounced due to the missing tooth visible through his open mouth. He showed her the prize. At the end of the rod hung a snake with a badly smashed head. She nearly collapsed on the ground with fear, while Jhumma stood smiling.

Being a man of the wild, Jhumma was instinctively alert to his environment. Though he had covered himself well with his old blanket, he had felt something move beside his feet where he lay on the floor. Forthwith, he had raised himself on his elbows to monitor the situation. There was no way that the rope-like thing, slithering up the foot of the cot, could have escaped Jhumma's night vision, sharp as a hawk's, despite his age. The bluishness patch of moonlight on its moving body was enough to send Jhumma springing into action to reach for the rod.

Saanvri went back to sleep far more relaxed this time. She had no doubt about the capabilities of her newfound protector-cum-friend. Not only did the sleep grip her faster this time, even the dreams that came streaming in were all sweet and soothing, after a while.

For some fortuitous reasons, an old woman kept on appearing in the dreams. She had a lissom body and a very compassionate face with a benign smile. Her long white hair flowed like a shimmering halo and accentuated the angelic quality of her luminescent eyes. Who was she? Saanvri wondered even through her dreams, one dissolving into another. Then, in the surrealistic montage of incomprehensible visions emerged snatches of a wedding activity—her wedding a few years ago. The old woman's lingering presence was more noticeable now. It was consistently a reassuring presence, even when the happenings seemed to be pretty sordid, otherwise. She recalled the old woman taking her in an embrace and folding her in her comforting arms.

Suddenly, Saanvri recognised her and woke up. It was not as dark as before in the hut. Soft sounds of a flute filled the atmosphere. Through the deep bluishness of the very early dawn, she could see a human figure outside the door. The shadowy person seated on a rock was Jhumma, lost in playing a soulful tune on a bansuri.

She got up. Wrapping the sheet around herself to ward off the early morning nip in the air, she went out and sat down on another small rock, facing Jhumma, to listen to his beautiful rendition. After some time, when he put down his bansuri, she told him about her dream and the old beatific woman who had appeared in it.

"Who could she be, any idea?"

"I think I do."

"Who?"

"I think she is my *marad*'s mother," she said speculatively.

"Your husband's mother…your mother-in-law?"

"Yes, my *sasu-ma*." She looked certain.

Saanvri recounted to him the incidents during her marriage, rather vividly. She recalled how it was not only her mother but also several other relatives, who remarked rather derisively how, ever since birth, Saanvri had always brought ill-luck to the poor woman. The cruel comment had not gone well with the only other, much-older woman present in the room, who happened to be her mother-in-law. She had immediately reprimanded others while pulling Saanvri in her protective arms.

"Have you gone mad, all of you? Don't you know what not to say," she had fumed. "You break the law and then blame the poor little girl for it. Lay off, all of you."

Saanvri recalled how she had then fondly kissed her forehead and had said reassuringly, "Don't you worry, *bitiya*, you are now my daughter. These four years will pass in no time, and then I'll take you away. I may even do that earlier."

Saanvri described, with her voice cracking with emotion, how her *saasu* then wiped the tears that had flashed in her eyes before tenderly kissing her eyelids and saying, "If there is any problem, you come over to me."

Jhumma sat silently for some time, pondering over the significance of Saanvri's recollection of her mother-in-law and her comment. When

Saanvri looked up, Jhumma searched her eyes and spoke, "What do you want to do?"

"I want to go to her." There was certainty in her eyes.

"Do you know the address? The village they live in, anything?"

She stared at him blankly for a couple of seconds and then shook her head. Her response did not surprise Jhumma. The atmosphere suddenly turned heavy. They sat absolutely still in their places with their heads bent down. Then Jhumma put the flute to his lips again.

Even as his lips worked wonders, weaving amazing ethereal symphony on the small, homemade bansuri, his eyes were restless—at time staring up heavenward as if looking for some divine intervention and then darting back to the diminutive figure of Saanvri seated in a forlorn state, with her head bent down in resignation. He noticed two drops of tears fall on her lap. He stopped playing the flute instantly and sat immobile in his place. Then, there were two more drops and he could not sit quietly anymore.

"Don't worry, I am there," he rattled quickly while tenderly caressing her head. "I shall go and search for the address, don't you worry, *mera bachcha*," he added reassuringly.

All of a sudden, Saanvri got up and surrendered herself in his arms, which opened up to hold her in a warm embrace.

Within a few days, Jhumma's pursuit bore fruit. Chhoti-Jhareli was a very small village, more like a small habitation among a cluster of hamlets, some 60 km off Mathania-Ummednagar main road. Thus, it was not difficult to pick up gossip about the disappearance of a local adolescent girl. All Jhumma had to do was to let his flock of goats stray away from the patches of jungle shrubs around his hamlet, Bilaina, to some 7 km away towards the *bawdi*, at the fringe of Chhoti-Jhareli. He had strictly instructed Saanvri not to venture out of the hut at all while he was out on his mission.

On the third day, in the afternoon, when some of his goats had jumped into the *bawdi* to drink water, he had a godsend encounter with none other but Dulli.

"Who are you, old man? You are not from our village, so how dare you bring your goats here to drink our water?" She had pounced at him.

"I shall herd them out, don't you worry. It'll only take a minute," Jhumma looked very apologetic.

"Are they any good for milk…your goats?"

"Yes, of course, want to try some?" Jhumma had taken out a much used aluminium tumbler from his *jhola* and said, "That is, if you don't have any reservation about drinking from this."

The little gratification extended by Jhumma through his goat-milk had done the trick. Three more instances of straying by his herd of goats, up to the *bawdi* of Chhoti-Jhareli, and he had not only found out about the village where Saanvri's in-laws lived, but also picked up amusing titbits about the amorous outings of the ASI to Ghumri's house. He also gathered that Ghumri had even gone to Saanvri's in-law's place once, looking for her. Not finding her there, she had made peace with her daughter's disappearance and managed her *khela* by engaging one or two younger girls of the village.

Now, the problem was that Saanvri's in-law's place was a good 300 km away. It was not possible for Jhumma to accompany her for he had the goats to look after.

"You don't worry about me; I can make it on my own." Saanvri assured him, putting on an air of confidence.

"How will you go, tell me?" He quizzed her on her false bravado.

"Asking for directions, from people to people," she spoke forthwith.

"People to people! For all the 300 km or so…and you think you'll reach the place?" he teased her.

"Yes." She nodded confidently.

"And how will you travel?"

"On foot," came the answer.

Jhumma was touched by her naivety and innocence. In the two weeks of her stay with him, he had become quite fond of the small girl, who could have been his granddaughter or maybe even a great granddaughter. Jhumma knew he was going to miss her sorely—her cooking in particular and her singing. Her songs always blended so beautifully with the music from his flute. Jhumma felt a tug at his heart, never experienced before. But there was no question of asking her to stay. He knew that she could be found by the *thanedar*, anytime.

Jhumma did a thorough job of finding out in bits and pieces the required direction to reach the place. Two days later, on a Wednesday, early in the morning, he put Saanvri on Daijar–Mandore bus, going via Mathania. It was the only direct service for that distance, plying three days a week. She was to alight at Phool-Birai, a small village some 7 km before Mandore.

Nobody on the bus took any notice of the frail and elderly looking woman, completely wrapped up in an old black shroud, revealing only her eyes through a slit-like opening. Saanvri managed to get down at her destination without provoking any curiosity.

Though Phool-Birai was also a small village, it was certainly a lot bigger than both Bilaina and Chhoti-Jhareli, and people seemed more helpful. Yet, she avoided seeking any help from the men of the village after getting down from the bus in the late afternoon. Instead, she sought direction from the small cluster of children playing about here and there.

It was well after six when she rattled the *sankel* on Dhania-bai's door. Though she had brought some rotis with her, she had not eaten anything on the bus. By now she was feeling extremely weak and famished; her head was reeling and her body going limp. Hence, as soon as the door was answered by the old woman, her feet turned to jelly and Saanvri collapsed right there, at the doorway itself.

Six

An involuntary light scream escaped Dhaniya's lips as she saw an unexpected visitor collapse at her feet. Impulsively, she searched for her hand in the folds of her cloak and found it to be rather cold. Then one by one she lifted her closed eyelids to check her eyes. Her pupils were dilated but they still had movement. Now Dhaniya ran inside to fetch some water. It was when she uncovered her face that she sensed something familiar about her. She sprinkled water on the innocent face and as Saanvri opened her eyes Dhaniya had no doubt about who she was.

Some days ago, Ghumri had been to her place looking for Saanvri. Whatever little Ghumri had told her during her unexpected visit, had raised doubts in Dhaniya's mind about the veracity of her version regarding the disappearance of her daughter. She had smelt something amiss and had become concerned about the little girl. She had taken an immediate liking to Saanvri when they had been confronted with the oppressive onslaught of the police some years ago just as the marriages were to be solemnised. She recalled the moment when driven by the maternal instinct in her she had instantly drawn the lonely looking girl in her comforting embrace.

And now when Dhaniya had almost begun to reconcile herself to the inevitability of the situation—of losing out on the certainty of the beautiful, tender girl entering her house as her son's bride one day—

most dramatically, the girl had landed at her feet out of nowhere. She sighed with wonderment at the strange ways destiny changed, and helped Saanvri get up.

Saanvri had barely found her feet, aided by Dhaniya, that a fresh surge of emotion triggered something in her and all her fears, insecurities and anxieties came tumbling out in a torrent of tears. She wobbled on her feet again. She was about to collapse on the ground all over again, when Dhaniya quickly reached out and held her in her comforting arms. She let the howling girl pour out all her aching, twisting torment over her shoulder. She tenderly caressed her back till her weeping subsided to shivers of occasional sobs and then led her inside to the cot in the small bedroom. But Saanvri could not be persuaded to sit or lie on the bed at all; instead, she sat down on the ground and stretched her arm on the cot for support.

Dhaniya sat down on a low cane-stool close by and patted Saanvri's bowed head reassuringly. No questions were asked and no explanations were given. But it was not an empty silence. An intuitive connection between the two had bonded them, despite the awkwardness of the situation, allowing a certain quiet communication between them without any exchange of words.

Dhaniya reached for the cloth bag that Saanvri still slung across her chest underneath her cloak and helped her to get it off. Inside she found a small *potli* with a few rotis and some pickle, which had not been touched. She realised that the girl had perhaps not eaten anything at all. She immediately got up and carried the *potli* into her small kitchen and in no time returned with the rotis, all warmed up, and some curry, in a thali. She placed it in front of her along with some water in a brass glass.

"Poor thing, you look so weak. Come on, eat now." Dhaniya said affectionately.

"But..."

"No 'but'. You eat first." Dhaniya was firm.

Saanvri read it in her eyes and gave in.

It was amazing that despite being an ordinary villager with no formal education or training, Dhaniya was not only a woman of the world. She was also a perceptive human being. Hence, there was neither any coaxing nor cajoling or 'leading on' of any kind, from her side. All was revealed during snatches of conversations over the next few days. Dhaniya felt rather proud of the young girl's grit to flee and was also very protective towards her for her vulnerability. Her daughter-in-law to be was also now her daughter.

Dhaniya worked in a local municipal hospital as a ward help. It was the job she had inherited from her late husband, who had died a couple of years ago in a road accident in the hospital ambulance van. Since he was 'on duty' at the time, the authorities had suitably compensated the family and offered a replacement job to the widow.

Dhaniya's departed husband had aspired for their son to pursue higher education and enter the medical profession someday. But Khoobchand had completely belied his hopes. Thanks to the bad company he had fallen into, he had dropped out from the junior school, barely managing thereafter to find a job as a car mechanic. Looking at Saanvri now, a glimmer of a dream re-emerged in Dhaniya's mind—her late husband's unfulfilled dream.

First of all, she enrolled Saanvri in a school to recommence her education, which had been interrupted because of Ghumri's ill-found belief in the old adage that it is a waste of time to send girls to schools—since girls ultimately ended up doing housework after marriage. Whatever little schooling Saanvri had managed to secure had been possible while her father was alive, and that too because primary education was compulsory in the state. It had been abandoned soon thereafter, at Ghumri's behest, and she had been pushed to perform the illegal *khelas*.

Then, Dhaniya started taking Saanvri to the hospital whenever there was no school, or even during the free hours after school. The medical officer was game in letting the girl assist her 'mother' or even tend to an odd little task now and then, as long as she was not to be paid for it.

Khoobchand was totally unaware of these new developments in his mother's household. He had not been given any intimation of Saanvri's arrival where he worked in Jodhpur as a casual car mechanic. Because of the considerable distance from Phool-Birai, he preferred to live in Jodhpur itself, sharing a small room in a tenement with two other odd-job handlers. He visited his mother for a couple of days every three or four months and sent an occasional letter to enquire about her wellbeing.

When he came home to visit his mother, after some months, he was naturally surprised to find Saanvri. He had hardly seen her at the time of the wedding; hence he had not recognised her. Though she had made no impression whatsoever on him at that time, he could see that the girl had something very arresting in her now. Of course, being a man of a somewhat lumpen disposition, his initial interest was limited to the physical attributes immediately noticeable. The fact that he was already married to her made him a bit smug about it and he bided his time to claim her bodily, especially since he like his other friends had always felt deprived of those pleasures of life and had to make do with alternate arrangements.

But the problem was his mother, who had a different value system. She firmly forbade him from getting any closer to her; not until the *gauna* was performed. That was still nearly eighteen months away, when the girl turned sixteen, considered legally an adult.

After the enforced celibacy for the first two days, Khoobchnad was already feeling sexually frustrated. In the evening of the third day of his stay, he ended up consuming a good quantity of alcohol in the company of some local boys. With his carnal fires further stoked he returned home late. Fearful of his mother, he made his way to the roof on his wobbly feet where he had been ordained to sleep. Mouthing obscenities he fell into the cot and was soon snoring.

During the night, when Dhaniya turned to adjust herself, she noticed, through her half-open eyes, the terrace door slightly ajar. The cat must have sneaked in as usual, she thought. But sleep sat heavy on her eyelids, making them give in to its seductive sensation and depleting her of the habitual urge to take out her stick from underneath her bed and go after the invading little beast. A dream immediately swept over—of her chasing the cat all over the kitchen, again and again, and not being able to catch her. Then she heard a sound.

Saanvri who was in deep sleep, woke up with a start. To her utter shock, she found a half-naked man beside her who was trying to place her one hand around his aroused organ. His other hand held her in place. A scream had hardly escaped her lips that it was stifled with a firm clasp of his hand around her mouth and a whisper into her ear that he was her husband and hence she should not struggle. As she tried to free herself with all her strength, the man pinned her down even more firmly. But then suddenly he shrieked in pain and fell away.

"*Argh*..." He swirled around reacting to the surprise attack. But immediately there was another blow, this time on his elbows as he tried to shield himself.

"Get out...Get out right now, you *jaanvar*," screamed Dhaniya hovering over him with her long stick. She gave him another strong lash on his side even as he sprung to his feet and quickly tried to gather up his unfastened trouser. "I had told you to keep away from her... didn't I?" She barked.

"Hold it, hold it Amma, what are you doing? Give me a chance to, at least, do up my trouser," Khoobchand pleaded as he tried to ward off another blow with one hand while struggling to hold together the flaps of his unbuttoned trouser.

Saanvri also sat up quickly, at once shaken by the unexpected onslaught as well as amused at the ludicrous sight of her husband squeamishly slinking away through the door like a beaten street pup. But above all what she felt was a sense of security, never experienced before, in the presence of her mother-in-law—she finally had a mother for real.

As the saying goes, in utter darkness hides light, or that a sordid happening might be a precursor to good portents in life. This instance settled the matter between the mother and son on the Saanvri issue, once and for all. Khoobchand understood clearly that he could not claim his husbandly rights over her till after the *gauna*. Till then, not only did he have to respect her chastity, he had to behave honourably towards her in every other way. Nevertheless, when he returned he was happy to know that some eighteen months later, like his other married friends, he too would have something to look forward to—a home to come back to and children of his own to proudly display. Essentially a simple man, he was beginning to see light at the end of the tunnel of his dismal living and felt happy in a way.

The intervening months had also ironed out issues between Saanvri and her mother—Ghumri. After being informed of Saanvri's whereabouts, she had visited her a few times. She had also been made to realise that she would no longer be able to exercise any control over her daughter. For that matter she was not too keen either, considering her sticky position with the random visitations of ASI Mangal and a few more, from time to time.

Eighteen months later, with a simple ceremony organised at her house, Dhaniya formally took Saanvri as her *bahu*, after the solemnisation of *gauna* by a priest. Other than Ghumri, only two or three very close relatives had been invited for the occasion. Ghumri's brief stay had been arranged at the house of one of Dhaniya's neighbours, which was also symbolically used as the bride's place for the initial part of the ritual.

The first night after the ceremony was the night of a bit of misadventure. Even though still in her teens, Saanvri was a fulsome young woman and in her bridal finery she looked strikingly attractive. Khoobchand had made elaborate preparations for the *suhag-raat*, also with different food for potency to match the calling of the moment. But his excitement for the evening got better of him and turned out to be an anti-climax.

Khoobchand was looking forward to entering his new status of that of a married man, that too with a beautiful young girl. He had already found a rented room for himself and his wife to start their life's journey together. It had a tiny attached space, under a tarpaulin shade with temporary walls made of iron grills, to serve as a cooking area, just outside the door. There was a common lavatory in the public compound, and so bathing and washing was usually managed in one corner of the main room.

A month after the final solemnisation of his marriage when he and Saanvri boarded the bus to Jodhpur, Khoobchand had dreams of a new life in his eyes and excitement of a young lad in his heart. She too was overwhelmed by dreams of happiness, but not without a niggling apprehension of a strange sense of loss. Though her eyes were taking in the adventure of the new life as they passed the trees, fields and buildings outside the window of the bus, her heart had not completely left her mother-in-law. Even though Dhaniya had promised to visit them from time to time, Saanvri was already missing her desperately.

Despite the initial awkwardness of a young couple, their relationship progressed well and in right earnest. Khoobchand was in fact, quite enamoured by his wife. If there were occasional scraps between the two, there were sweet making-ups too. Khoobchand was adept in making light of tricky situations and was always on the lookout for opportunities to entice his wife.

One day, well after Khoobchand had left for work, Saanvri settled down for a bath in the little enclosure behind a low partition in the corner of the room. She had barely started pouring water over her head when the room suddenly plunged into darkness. Driven by instant panic, her hand holding the *lota* (tumbler), stopped in its tracks. She suspected someone had entered the room. The window, which was the only source of light during the day, had been shut by someone from inside. With a touch of fear in her tremulous voice, she spoke aloud:

"*Arre*, who is there?"

As no one responded, her panic grew and in an involuntary reaction, she quickly pulled up her wet petticoat over her large breasts and turned around to demand again, her voice quavering a little bit more.

"Who shut the window?"

Khoobchand had quietly sneaked into the room with his own key and had soft footedly made his way to the window. She had not noticed him because of the divider. Her bare back presented a tantalising spectacle, which made him even more mischievous.

"Stop! Who are you?" she screamed in fear as she noticed a shadowy figure rise up and advance towards her.

"*Arre*, who else would be there," Khoobchand spoke playfully, "It's me, your *saajan*."

"Why have you closed the window?" Saanvri feigned anger.

Khoobchand took smug steps forward while saying even more playfully.

"Amma had instructed when we left, that since I was taking my *bahu* to town, fresh after *gauna*, I should keep her away from people's prying eyes, or their jealous stares can have a bad effect on the attractive new *bahu* in the neighbourhood." Turning her around to look at her buxom body from the front he tweaked at her wet cheek.

Feeling flattered, Saanvri, holding her wet petticoat up to her breasts, teased him shyly.

"And you…what do you say?"

"What do I say?" For a moment Khoobchand seemed lost for words before a flash of mischief danced in his eyes again.

"You are something special as it is," he said lasciviously, pouncing at her. Grabbing her, he lifted her up. Quickly and gently, he dropped her on the bed, pushing her to lie back. Swiftly he released the edge of her petticoat from her easily yielding grip. With his one hand trying to pull the stuff down, his other hand reached for her breasts, while he muttered in a lusty growl, "I…I prefer getting on with the real thing."

"What…what are you doing?" She put up a mock protest while trying to hold his hands, though more facilitating than restraining.

Khoobchand swiftly removed his shirt and once again lowering himself over her, he said, tongue-in-cheek:

"I am just shielding your beauty with my body."

He had just about commenced fondling her breasts when she pushed him aside and suddenly sat up.

"Alright…but first you promise me something." She sounded solemn.

"What?" Khoobchand looked confused and slightly irritated.

"Promise me that you will let me pursue my studies."

"Let you pursue your studies?" He looked even more confused.

"Yes! I have to study further…I have to become a doctor." There was resoluteness in her eyes before an avenging gleam took over as she continued, "My mother wanted to throw me away as a disposable waste…I refuse to remain that. I have to show her that I can become something. That is why I have to pursue my studies."

Khoobchand also turned serious and looked deep into her eyes. He saw a certain firmness and determination in them. He met them with an empathetic expression in his own eyes. But within moments he was back to mischievous and lascivious self.

"Alright, sure…go ahead with your studies. But right now, allow me to continue with my study." With a gentle peck on her head, he nudged her and lay her down again. Agreeably disposed now, an inviting gleam appeared in her eyes.

The first few months of their married life passed fairly happily in enjoying new exciting things like discovering Jodhpur, a town rich in history and culture; paying obeisance to gods in temples of eye-popping dimensions; learning the conflicting ways of a society, at once feudal and yet struggling to be modern. The heartburns and fissures appeared mostly on account of the company Khoobchand kept and the loathsome habits he acquired from them.

Most abhorring of all was his weakness for alcohol. Whenever he had a 'little evening out' with friends, which of course was far too often, he came home drunk with a repulsive demeanour. On a pay-day or for two or three days after that, he would still be tolerable, for he would drink some so-called English *sarab*, a product of some proper Indian distillery, But after that he would come down to awful smelling desi *tharra* as his funds depleted. He would often be found lying drunk by the wayside. Even if he made home somehow, it would not be uncommon for him to have collapsed at his doorstep after being thrown out by Saanvri, after a midnight brawl between the two.

Despite this, within the first three years itself the family had expanded with the arrival of a son and a daughter. It invariably began to have a toll on the household finances. Though on one hand, it had made Khoobchand very proud and happy, on the other this became an excuse for him to have a little celebration with drinks. That produced a heavy strain on a still young Saanvri. However, once again her mother-in-law, Dhaniya, rescued her from abject misery. With good references from her own bosses, she secured Saanvri an orderly's job in a local hospital.

Saanvri worked hard and with remarkable industriousness. Not only was she very diligent with her job at the hospital, she also enrolled herself for the junior nurses training course. She had already acquired requisite education up to the higher secondary at Phool-Birai and then at Jodhpur itself. She was equally attentive and responsible in caring for her children and towards other duties of the house.

She had realised by then that due to his indulgences, Khoobchand could not be depended upon for his obligations as the man of the house. On the contrary, it had become a bit of a usual habit for him to sponge on her for money midway through the month; this led to bitter quarrels. Even the physical fires between the two had almost extinguished. The resultant celibacy was, in a way, a much needed refuge she sought out of revulsion for Khoobchand's detestable habits.

•◆•

Another three years passed in this kind of uneasy status quo. Saanvri's son, Neelesh had turned six and her daughter, Basanti had completed four years. Guided by her mother-in-law, Saanvri had put Neelesh in a primary school when he turned five and kept an eye on him right from the start, so that instead of loitering around with other children of his age, he engaged himself in studies. Saanvri herself devoted a lot of time, to help him with his school work. It was not uncommon when after a day's hard work both mother and son would be found asleep over books they had been working upon through the night, only to be awakened by the milkman knocking at daybreak. Saanvri had also, by now, successfully completed her training and been appointed as a junior nurse and then, after acquiring further training, promoted to a full-fledged nurse in the same hospital.

Saanvri felt very secure and comforted whenever her mother-in-law visited them and there would be all kinds of emotional blackmail to delay her departure as it came closer. Yet, such was not the case when her mother Ghumri came. Invariably, there would be heartburns, arguments and sometimes even small showdowns due to clash of values between mother and daughter. Thankfully Ghumri's visits were not frequent.

When Saanvri's daughter Basanti was to turn four, both her mother and mother-in-law visited the family at the same time—a rather rare occurrence. Driven by her foolish enthusiasm that she would perhaps be praised for it, Ghumri would often engage Basanti to learn the acrobatic craft of *khela*, much to the un-expressed disapproval of Dhaniya who preferred that in time, just like her brother, the little girl too should attend school.

Ghumri would go about her mission only after Saanvri left for work, under the belief that the surprise discovery of the little girl's accomplishments would ultimately bring her credit too. Dhaniya chose neither to voice her views nor complain about it to Saanvri.

One day, Saanvri returned from the hospital a little early. She was still in her nurse's uniform when she got down from the cycle-rickshaw outside the door of her new two-room house. She picked up her knick-knack and paid the rickshaw puller before pushing open the door which had been left ajar. When she stepped inside she was left aghast.

Right across the front yard of the house, a rope had been stretched, about five feet high in the air, tied at two ends to two large nails in the opposite walls. Basanti stood on a small-wooden platform while Ghumri nudged the child to step forward on the rope.

"What are you doing, Amma?" A furious Saanvri lashed at her mother from the doorway where she stopped in a state of shock. Basanti, who had already taken the first step on the rope, retracted it. A startled Ghumri turned around to look at Saanvri, who immediately sprung forward in rage

"Whenever you visit me, you do such things," she lashed out. "I had forbidden you…had told you absolutely clearly…not to teach all these things to my daughter…didn't I?"

"So, what is so wrong in it. If a *nati's* daughter will not learn gymnastics and dancing, who will?" Ghumri tried to stand her ground.

"My daughter will not jump about and perform *khela* and all that on the roads like you. She will go to college, acquire education and become a doctor." Saanvri said confidently.

"Oh, ho." Ghumri responded sarcastically, "Like you have become one."

"How does it matter if I didn't become a doctor. At least I have become a nurse," Saanvri burst out. "If you had your way, you would have dumped me or put me in the *bajaar*, for people to play with."

Though Ghumri was too stunned to say anything for a few moments, soon she gave back.

"Look at this girl's tongue. How she speaks. Family occupation has become dirty, *bajaroo* now."

Turning to Basanti, she said with undiminished sarcasm, "Let it be, *chhori*." She reached out to bring her down and stealing a look at Saanvri she continued, "Your amma has become too big a person."

This incensed Saanvri even more. "I shall become, that too. You'll see…I am not going to be a slipper in anyone's foot. My children and I will sit there," waving her hand high in the air, she screamed, "High, very high…where you can't even imagine."

Ghumri would not to give in yet. She put a finger to her cheek and rolling her face mockingly she taunted. "*Oye hoye*. You go and sit wherever you please, but you are going to remain a *nati* and only a *nati*. Go and write down somewhere what I have said, lest you forget."

"I won't remain a *nati*!" Saanvri screamed aloud and then lashed out savagely, "Saanvri won't dance for anybody; she'll make people dance…" Trembling with anger, she swayed her body in a mock dance, while also moving her finger in a circular motion and said, "Like this… like this…"

The doors to the inside rooms were flung open and Khoobchand, Dhaniya and six-year-old Neelesh burst out into the *aangan*, startled by her hollering. Meanwhile, Saanvri pounced on Basanti and grabbing her arm stormed into her room and slammed the door behind her.

Seven

The long conical *kalgi*, atop the gleaming golden dome of the majestic Chamunda Mata temple, pierced the vast blue cloudless sky like a raised spear in the hand of a charging warrior. Despite being a working day, the enormous courtyard as well as the large hall outside the main sanctum-sanctorum, housing the presiding deity, was full of people. Serpentine queues of devotees, as usual, moved at a snail's pace. Here and there, priests performed smaller rituals for the benefit of engaging the *jajmans* (patrons) in a personalised service.

Away from the milling crowd, Rana Suraj Bhan and his wife Madhvi were led directly into the sanctum-sanctorum through the VIP chamber alongside it. Promptly, one of the young priests—among the three or four, aiding the head priest—who had been nudging the people to move quickly, took charge and helped them perform the brief puja in peace, before handing them again to the escort. Accepting reverential goodbyes from the personnel of the Chamunda Mata Temple Trust, Rana and his wife passed through the VIP waiting room into the courtyard.

Negotiating their way, with great difficulty through the thick congregation of people milling all over, they moved across to the other side to access the stairway. The temple was built atop a plateau with a long flight of steps carrying devotees from the bottom. Rana and his wife climbed down gingerly along with the ant-like queues of people—

one going up and the other going down. Madhvi held the puja thali in her hand, while Suraj Bhan distributed alms to the poor, seated every few feet, on either side of the stairway.

It was even more crowded down at the bottom of the stairs with a cheery atmosphere around the stalls selling puja stuff and mandir related memorabilia on either sides of the pathway. There was no way that their vehicle could have made it up to the stairway through the thronging crowd, hence they had little choice but to walk barefoot all the way to their car, a good distance away. There were long rows of four wheelers and auto rickshaws and oddly parked motorcycles, all along, leaving little space for movement.

Immaculate in his white uniform, the old driver who stood leaning on the big car, rolling tobacco in his palm, with fond ministration of his thumb, sprung into an alert position as soon he noticed Rana and his wife making their way through the pedestrians. He cursed under his breath as he had to let go of the tobacco that he had so lovingly crushed and rolled and was about to toss into his expectant mouth. The frustration was compounded because it was an expensive brand of tobacco. He quickly opened the rear door of the car and swiftly withdrew their footwear, placing them on the pavement, for them to wear. Rana and his wife put on the shoes and boarded the rear seat. The driver promptly and softly closed the door before taking his own seat at the front. The car moved off, with a groaning engine

But they had hardly gone any distance when the engine died on its own. The driver tried to revive it with false starts while still in motion, but to no avail. Exasperated, he stopped the car and got out to check the engine first. A few minutes later, he walked to the rear door and addressed Rana, rather apologetically, who having lowered the window, awaited him with piercing eyes.

"Hukum, I have to go and fetch a mechanic."

"How many times have I told you to check the car properly before taking it out? You don't seem to understand," Rana growled.

"I'll fetch somebody in no time, huzoor." The driver said bowing down, as was the custom.

Rana grunted indifferently. The driver took off and melted into the crowd. Rana got down from the car and slammed the door after him. He stretched himself and then mumbled to his wife. "Do you want a *paan*?"

She declined. He walked across the street to the *paan* shop on the other side.

The car mechanic that Lachhman had spotted at the small roadside workshop, was none else but Khoobchand. His eyes glazed, he was pottering around in his little shop in what seemed a drunken stupor. But Lachhman had little choice. There were no other garages anywhere close by.

The mechanic insisted that he was proficient with any make of car, especially the imported ones. Of course, the old fellow continued to mumble *Hanumaan Chaalisa* under his breath, lest anything went wrong at the hands a country bumpkin.

But as soon as he started working, Lachhman knew that the guy was a genius. A few times back and forth from the dashboard to the bonnet, and another ten minutes of focussed tinkering under the bonnet, the car seemed ready.

"Start it." ordered Khoobchand, coming out from under the bonnet.

"Wha…what?" Lachhman seemed surprised.

"Start it. Turn on the ignition." Khoobchand said coolly.

A little unsure, Lachhman sat in the car. Rana crossed the street and came over by then. With a nervous hand, Lachhman turned on the ignition. Sure enough, the engine purred into life. Lachhman throttled the engine and it roared like a beast.

"Now turn it off and then start again." Khoobchand said confidently.

Lachhman exchanged a quick look with Rana and did as told. Unhesitatingly the engine obliged.

"Hmm…He knows his job well, pretty well, I must say," remarked Rana and then turning to the driver instructed Lachhman to pay him a little extra.

As Rana took a step or two to the rear door, Khoobchand hurriedly followed him with folded hands.

"Hukum, I don't need the money, sarkar...Please give me a job, malik."

"Job...What job can you do?" Rana asked, his hand already on the door handle.

"I can also drive, sarkar; have driven for years. I also have the full license *malik.* You can take a trial, sarkar."

Rana turned to face him properly. His eyes gazed at Khoobchand for a few minutes.

"Alright. Come and see me at the haveli someday." With this he slid inside and shut the door.

"May the world sing your praises, hukum...*bahut bahut jai ho*!"

Providence had done a good turn to Khoobchand by way of this unexpected encounter with Rana. He was immediately assigned to Rani-sa, Madhvi's duties. It did not only entail a good and regular income, it also meant better food while on duty, an occasional gift and a healthy overtime allowance. The only compromise he had to make was foregoing the alcohol, which was a complete no-no on Rani-sa's orders. But the craftiness in him always found a way out.

Saanvri had a late shift at the hospital that night. When she got down from the rickshaw outside her house, in the middle of night, she barely had the strength to pick her bags and move to the door.

"Tomorrow, what time?" The rickshaw puller asked her just as her hand reached the door knob.

"Oh, I completely forgot...It's an early shift again tomorrow. You'll have to be here at 6:30 am, Rehmat," she said apologetically.

"I shall be...but you take good rest, *bhabi*. You look run down," Rehmat said sympathetically.

"I shall be fine, Rehmat *bhaiya*." She smiled and went in. Rehmat also drove away.

Closing the door behind her she moved towards her room. Without turning on the light she put her stuff on the small side table, underneath a half-open window. A shaft of dim light from outside fell on the table through it. She tiptoed up to the bed in the corner of the room and rearranged the sheet over her son and the daughter before bending over and softly pecking them on their cheeks. As she straightened, a fond glow appeared in her tired eyes. She continued to stare at them lovingly, for a while.

She then went to the closed door at the other end of the wall. She adjusted a lock of hair that fell on her face, then softly pushed open the door to the adjacent room. She could hear uneven breathing of someone sleeping in the far end of the dark room. She went up quietly, then bending down at the edge of the bed gently touched the forehead of the person who breathed with a mild groan.

"How are you feeling, Amma?" She tenderly addressed her mother-in-law.

"A little better than before...even slept a bit...off and on." Dhaniya said with a grimace.

"Took the medicine?"

"I will take in a while," Dhaniya mumbled, lowering her eyes guiltily.

Saanvri looked at her with mock reproach and then affectionately stroked her forehead, saying, "I'll give you the dose...You'll have a good sleep and will be better by morning."

She then proceeded to give her a dose from a bottle of cough syrup, placed on a small wooden stool nearby. After settling Dhaniya into a comfortable sleep she came out and pulled the door shut behind her.

She went back to her room wearily. Her hands involuntarily went to her white uniform, unbuttoning it one by one. She disrobed herself mechanically and dropped both the shirt and the long skirt on the bed. She then sat down to remove her shoes and the socks.

After a few ponderous seconds, Saanvri staggered up again, and now wearing only her bra and the slip, she walked stealthily to another corner of the room while unpinning her long hair, which fell around her shoulders. She reached for a large alcove, set deep into the wall, with a mirror in it. She turned on the discreet soft light, set inside the alcove, dimly illuminating her face and the knick-knack for makeup. She put down her hair clips and watch on the small platform of the alcove before giving a few slow turns to her neck to soothe her nerves. Then she stood in front of the mirror and ran her finger on her face slowly and thoughtfully, staring back deep into her tired eyes. She noticed the dark circles under her eyes and her expression turned sad and wooden.

Just then, a sound at the main entrance distracted her and she turned to look. Someone fiddled with the key with unsteady hands and the door opened to reveal a human figure. Irritated, yet anxious she demanded in an admonishing whisper, "So you've come?"

The dim light from the alcove caught Khoobchand laughing stupidly as he took another couple of steps forward. Saanvri, now flushed with anger, reprimanded in a hushed voice, "You have no shame, you burnt mouth. Children are alone, your mother is ill…and you knew that my duty would not get over before late night, yet you went out."

Khoobchand, who had already been swaying on his feet, almost doubled up to the ground, bending down on his feet in pretended remorse. "*Sho-ree, sho-ree, sho-ree,*" he mumbled in false self-reproach with his hands halfway under his partly folded knees.

Being used to his antics, Saanvri reacted with a dismissive smirk. Hearing no further reprimand, Khoobchand straightened again and with a cryptic smile proceeded to search for something in one of his trouser pockets. Dramatically, he withdrew something and playfully advanced towards her, dangling two tantalisingly beautiful chandelier earrings before her.

Now being a young woman that she was, Saanvri's eyes brightened up a little and she asked, "*Jhumke?* For whom, me?"

"No, for Sridevi," he said tongue-in-cheek.

She was stumped for a minute. But as usual, he was quick to better his flattery, "You only are my Sridevi."

"*Chal harami*...trying to flatter me!" She responded with mock reproach. But it had done the trick. She eased out of her surly mood and going for the chandelier-like earrings from his hand she said, "Show."

She turned to the mirror again and began to take off her ordinary *balis* (earrings). Her mood had changed considerably by the time she wore the *jhumkas*. An enticing gleam appeared in her eyes as she took an admiring look at herself in the mirror.

Khoobchand, who had been watching the whole thing with fascination, was now back in his element, as he swayed forward a couple of steps, saying aloud romantically, "*Ha-ye meri dhakdhak*, you are looking both like Sridevi and Madhuri."

The comment had the desired effect. Saanvri responded with a come-hither look, which made him a little more daring. He moved closer and drooling over her, tried to kiss her on the cheek. A big whiff of cheap liquor brought Saanvri back to earth, instantly. She rudely pushed his face away immediately and retorted angrily, "You've been drinking again?"

Khoobchand nodded while laughing stupidly. Saanvri was a different woman all of a sudden.

"Get out of here," she hissed with fury.

Continuing to laugh, Khoobchand tried to humour her.

"Why are you getting angry my sweetheart, I drank only in celebration of these *jhumkas*, *meri* rani." He lurched forward again, trying to embrace her.

"Don't you touch me!" She muttered under her breath, with her eyes blazing.

Khoobchand stopped in his track, frozen by her fiery stare. Not daring to move, he mewled from his place: "But you are my life partner, rani of my heart. If I won't touch you, then who else would I touch?"

"If you come home after drinking, I won't let you enter the house," she threatened uncompromisingly. "Do you understand?"

Khoobchand quickly reverted to his old tactic of abject surrender. He held both his ears in his hands and bent down a little. Then, pretending to be remorseful, he said dramatically: "*So-ree bola na...* It's been a mistake. In future, I won't ever come home drunk." He straightened and continued his tone of appeasement saying, "Is it fine? At least now, let me have the *pappi*." And he again made a go for her.

"Get off, you *harami*." Suddenly enraged, she pushed him off forcefully, "Dare not touch me until you stop drinking." He went off balance for a moment. She was unsparing:

"You have no shame whatsoever...what hard and long hours your wife has to work to save a few paise, so that it helps making a decent life for the children; so that they get educated in a good school...and you come home drunk rather than helping." She stopped for only a few seconds while glaring at him with anger and fumed again:

"When you got a good job at Rana-ji's place, it never occurred to you to request him to get me transferred to a nearby hospital? So much money is wasted on travelling alone, we could have saved a few paise as well as some time in travelling long hours."

Khoobchand lowered his eyes. She fell silent. She continued to stare at him like an adversary. Misunderstanding her silence for truce, he raised his eyes and stupidly took a step closer to speak solicitously.

"Don't be angry...I shall talk to him tomorrow itself." He moved his face towards her mouth and rounding up his lips said, "Come on... now let me have a kiss."

But something had snapped within her. A fuse had gone off. Charging like a lioness, she kicked him with full force on the chest, sending him tumbling out of the door, which was still open. At the same time her fiery voice rang out loud, not bothered of her children and mother-in-law or even the neighbours.

"Get the hell out *madarchod*." Just as his back crashed to the ground, she screamed again on top of her voice, "Don't you speak a word after this." And with that she slammed the door of her room behind him.

EIGHT

Just as the car left the main road to turn into the narrow lane, Madhvi shifted the puja thali to hold it securely with her left hand. With her right hand she picked up the cell phone lying beside her on the seat and dialled a number. On hearing the voice on the other side, she merely mumbled, "We are here," and then dropped the instrument into her open bag, which lay on the seat. The car had barely traversed the small and almost empty street to the T-junction that two huge flanks of an imposing gate opened up as if on their own.

The red Honda Accord slipped in and went into the large yard, stopping not far from Rana's white Mercedes that stood in readiness, close to the inner door of the haveli. Khoobchand, attired in a driver's uniform, swiftly got out to open the rear door to help Madhvi alight. He was no longer the clumsy and languorous person that he was in his drunken state but alert and strident in his demeanour as he held the door open for her to step out. She carefully balanced the thali containing the puja paraphernalia in her right hand. When she was about to move, he pleaded with folded hands:

"Rani-sa…hukum."

"Yes, Khoobchand," she stopped and turned to him.

He bowed down a bit and pointing at the white Mercedes from his eyes said with great regard.

"It appears that Bade-sarkar is just about to leave. If you could please recommend my matter once."

"Let me see what I can do. Will do something," she said emphatically and moved off.

She reached the door already held open by the sentry for Rana, who was coming down the short corridor. Just as he stepped out, she addressed him: "Khooba was again begging for the same thing while returning from the temple. Can you not please do something for his wife's transfer and get him off my back?"

Rana gave her a long look and then his eyes fleetingly ran across Khoobchand before he addressed Madhvi, "Let me see. I'll try and do something."

As he walked towards his car his eyes casually went to Khoobchand, a good distance away. Khoobchand immediately responded with an exaggerated motion of bowing down with folded hands. Before entering his car Rana stopped abruptly at the door, held open for him by Lachhman, and summoned Khoobchand with his finger, who scurried up to him.

"Malik," Khoobchand huffed subserviently with folded hands.

"Tell your wife to come and meet me in my office tomorrow. Ask her to bring along her application, her certificates and a couple of photographs."

"Yes, malik. So very kind of you, malik," Khoobchand bent down again with folded hands.

Rana did not say anything more. He moved towards the camel in the corner of the compound, leaving Lachhman holding the door of the car open.

Mohak Chand Jhaveri & Sons, one of the oldest jewellers of Jodhpur, had an imposing showroom in the Tripolia Bazar on Nai Sarak. The next day, as Rana's car travelled down the main street after arduously negotiating the dense melange of vehicles, push-carts and a stream of people, halfway through it turned into a narrow side lane. Skilfully manoeuvring through the chaotic stream of hawkers, shoppers, office workers, badly parked cars, vans and cows, blocking the road, the driver went around to the back of a building, into an even a narrower lane.

Rana alighted and pressed a tiny doorbell, built into the door-frame of an inscrutable small door of an old building. As he took a step away, unknown to him, a miniature camera fashioned into the eyepiece of the door relayed his image on a monitor in the security room of the building. Within seconds, there was a sound of footsteps climbing down the stairs. A turbaned security man opened the door and led him up a narrow stairway covered with a jute carpet. A short flight of steps delivered him to a different world altogether. It was an expensively carpeted broad corridor with wooden doors on both sides, interspersed with well-upholstered modern couches for visitors. He was led to a small lift.

On the top floor of the building, a beautiful girl in her mid-twenties, dressed like a princess of yore, waited for him. She greeted him in clipped English and led him into a room at the other end of an even broader and far more expensively furnished corridor. It was a large, tastefully done up office with modern trappings and two sets of expensive sofas in different corners, beside a medium-size mahogany desk along one of the walls. A short and slightly plump man of nearly Rana's age, dressed in a perfectly fitted suit and tie, was seated behind the desk. He almost jumped up and hurried towards Rana as he stepped inside the room. He clasped Rana's hand even before it was extended. The younger man ducked and bending to touch Rana's feet greeted him.

"Pranam hukum...*Padhariye*, sir."

"Hello Ramnik, how are things?" Rana patted him on the arm.

"Fine, hukum, absolutely fine! Come, sir...Please sit," he said, ushering him to the visitor's chair. "What will you have, hukum?"

"No, Ramnik, I don't have the time today. There is a very busy day ahead. I would rather just have a look at the piece and leave." Rana pushed back the chair pulled out by Ramnik, reached the inside pocket of his Nehru jacket and brought out a packet wrapped in plastic and proffered to Ramnik.

"These are two lakhs for now…rest after the setting. Fine?"

"There was no hurry for that, hukum," said Ramnik, even as he took the packet. "You have a look at the beauty first, be absolutely satisfied, then only we should go for the setting." With this he swiftly went behind his desk again.

He bent down to open a side drawer of his desk and picked up a manila envelope. He straightened and withdrew from inside a small cloth bag, fastened with cotton drawstrings at the mouth. He put it down on the desk and undid the knot to gently stretch open the constricted mouth with his pudgy fingers. Rana leaned forward as Ramnik produced an egg-size rock, which sat in the cushion of his flashy palm, emanating bright glittering rays from all sides. Bitten by its paralysing beauty, for a moment, Rana froze in his place. Ramnik, who had read Rana's immobile stare, said:

"Hukum, you take it today just as it is, show it to the lady." His eyes betrayed a smack of a secret that he shared with his client, as he proposed, "We can get it set easily, with total love and care, later."

"But then…" The spell was broken for Rana.

"Take it, Rana-ji, carry it with you today. We won't take too much time after that, I promise, sir."

"Are you sure, I haven't even paid you fully yet."

"Money is not running away anywhere, Rana-ji. I still have to do the setting and all that, so don't worry about that. Keep it with you a few days; show it to the lady or any one closer to you. We shall then get on with the job, nice and proper," Ramnik was insistent.

"Fine then. I shall bring it back soon."

"Fine, hukum. I'll have it put in a nice box."

Minutes later, as his car was travelling down the Sardarpura Main road, Rana was already fantasising the promise of a carnally vibrant moment in the sensual arms of the intended beneficiary of the expensive rock. The heat in his loins persisted till his car left the busy road to enter the compound of his imposing, multistoreyed, glass-panelled commercial complex and came to a halt in its fore court. A cryptic smile sat on his lips as the attendant security-man opened the door for him. There was a bit of a spring in his feet as he climbed the steps to enter the reception lobby.

In his personal office-chamber on the top floor of the modern building, as usual, the first thing he did was to light the *agarbatti* (joss stick) on the bracket below the framed picture of Durga, on one of the walls of the large room. He had barely finished the chore and was pushing his feet back in his designer shoes, that there was a gentle tap on the door. His secretary, a middle-aged man of nearly his age, wearing a broad smile, entered on being beckoned.

"Good morning, hukum. Hope everything is fine sir?"

"Of course, it is. Who all are there?" Rana asked, descending into his chair.

"There are only three or four party workers, hukum. Then there is a woman…someone called Saanvri. Khoobchand has sent her. She's been waiting for quite a while."

"Okay Gupta-ji, you send this woman first. We'll clear her quickly." Rana said indifferently.

"That's fine, sir."

Rana took out his cell phone and placed it on the table. He had hardly stretched back in his chair to brace himself for the long and futile exercise of meeting the party workers, that the cell phone started ringing. He picked it up with a frown on his face. But having recognised the phone number, his eyes lit up.

"Hello, hello Munni-jaan, what's up? How come, you remembered *us* so early in the morning?" He said playfully, using second person plural 'us' for 'me' as royals do.

In a tastefully furnished spacious bedroom of an upscale apartment, an attractive young woman in her mid-thirties reached for the regulator of the ceiling fan and turning it to high speed, she said feigning a complaining tone: "Now, if you won't remember *us*, that doesn't mean we won't remember you either," she mimicked Rana.

The woman, who was attired in a tracksuit, unzipped her top with her free hand and lowered herself on the large bed while unpeeling the garment off her body. She was bathed in sweat and purred with a welcoming sigh as the gust from the fan hit her.

"*Aaye-haye*. Even while complaining you have that seductiveness," Rana teased her. "How come your majesty is breathing so hard?"

Balancing her cell phone between her shoulder and the ear, she reached back with both her hands to unhook her bra and tossed it aside before reclining back on the backrest. With her sweat smothered fulsome breasts freed of any clothing, she spoke with a touch of seductive playfulness: "Was on the treadmill. It's been a bit too much today. Am underneath the fan right now, drying up the sweat."

"*Aye haye-haye-haye, seena aur paseena*; is it all uncovered?" Rana teased further.

"How else will I dry up?"

"*Haye-e-e*," he made a mischievous sound as if he had been impaled by something piercing and then said in a lusty voice, "Shall *we* come over to dry up the sweat?"

"As if you will come? You just say such things. " Her tone was even more complaining and seductive.

"This time when *we* come, *we* shall come with your thing. It is already with *us*," he said mysteriously.

"But when?"

"Just wait another couple of days or so, *janeman*. *We* have purchased it already this morning, but one has to get it set also. After all, the diamond has to heighten the glory of your beautiful neck."

"You've bought it? *Hai* Allah," she said excitedly. "How does it look?"

"This will depend on the placement, *meri-jaan*, as to where it rests in the valley below your neck."

Munni's hand went to her naked breasts in an instant involuntary reaction to cover them, as though from an unwarranted onlooker ogling at her.

"*Haye-e-e*! How much you trouble me." She feigned unease and said in even more of a complaining tone, "You put me in so much discomfort…honestly."

"*Lo*. And what about *us*?" he too adopted a complaining tone and said. "Howsoever tight we may tie the string in the trouser, the tent still rises up."

"*Hatiye*," she beseeched him teasingly, "Don't be naughty. Let's talk about the diamond."

Rana laughed with abandon and reached into the pocket of his blazing white starched kurta and withdrew a small box. He opened it carefully with the same hand without putting down the cell phone and fondly picked up the large rock. He held it between his thumb and the index finger and turned to the open window in the side wall some distance away.

"Gosh, what an exquisite piece. You'll be bewildered, Munni-jaan when it sits around your neck," he said, gazing at it. Once again a lustful film spread in his eyes as he continued, "Absolutely unblemished. What superb cutting. Each image through it looks so perfect that you cannot say which one was real and which was unreal."

Lost in admiring its beauty, he revolved back on his chair to once again face the open space in front of his desk, towards the entrance door, while still holding the diamond high in his hand, between his index figure and the thumb. But as his field of vision reached the space around the door, he was entranced by a new image. A captivating figure of a woman and her shimmering illusions materialised through multiple surfaces of the diamond. Astounded by the bewitching intrusion, he abruptly brought down his hand and found himself face to face with Saanvri.

Time stood still for a second or two. Saanvri's hands went up hesitantly. She folded them respectfully and mumbled, "Pranam."

She looked quite lost though extremely desirable in a figure hugging white salwar-kameez and a matching orange transparent cotton dupatta. The red bindi on her forehead made her look disarmingly simple, yet mysteriously awesome. Rana was so mesmerised for a moment by her beguiling beauty that he did not even offer any response to her greeting. Instead, he urgently murmured into his cell, "I'll call you little later… Somebody is here…Ah…I mean someone has come in just now." He quickly turned off the cell phone and put it down on the table.

Unable to make out anything of his reaction, Saanvri brought down her hands and lowered her eyes. Rana, still flabbergasted, gawped at Saanvri, who with her long hair, partly falling over her well-endowed front, looked ravishing and sexy in a very earthy way, even though she was not inappropriately dressed. She herself broke the spell as she raised her eyes again and said apologetically, "I am Khoobchand's *lugai*, sahab. Rani-sa had spoken with you."

"Yes, yes. She had spoken, she had spoken. You have brought your application and the certificates, haven't you?" He said regaining his composure.

She nodded. Rana stared deep into her eyes as if for an eternal moment, with a look that was at once probing yet communicative—communicative of what had stirred inside him—before shifting his eyes to the intercom. With a slight uncertain movement his hand reached the button and pressed it.

"*Ji*, sir?" Mr Gupta's voice rang out through it.

"Will you put me through to Kaushik-sahab, in the Family Welfare Ministry?" he said in an officious tone.

"Yes, sir."

In no time the call was put through. The predator in him had gone into overdrive. It searched for ways to extend her presence in his office. But before he could engineer anything, he was outmanoeuvred by the unexpected efficiency of his secretary to attend the mandatory meetings with the waiting party workers. He had to let her go after taking her papers and assuring her that she would soon hear from the ministry. But, surely, she was not going to vacate the space in his mind in a hurry.

And surely, what was in his mind had not remained quite unread by her, either. Having risen from the ranks through sheer hard work, she had developed that acute sense that enables an alert woman to see through a man even when he may have not been overtly expressive about his intentions. But strangely though, for the first time she did not feel the indignation that usually rose in her when she sensed any amorous vibes emanating from a man.

Barely three weeks later, when she received the desired transfer order for her placement in a neighbourhood hospital, Saanvri immediately agreed to Khoobchand's suggestion that she herself should go to present a box of sweets to Rana-ji. She even became amenable to his insistent persuasion that she dress up in the glamorous *joda* he had bought for her as a bridal gift years ago, which she had never worn except once for his friend's wedding. Khoobchand prevailed upon her in the face of her reluctance to wear such a low-cut kurta in the presence of the many men she would have to face during her visit to Rana's office. She could not be sure if it was Khoobchand's glib spiel of how being "modern" was appreciated at such places, or something else brewing within her that made her surrender at last.

Alighting from the auto-rickshaw as she crossed the lobby of Rana's office building, she was acutely conscious of the sly gazes of the people milling about, some of whom were even audacious enough to turn back and stare. She darted into the first available lift and quickly pressed the button. By the time the car reached the seventh floor, she had composed herself remarkably.

As the doors slid open noiselessly on the posh top floor, Saanvri, the sole occupant, leaning on the rear wall of the car, stirred from her place. She was now a different person. Attired in a deep red silken salwar-kurta with a broad and low cut neck, she brandished blatant sexuality. The thin gold dupatta in sheer material was insufficient to hide the swell of her breasts that were enhanced further because of the tightness of the kurta, which was a size too small now.

With the first step out of the sliding door of the car, her gait had changed. She raised her right hand, which held the parcel of sweets, right up to her chest, pressing it slightly on her defiant breasts like a shield. But to her consternation, she could still feel them bounce because of her wired bra, as she balanced herself on the high heels she had worn.

However, within a couple of seconds, she had composed herself sufficiently and now her eyes were beaming while a bewitching smile appeared on her lips as she walked through the corridor in between the work spaces. Her walk had acquired a cool panther-like quality, indifferent to the gawking faces stealing glances at her, as she, almost with practiced ease, turned corners from one short corridor to another, till she reached the desk of Rana's secretary.

"I've brought these sweets. I had called you earlier," she said, raising the parcel higher in front of her chest.

Mr Gupta looked up. His eyes scanned her up and down in a quick glance and spoke with an officious reserve.

"You can go in," he said, pointing at the door to Rana's chamber. "I have informed sahab already."

Saanvri looked at him ingratiatingly and walked to the door. After a soft knock, she entered. Suddenly, she was gripped by a sense of panic as she stepped inside. With the hydraulic door having automatically closed behind her, she felt uncertain about her entire bearing, especially the dress, in the face of the oppressively vast and formal setting of the office. Rana stood by the window on one side, immersed in a call on his cell phone. His back was turned towards her as he conversed while looking out at the cityscape below.

Self-conscious and nervous she made no attempt to move from her place or utter a sound. Rana concluded his call and turned. Immediately, the box of sweets went even higher in front of her chest, as if in self-defence. Rana's eyes lit up. He moved towards the table while acknowledging Saanvri enthusiastically.

"Oh, Saanvri! Come, come."

A confused Saanvri moved from the door and went straight for his feet. As she swiftly bend down to touch them, Rana too put his right hand on her head in an act of blessing.

"*Khush raho, khush raho*. So you got what you wanted?"

Saanvri straightened up and said gratefully with mild excitement, "Yes, hukum. All because of your blessings. I have already received my transfer orders." She quickly proffered the box of sweets to him, "This is for you, hukum."

"Oh ho! You've brought sweets? Then, what are you waiting for. Come on, open it."

Saanvri quickly went about opening the box. As she did so, Rana's eyes travelled to her slightly undulating breasts, which had now lost their cover. For a moment, he was caught unawares, as Saanvri enthusiastically extended the box towards him. He quickly raised his eyes and picked up a sweet and took it to her mouth.

"First, you take one."

Though slightly embarrassed, she opened her mouth. He put the sweet in and then softly patted on her cheek, in a gesture that was at once patronising as well as personal. Covering her mouth partially with her free hand, she shyly munched on it for a couple of moments, before proffering the box to him again.

"Now, you too have hukum. It is you who got it done for me."

He did not take the box, but picked up a very small piece. Even from that he took only a small bite, saying, "Good, it's very good." He held out the rest towards her, going for her mouth. "Have the rest. Open your mouth. Come on."

"What are you doing, hukum. As it is you've hardly taken any." she tried to dodge his hand.

But he grabbed her arm to restrain her, insisting, "Open. Open your mouth." She relented and he pushed the piece through her parted lips before continuing, "I'm not allowed, you see. You should eat. You are young and beautiful. You'll do more justice to such rich sweets. I'm after all a man of advanced age, forbidden to eat so many good things in life."

Saanvri was perplexed. By forcing in her mouth that piece of sweet, which had been partly eaten by him, Rana had breached the air of formality and protocol so unexpectedly that she did not quite know how to react. He had established an uneasy familiarity that could be saying a lot, and yet it could be misconstrued easily. After a moment of uncertainty, she slowly began to chew over the piece.

He moved around his desk to sink into his leather bound swivel chair. Just as he lowered himself in it, he said, almost as an afterthought.

"Oh yes, I could benefit from your visit, couldn't I? You could check my blood pressure, right? I won't have to go to the doctor from now. What do you say?"

"Yes, I could do it, but," she said with a slight reserve after a moment's hesitation, being unable to fathom the situation. "Where is the blood-pressure gauge? Mine is in the hospital."

"That's not a problem. We shall have it fetched right now," he said. "There's a chemist's shop, down in the market."

He straight away went for his intercom. Just as his PA answered, he injected sufficient informality in his tone as he spoke:

"Yes Gupta-ji, *arre bhai*, please get a blood-pressure gauge from the chemist below. It would be a gift for madam from our side and, and she'll oblige us by checking my blood pressure with the same." He replaced the receiver even before Mr Gupta could acknowledge his instruction.

Then he turned to Saanvri to say with a meaningful twitch in his eyes. "But there is one condition, that...that you'll come over to check my blood pressure, whenever the need arises."

She too held his eyes, which gazed deeply in hers, before a tiny smile appeared on her lips and she lowered them, nodding in assent.

"Now, what about some tea?" He said even more effusively and once again he reached for the intercom.

But Rana was a wily hunter. He entreated her with disarming foxiness, to slowly and slyly engineer the lowering of her defences, rather than pouncing upon her like an animal on a prey. He surprised her with his civility and classiness. Right through the tea, he engaged her as a VIP. With impeccable finesse he stirred sugar for her in a bone-china cup, before pouring for himself, and steered an unhurried, yet sufficiently intimate, conversation between the two.

In twenty minutes or so, he had gotten enough information about the severe glitches in her marriage. He had also let out in right measure and right refrain the disquieting and despairing elements in his own, which many men cleverly invent to seek out empathy from gullible females.

Ready with the machine to check his blood pressure, Saanvri asked Rana to shift to the couch. Sharing the same space with him, as he rested on the couch with his hand around a large cushion positioned by an armrest, a level of easy familiarity had already been reached between the two. Unlike a professional nurse, her touch, with her nimble fingers, was that of a caring friend and they shared a tease here and there about matters of health.

After wrapping his arm with the cuff, as she put the earpieces of the stethoscope in her ears and proceeded to pump the air, a habitual solemnness descended automatically on her face, making it dignified and even more attractive. Her eyes, of course, were fixed on the rise of mercury in the column, but his were, instead, focused on the enticing swell of her breasts, which were now in clear line of view, with her dupatta having risen high up to her neck due to the movement of her arms. Unknown to her, a latent desire betrayed his eyes, as he gazed unashamedly at the unsettling gorge between her large breasts. Happy with the reading, she bled the air from the balloon and with a broad smile, reaching for the earpieces, said, "Everything is fine. It's absolutely normal."

But just as she removed the earpieces from her ears, Rana reached out and grabbed them from her hands. Ignoring her look of bewilderment, he put them in his ears. Then, he picked up the round chestpiece. For a moment he seemed to play with it idly while she watched him somewhat curiously. Suddenly, there was a spark of mischief in his eyes and leaving her astonished, he put the chest piece on her bulging left breast. A gasp escaped her mouth.

"It's beating…beating fast…" he said softly, yet meaningfully.

Her mouth remained open even as her shocked eyes were arrested by his sparkling ones. Moments passed. Her mouth closed slowly, but eyes remained lost in his. Written in them were many stories, many promises, many adventures. They both knew that they were going to read them together. An electric wave travelled between the two.

The spell was broken as he took her right hand in his and slowly brought it to his lips. After another deep gaze in her eyes, he put a tender kiss on its fingers.

"Gone cold, so suddenly." He seemed surprised and then said reassuringly, "Don't you worry even slightly, won't let you be in any trouble whatsoever."

And then, he surprised her yet again. Without letting go of her hand, he helped her rise from the couch before getting up himself. His actions were chaste without the slightest perfidy that could be sexually suggestive.

"How will you go back?" he asked as he rose up.

"I'm sure there would be some rickshaw on the street."

For a second he considered her reply with a benign smile, before he walked across to his desk. Reaching behind it he picked up the intercom again. His secretary's voice crackled.

"*Arre bhai*, Gupta-ji, please ask Lachhman to drop Saanvri-ji at home. She has waited so long to do my check-up. Where will the poor lady find a rickshaw." He was casual yet gracious, without any trace of condescension.

Saanvri was not quite herself when she travelled back in Rana's car. Suddenly, many wires had been touched inside her, but none had short-circuited. She was not overwhelmed...at least, not yet. With her thoughts all jumbled up, she reclined on the back seat of the car and shut her eyes.

The strange state of disorientation lasted all evening. Nobody was at home when she arrived. Her children back from school had gone to play in the neighbourhood. Having fully recovered, Dhaniya had already returned to Phool-Birai, to rejoin her duty. Even so, for a good length of time, without changing her clothes, Saanvri remained seated on Dhaniya's cot. Perhaps sub-consciously, though absolutely unintentionally, in her state of turmoil she hoped to gain a subliminal anchorage from the notional presence of her mother-in-law even though she was physically absent.

Later on, even with all the rejoicing and merrymaking initiated by Khoobchand, she had not quite succeeded in shrugging off the uneasiness that had seeped into her. His hopes were also belied when in the middle of the night he tried to make a foray into her bed. Now that she was happy with the new job and since he had refrained from drinking, he had hoped that she would be generous enough to let him have a long-denied release of his carnal needs.

The disquiet in her mind tapered off in a couple of days in the face of vigorous activity related with the formalities of leaving the present hospital and joining the new one; familiarising herself with the fresh environment. Strangely, what had caused anxiety to her moral equilibrium was exactly what she began to miss within a week of undisturbed routine. So when the call came some ten days later, she was somewhat a willing conspirator in challenging the placidity of her emotions.

The car took her to a newly built, high-rise building off Pali Road. She had never entered such a posh residential block before. The flower beds along the small driveway, the gleaming lobby, the swift lift and a luxurious apartment on the twelfth floor; was like a dream to her. She felt both a sense of awe and a tinge of jealousy in her heart. For the first time, a repressed sense of longing began to stir within her. She found Rana, dressed in a casual cotton trouser and a collarless designer T-shirt, seated alone at the small bar in a corner of the sitting room. The driver of the car, who had ushered her in, put down her bag along with the blood-pressure monitor and the stethoscope on a side table by the sofas and left. An office-assistant type of a young lad who had opened the door for them also excused himself.

Rana rose up from the stool leaving his glass of wine and approached her enthusiastically.

"Come, come Saanvri. *Kaisee hai?*"

"*Tharo aashirvaad*, Bado-hukum," she said submissively reaching out to touch his feet.

But Rana quickly stopped her midway. Taking her in a bear hug he said generously, "*Jeete raho*."

He pressed her against his body and then gave a peck on the cheek with great familiarity before releasing her, but still held on to her hands in his.

"What is it, why are your hands so cold? Was the A/C too high in the car?"

"No, no. It was alright, there is nothing to it," she tried to make light of the situation, looking suddenly nervous and self-conscious. "It happens to me sometimes...blood pressure plays up a bit...please take no notice." She sounded flustered.

"Blood pressure? Is it that I shall have to check your blood pressure first? But you'll have to teach me, I haven't checked anybody before and certainly not anyone as pretty as you," he said in a tongue-in-cheek tone.

Both burst into laughter. The atmosphere having turned light, he led her to the sofas.

"Come now, sit and relax."

"But, your check-up?"

"Yes, yes that'll also happen. You relax first." He almost pushed her on to the settee and then lowering himself on the one opposite her, he asked, "Tell me, what would you have?"

"A glass of water will do."

"Now that's a difficult one. For that I'll have to travel up to the kitchen and fetch it from the fridge, whereas the wine is right here on the bar," he said mischievously, pointing at the bar nearby.

"Why will you do it hukum, I'll help myself." She leapt up to her feet. "Which way is the kitchen?"

"There, through that corridor, from where you entered, near the main door," he said pointing in that direction.

"I'll just come," Saanvri said and went to the kitchen.

In a couple of minutes, she reappeared with a glass of water placed on a small tray and went up to Rana.

"Will you have some, hukum?" Bending down a little near his sofa, she offered it to him. Fascinated by her domesticity, he took the glass.

"Now that you've brought it with such feeling, I might as well take some," he said reaching for the glass.

"Are there no servants here? You live here too, hukum?" She looked around curiously.

He emptied half the glass and then got up, saying, "This is not my apartment…belongs to a friend." He then walked up to the bar a little uncertainly to put the glass on the counter rather than on the coffee table, which was nearer, and said, "I only come here sometimes; whenever I feel like being by myself."

She watched him with an amused look while still holding the tray in her hands. As he approached her now, his eyes had a glint in them.

"Now, first of all put this tray down here." He took the tray from her hands and placed on the coffee table while continuing, "You look like a waitress, waiting to take an order." Then, looking at her face curiously, he considered her for a moment before reaching out his hands to her head, "And now remove this nurses' head gear…makes me feel like I am in a hospital."

She gave a broad, agreeable grin and her hands went to her head, immediately, to unpin the cap. He helped her take it off and put it on the coffee table. As he straightened, he found that she had also shrugged her hair loose, which then cascaded down to her waist. He was stricken by the earthiness of her beauty.

"What beautiful long hair. Do you realise how arresting you look?"

She melted with shyness and lowered her head. He reached out to caress her tresses.

"Silken and sensuous," he slowly passed a clutch of her hair over his face as if to seek some kind of intoxication. "Smells so good too." He let her hair go and instead, pulled her closer to him, to fall into his easy embrace. Brushing his lips over her temple, he murmured mischievously, "Which shampoo do you use to make one so dizzy?"

"What shampoo, hukum? I can't afford shampoos. I use only *desi reetha* to wash my hair." She was humble, yet teasing.

His arm continued to hold her close as his lips caressed the side of her eyebrow, the forehead and her ear before kissing her hair on the head. Just as the proximity was beginning to send her into raptures of excitement, he released her and said in a matter-of-fact way:

"Let me get you some wine first. Which one, red or white?"

"But I don't drink…never had any liquor in my life!"

"Wine is not a drink…have a little." He turned towards the bar.

"Hukum, honest," she touched her neck with her two fingers as a gesture of swearing. "I'll pass out for sure."

Rana turned around again and said persuasively, "*Arre*, don't talk like a fool. Nothing will happen to you, I promise. It's not liquor like whiskey, rum or gin. It's more like a relaxant, you'll feel good. And I am not asking you to take the whole bottle. Just try a couple of drops and then tell me." He once again turned to go to the bar.

"But what about your blood pressure, hukum? Let me first check that at least," she said plaintively.

"Oh *yaar*; alright," he stopped abruptly midway and turned all over again saying, "Let's do that first, if you insist."

"It'll be better if you recline some place. Where?" She said even as she reached for the case containing the blood pressure gauge.

"Well either here on the settee or may be on the bed inside, which of course would be more comfortable; what do you say?" The question in his eyes had a stoic calmness despite the underlying potent mysteries it held.

Saanvri, who had already stood up facing him by now, remained still for a long time with her equally calm eyes arrested in his, before she uttered softly, "Wherever."

Strange, how a word that merely denoted another location in the same overall space could have such an intense effect in the given context or circumstance—the word was "bedroom".

Gripped by sudden self-consciousness, they moved silently to the bedroom. Like any patient, Rana lay down on the bed, partly supported by the backrest. Saanvri was again taken by surprise. She was amazed at Rana's instant capacity to shift gears. While the environment was heavy with wild anticipation, he was behaving completely out of character as he did during the check-up. Not a twitch out of turn. He could well have been on a bed in the ICU of a hospital.

Even Saanvri acted with remarkable dexterity and professional placidity, despite feeling weak inside. It was only when, just as before, she started removing her earpieces of the stethoscope that he made the first move.

"Will you do that again?" He sounded enticingly mysterious.

"What?" she gaped at him.

"What you just did!"

"You mean take your blood pressure again?"

"No, not the whole thing; just the last bit. I mean taking off the earpieces bit and whatever you said with that."

"What did I say?"

"Whatever. Just enact it again. Please." He said persuasively.

She looked very confused and put on the earpieces again.

"Like this?" she had an amused look on her face.

"Hmm. Go on."

A brightness appeared in her eyes as though to enjoy the act, and after exchanging an agreeable nod with him, she proceeded to once again remove the earpieces and said with a smile, "Absolutely fit. Completely normal."

"*Hai mar dala*," he exclaimed.

She went red on the face, having noticed the mischief in his eyes. He continued with the tease, "Now I know why your patients are so fond of you."

Anticipating more leg pulling, a questioning look appeared in her eyes. He sat up straight and held her arm before slowly pulling her closer and saying, "The fault lies with your lips."

She looked bewildered. He leaned forward while pulling her yet again to a dangerous proximity and whispering, "The smile that you bring to these lips; nobody has any chance."

Before she could react any which way, his lips were pressed on hers. The moment had in one go undone the equilibrium and redefined everything. Yet, it was a moment that was neither completely unanticipated nor resented for its audacity. Nevertheless, for her, total stillness was the best alternative, lest she unwittingly triggered something beyond her. Slowly the numbness of the moment began to give way to life. His lips first moved just tentatively; up and down, sideways, and even tender pecks once or twice, while he mumbled: "Soft and luscious, like rose petals."

As her nose began to emit slow and small bursts of heat, his lips moved upwards. He kissed her nostrils, the bridge of her nose, pecked her softly on her closed eyelids, her forehead and her temples before returning to her lips again, which had by now parted slightly with gasps of desire escaping of their own.

Slowly, they let go of their restraint. He claimed her lips aggressively, sucking on them with abandon. And her lips were not far behind either. They retaliated with equal ferocity, grabbing his lips, even biting them now and then. It was a duel which she had not started and the response was not consciously engineered either. Their tongues charged savagely like lances into each other's mouth, searching, attacking, entwining.

A sudden slapping sound diverted their attention. The lid of the blood-pressure gauge had snapped shut. The physical excesses of the two bouncing bodies on the soft mattress had unlocked its lever. The unexpected interruption had stopped them in their tracks. Shocked, they looked at the appliance. Then realising what had happened, they burst into a laughter.

Saanvri immediately got busy in packing her equipment in her bag with all the seriousness of a professional. But as she rose up and turned around to move with the bag in her hand, she once again found herself face to face with Rana, in touching distance.

She looked up slowly to meet his eyes which gazed into hers, emitting unsettling sparks. Slowly and without shifting his eyes, he took the case from her hands and dropped it to the ground. He put his hands on her shoulders, without letting go of her eyes. Then he slowly turned her around and brought down his arms to slide up from both sides of her waist, locking her in a hug from behind.

His lips went to work again. Hot with passion they triggered sparks wherever they touched her skin. He gently pushed aside the cascade of hair and kissed her on the nape, on the temple, on the ridge behind her ear, his tongue probing inside the lobes. Then his lips slid across the side of her face, pecking on her cheek before straying to the edge of her gasping mouth, which turned towards him on its own as if to ensnare him for more. They did not stop. With electrifying caresses they brushed her partly open lips only to inflame them and then moved down to grip her chin. They continued their journey down her neck, tingling with expectation, till they rested at the bridge of her collar bones.

His hands now moved upwards, undid the buttons of her uniform and then slid it off her shoulders and dropped it on the ground. His fingers caressed the edge of her slip over her breasts before moving to its straps resting on her shoulders and sliding them down. Still holding her from behind, he eased her out of the slip. He kissed her shapely shoulders, sending a shiver through her body. He helped her out of the pile of clothes at her feet and gently led her to the dressing mirror close by.

Now dressed only in her undergarments, she looked irresistibly seductive. His rebellious organ shot up on its own and prodded threateningly between the cheeks of her buttocks. His hands were not done yet. His fingers skilfully unhooked her bra from behind, before nimbly sliding off the straps from her shoulders. Desire danced unashamedly in the reflections of the eyes of both just as his hands held her tantalizing breasts, fondled them gently before tenderly tweaking her nipples. That did it.

Retaliating with fury, she swung around and went at his clothes with rising urgency. Holding its hem with both her hands, she yanked his T-shirt over his head and raised hands, in one sweep. Her lips grazed the hairy span of his broad chest, clung to it as if to seek succour, before beginning to suckle his bead-like nipples. A repressed groan escaped his clenched teeth as he seethed with desire. His fingers trembling, fumbled with the belt of his trouser. She beat him to it. With fiery eyes, she unclasped it before quickly unbuttoning and unzipping his trouser.

With equal frenzy he was shorn of everything. After a moment's uncertainty, just as his organ sprung up threateningly, she fell on her knees as if to pacify it, kissing it repeatedly and finally enveloping it inside her hungry mouth. But the wetness of her mouth aroused him more, fuelling his passions further. Groaning, he looked down disbelievingly with glazed eyes, at the unsparing ministrations on his entrenched weapon. In a claw-like steely grip, fingers of his hands clasped her tresses before pulling her head away with a loud and admonishing groan, rising from deep inside his gullet. She looked up like a fiend with matching fire in her eyes. As they both stared at each other amid wondrous gasps, their eyes melted into a strange tranquillity.

Slowly he helped her stand up and led her to the bed. He sat down at its edge and positioned her to stand close, facing him. His hands, once again amazingly soft and tender, rose to hold her fulsome breasts. He fondled them tenderly and drank passion from her bulbous nipples, before surrendering his face into the deep valley between the heaving hills. She too put her arms around his head protectively.

Like the changing notes of a symphony, when he raised his head his eyes illuminated with a longing of a different kind, deeper and soulful. She leaned forward and claimed his lips, engulfing them in her mouth and probing with her tongue with no less passion but much less belligerence. He responded equally ardently. His hands traversed down to reach her panty and slowly relieved her of it. But his mouth was hungry. It went to the humid furriness between the summits of her thighs and drank on its musk, even licking at the flashy wetness of the crack.

The sensation was unbearable for her. She writhed in pain, at once excruciating, yet sweet, which was evident with her thighs breaking into mild tremors now and then. His body ached with desire too. The moment had come. He rose to it. Lifting her up in a smooth and swift motion he put her on the bed, like a devotee placing an offering on the altar for prayers. He then climbed in and for a moment sat on his knees admiring her bewitching nudity before climbing astride her.

Though at first it was only tentative, she felt scorched right through as soon as his organ touched the rim of hers. It was cruel too, as it made no attempt to enter what it had come to conquer, just sashayed arrogantly and ignited a million fires. All the pores of her folds opened up, emitting a flow of secretions as if to douse the uncontainable flames left in its wake. And when it entered the mysterious cave, it was a heavenly sail; at once searing, yet fulfilling. Her walls immediately closed around it, seizing it to a warm embrace. But it had other intentions and retreated to the mouth, teasing once again. Then, just as she eased her clench, it came again, and again. But only in a slow trot, a kind of initial fine tuning of a musical instrument, which has to get to vibrant notes soon.

The charge did not come uninvited. With her arms pinned down on the sides with his steely hands, the slow fire that he had initiated soon became unbearable with each of his gradually intensifying thrusts and relentless suckling of her nipples, inflaming her to a gurgling scream.

"Take me, take me, please take me hard," she begged.

And he obliged. The pounding that began was unrelenting. A steadily building crescendo resulted in a volcanic eruption in both, within a split-second of each other, its tremors lasting till eternity. They lay entwined; spent and feeble, also at the same time completely satiated, before he slid off and settled contentedly beside her. Soon sleep took over them.

When Rana woke up after some time, he did not find her beside him. His concern grew as he could not find her pile of clothes on the floor, where they were left, either. He quickly put on his underpants and trousers and hurried out of the bedroom, wondering if she left without saying goodbye.

He felt a sense of relief seeing her leaning back on the frame of the French window connected to a broad balcony, overlooking a stretch of green and the lake. Dressed only in her undergarments and a slip, she looked sensuously ethereal with her face turned away, admiring the light drizzle outside. The dim daylight, partly illuminating her shadowy figure at the far end of the large sitting room, presented a very captivating spectacle.

Barefoot, he tiptoed up to her. Lost in her thoughts, she did not notice him till he had leaned over her on the door-frame and turned her chin towards him. He responded to her angelic smile with a soft kiss.

"Aren't you feeling cold?" She remarked, looking at his bare body. He fondly gathered her in his arms and pulled her in an embrace.

"Now I don't," he whispered into her ears.

"I do feel a bit though…don't you think, there's a…"

"Yes, there's bit of a nip in the air," he cut her short and then taking hold of her hand, he headed towards the bar. "Come; let me offer you something to warm you up."

"But…" She tried to put a mild protest.

"*Arre*, come *na*…You'll like it." He pulled her.

He poured red wine in two glasses, little less for her but a full one for himself.

"Not for me, please hukum." She was still disinclined.

"Don't be foolish," he chided her, and then handing her the glass he said, "See, it is so little. As it is, nothing will happen to you."

Continuing to look reluctant, she took it. He held his glass and said, "Let's raise a toast."

"I didn't follow." She looked lost.

"Bring your glass closer," he demonstrated by taking his glass halfway in her direction. "Like this." She followed suit.

"Now, let's touch our glasses lightly to each other's…like this." He demonstrated by lightly clinking the two, "Cheers…Say, 'cheers'." He nudged her again.

"Oh…Cheers." She looked flabbergasted.

"Now drink."

"Nothing will happen to me, *na*?" She looked quite nervous.

"Actually, yes a lot will happen." He was suddenly grim and apologetic. "You'll start breaking the furniture, smashing the bottles, lamps, crockery, tearing the cushions and curtains apart…you'll get stark naked and run amok on the road, hitting passers-by, abusing them at will…and…"

She burst out laughing with him joining in. The atmosphere turned light. She took a small sip, made a face. Seeing the mock anger on his face, she took another. Soon an easy affability settled in.

After a few minutes, she turned quiet and contemplative.

"So quiet, what happened?" He patted on her cheek.

She smiled shyly and then said diffidently, "I'm thinking of learning music."

"Music! How come…so suddenly?"

She turned even more self-conscious before saying, "Just like that. I used to think about it sometimes. But today…I don't know…I just felt that I should learn it properly."

He stared at her before asking. "What? Vocal or instrumental?"

"Why not both?"

"Sure, why not both?" He still had a curious look in his eyes. "Join some music school. There are many on Pali Road. Find out how much is the fee. I shall pay," he added ligh-heartedly.

"No hukum, why will you do that? That was not the reason I mentioned it. It occurred to me a minute ago, as I stood there at the balcony watching the drizzle. I said it just like that, honest." She seemed a little offended.

He gazed at her even more curiously. Then leaning forward gave her a gentle slap on the cheek and chided, "Why will I do that? Hmm? Because if I encourage several other students by sponsoring their training in various things, why will I not do that for you?"

"But…"

"Now shut up, or else you'll get one." He flashed his hand in a mock threat.

Travelling back in the car, a short while later, not only was she a little tipsy, she was quite fuzzy in her mind, her emotions going topsy-turvy. Not only his suaveness, but also his gentleness touched her deeply.

Yet, the very next time they met, he was a different man. As soon as they were by themselves in the bedroom, he grabbed her, crushed her lips with his teeth, and almost ripped her dress apart, snapping off one or two buttons in the process. And as she staggered back a little trying to hold together the strap of her slip, which he had torn, he pounced at her to pin her body to the wooden closet and ravished her breasts hungrily. She too responded equally ferociously. Sucking, kissing, scratching, biting—a fearsome duel, seething with lust and obscenities. Unforgiving, he flung her over the rug and mounted her like a raging bull. An animalistic plunder followed, both equally aggressive, leaving them both hungry and satiated at the same time.

Later on, even as they stood together under the shower, the fury returned. There itself they took each other again, quenching the passion inside, while continuing to brave the lances of water outside on the freshly created scratches and bite marks on their bodies.

More surprises were in store on the visit after that. Rana was charm personified. Tender, soft, sensitive and caressing; every bit of his move was a lesson in seduction. The entire act, right through to the final fusion was poetry in love making. And sure enough, just as she had begun to think that this essentially was 'him', a lover of class and panache, he was to take her breath away all over again, with his beastly onslaught a couple of weeks later.

Just as she faced him after putting down her bag on the sofa, he grabbed her face in his claw-like hands and sent his tongue lashing inside her mouth. Raised to the occasion her tongue retaliated in equal measure. Then suddenly, he had a go at her new uniform, in one sweep snapping off many of its hooks, ripping apart her silken slip and sucking hungrily at the voluptuous breasts, before lifting her up and roughly dropping her at the top of the large dinner table. Unmindful of the pile of plates and a box of cutlery on the table, he mounted her there itself. The sound of the plates and the cutlery crashing on the floor due to the savage pounding she was subjected to, were no deterrence to them in the throes of passion, caught up in their wild and lusty love duel.

At night, after her children had gone to bed, she sat mending the torn buttonholes of her new uniform and pondered over her journey with Rana—how far she had travelled from her moorings. She was acutely conscious of the change she was going through. The churning that used to grip her in the face of conflicting emotions in the beginning, had turned to acquiescence of convenience with an element of anxious anticipation accompanying every amorous encounter.

Yet, she knew the reality—the reality that no dreams could be woven into anything finer. It was and had to be a relationship of trade-off. She was at best a 'keep', a 'golee', a concubine for Rana. Not even a 'mistress' in the glorified sense of the status. Probably, she was not even at par with 'Munni jaan'. And 'if it was so', 'had to be so', then, she resolved: *why couldn't she accept it and benefit from it?* She decided to accept the transformation without a grudge. That night she slept easy.

A pattern had been set. Every couple of weeks or so Rana's car fetched her from the hospital on a day when she would be on an early shift, and took her to the same apartment. Soon, an easy familiarity set in into their relationship. Not only were their bodies completely comfortable with each other, their temperaments were equally so. Both knew the score, despite never expressly spelling it out. This meant that they truly made the best of their stolen moments of togetherness.

Whenever they met there was bonhomie, fun, humour, unrestrained leg-pulling and even harmless teasing, and of course, huge doses of sizzling sex during their adulterous escapades. True to her acquired sense of diplomacy, she never put any awkward questions before him, just as he never did to her. But one day, after the vigorous love making, in a lighter vein she let out what had been niggling at her for some time.

"The way we both come here, suppose somebody got the wind of our little *leela*?" she said teasingly, as she picked up her uniform, lying on the settee nearby, and started buttoning it up.

Reclining by the bedrest, a bare chested Rana, still naked underneath the sheet, took a drag on his cigarette and slowly releasing it said, "*Arre*, how will anybody come to know? The guy to whom this apartment belongs is a very trusted man."

"But who is this man? Doesn't his family say anything? That day, those plates had fallen down from the dining table and were left broken."

"I've done so many things for him that he feels indebted. I got his job fixed at the Sachivalaya too. He is alone these days. His family has gone to Bihar."

Having dressed up, Saanvri went up to him and sat at the edge of the bed, facing him. She pulled out the cigarette from his mouth and planted a kiss on his mouth before saying.

"But his family will come back some day or the other. What will you do then?" She took a puff from his cigarette and coughed, displaying amply what a novice she was. She quickly handed back the cigarette to him.

Rana took another puff and releasing the smoke, he said, "Yes I know. I'll do something. Will make some arrangement soon."

Saanvri stretched forward. Placing her arms on either side of his body and balancing them, she reached right up to his face. She gazed deeply and suggestively in his eyes and then rubbing her lips on his lips, she said in a slightly teasing tone, yet with a trace of nonchalance: "You were talking about getting a better house allotted in my name as well, hukum."

"Yes, yes that too. I'll get it done. Ask Khooba to fetch the forms and see me," he too planted a peck on her lips before returning to his cigarette.

With gratitude writ large in her eyes as Saanvri withdrew and got up to fetch her cap from the settee, her eyes went to the blood pressure monitor placed near her head gear. She picked it up and turned around to say mischievously, "This machine is cast aside, crying for attention every time…At least once in a while you should let the poor thing be put to use, Rana-ji."

Rana sprung up from the bed like a panther. In a quick sweep, he extinguished the cigarette in the ash tray placed on the bedside table and grabbed her from behind. He undid her two top buttons and lifting her exposed breasts, he said playfully, "Write, the upper one is 120 and the lower one is 80. It's normal, absolutely normal."

Despite the equation of that of a benefactor and the beneficiary having been well and truly established between them, Saanvri was fiercely possessive about her individuality, which always had been an inherent trait of her personality. She zealously kept some of her cherished aspirations in her personal domain, instead of seeking monetary support from Rana in pursuing them. Driven by her fundamental streak of defiance, she chose to proceed on her own for learning music. She joined a music school without letting Rana get wind of it or seeking financial patronage, as insisted by him, when she had first broached the matter.

But there was more to it. And that was not at all easy to comprehend or understand. Essentially, it was something that was still traversing within the deeper recesses of her heart and yet was sufficiently disquieting for her sense of emotional equilibrium. It was a kind of a deeper urge that motivates a person to seek approbation from someone special for his or her achievements or pursuits of merit. Whereas a part of her was pragmatic enough to not let this feeling brew into an emotion, the other part was still tempted to surprise Rana, one day, after having acquired a level of proficiency as a singer and a musician—for it was after consorting with him for the first time on that beautifully bewitching rainy day that the desire to learn music had germinated on its own in her mind.

Months had passed. Rana had returned to Jodhpur that very day after a prolonged stay in Jaipur on account of the Assembly session as well as long spells of travel within India and abroad as part of various state committees and trade bodies. At night husband and wife went to attend an important wedding. It was their first outing together after a long time. Days of denial, impelled by straitjacketed official state travels and the extended stay in Jaipur, had made him sexually ravenous. Being at a private social gathering the embargo on spirits was thankfully absent. Equally demonstrative was the free spirit within the assembled men, especially in him. Soon his roving eye was at play.

Madhvi, his wife was familiar with every little twitch of his eye and every single ripple of his body. She cornered him just as he bumped into her again after repeated forays of 'just connecting with old chums'.

"Let's leave now. We've been here long enough," she said in a low chiding tone. "And you have already had too much to drink. Besides, we have to drop her home as well." She pointed at the old lady among her clutch of friends.

Rana looked bored at his wife's suggestion. In the sway of his high spirits, he took an exasperated look around him and then said in a repressed whisper, "You do one thing; take the car and leave. Drop her on the way. You reach home; I'll come after a little while."

"How will you come later on?" Madhvi was even more indicting in her retaliation, though also in whispers.

"I'll make my way, *yaar*. Anybody will drop me later on."

"But what is going on." She was intrusive and suspicious. "Whom do you have to meet on your own?"

"Nobody, *bhai*. You're always suspicious about everything," Rana said with an evasive smile before continuing, "The CM's brother is expected to come soon. I'll just say 'hello' to him and come home."

Madhvi's suspicious eyes bore even more sharply into his and she said with finality, "You don't have to take a lift with anybody. I shall just ask Khooba to come and fetch you in my car. You come with him."

"*Jo* hukum," he responded sarcastically before emptying his glass in a gulp. As he moved towards the bar he said to her trifle apologetically, in a tone which was not any less dismissive, "I'd just get a refill." He waved the glass and walked away.

But unfortunately the evening was not kind to him. It being a wedding party, everyone came accompanied with their spouses. He had to restrain his eyes from overstaying on the young luscious ladies, none of whom seemed to be alone, as if by design. Though among the assembled guests there were a few who beneath the facade of false marital respectability had had a scene with him in the past, today the conspiracy of circumstance had cruelly kept them out of bounds; depriving him of even a bout of flirtation. In his state of carnal deprivation, alcohol was what he took recourse to, but with each gulp his frustration increased. By the time he was picked up by Khoobchand, in Madhvi's Accord, he was rather sozzled.

Turning at the main road, Khoobchand once again looked with trepidation at the rear-view mirror to sneak a look at Rana, sprawled at the back seat of the car in an inebriated state. He had looked hostile as he had staggered into the car and sprawled across like an injured animal, which had prevented Khoobchand from daring to ask anything. Suddenly, in his state of drunkenness, Rana burst into an exhilarated mumbling of some romantic Rajasthani folk song. This gave Khoobchand the courage to plead with Rana:

"Bado-hukum, can I make a request?"

"Hmm." Interrupted in his mutilation of the love song, Rana scowled, "What?"

"Malik, if you permit me, can I pick up Saanvri? Her hospital is on the way. I can drop her on the way, hukum." He turned his head to look back at Rana and said in a pleading tone, "It will not take any time."

A brief silence followed, broken by the unmelodious massacre of yet another line of an otherwise soulful song. All of a sudden Rana stopped his gross rendition of the song and, though still in his stupor, said flirtatiously in the same sing-song tone:

"Alright, Khoobe. Let's pick her up. Surely, let's pick up Saanvri-ji as well."

Khoobchand was slightly alarmed by the sarcastic edge to Rana's response, but unable to fathom anything, he looked back and spoke aloud gratefully, "*Bahut, bahut meharbani, malik.*"

What he could have not known is that the mention of Saanvri, in Rana's ravenous state had ignited not only a bit of fire in his loins but also an element of suppressed fury, which he had been subconsciously feeling for some time at her streak of independence, quite unlike many other concubines he had as playthings for himself. Her declining his offer to pay for her music lessons and then the news of her surreptitiously going on her own, to obtain the training, had not done any good to his ego.

Some ten minutes later, after picking up Saanvri, the car travelled down a deserted road with a pervading sense of gloom. The couple exchanged tense looks in the front seat, hearing Rana make all kinds of strange noises from the rear, every now and then. They couldn't have guessed the game. Neither could they have seen the serpent of wickedness set out to play in Rana's head, nor the avenging gleam widening in his eyes as he continued to groan occasionally and made restless sounds, pretending to be in pain. Sure enough, soon he spoke out with a contorted face letting out another grimace:

"*Arre* Khooba, I am feeling some kind of a pain in the chest for quite a while. Can your wife come here in the back and check me? What do you say, Saanvri?"

Khoobchand exchanged a confused look with Saanvri, who had no expression on her face. He looked back and said in a capitulating eagerness.

"Sure, sure malik. Why not, sarkar?" He turned to her again and mumbled persuasively, "Saanvri..."

Khoobchand slowly applied the brakes. The car came to a smooth halt, and the front passenger door opened. Saanvri got out, opening the back door to slide in beside Rana and then pulled the door shut. The car moved on again. All this might have seemed routine, but it carried an oppressive, yet meaningful silence about it.

Rana said coolly: "Carry on driving, Khooba. You carry on driving the car!"

Gradually, the car picked up speed and went ahead on the dark road, lit only by the two cruel sharp beams of the vehicle. The faint reflection of the greenish illumination of the instrument panel on his face had heightened the brooding darkness invading Khoobchand's mind and spirits. Slowly, he once again shifted his gaze from the road to the rear-view mirror to steal a glance at the backseat. The darkness there was not impervious enough to hide the brazen display of incivility and insensitivity of one reared in feudal brashness towards lesser mortals.

Even before Saanvri had slid beside him, Rana had already undone the buttons of his long Rajasthani kurta and the string of the pyjamas. The first thing he did was to grab her hand and move it caressingly over his chest, uttering, "Here Saanvri, here."

Disregarding the whirlpool of conflicting emotions she tried to fight, Rana masterly manoeuvred her hand on his erect penis, leading her to fondle it. Then he whispered acerbically in her ear, "You think you can do things on your own, disregarding my offers? Don't you forget you belong to me now…completely."

It did not come as a great surprise to her as she heard his lusty tremulous voice and felt his trembling hand over her hand, encircling his organ. Strangely, it even gave her a sense of one-upmanship, realising the effect she was able to have on the ego of the man who thought of her only as a plaything. In the process, he had exposed much of himself for her own play. But she was deeply affected by the spineless capitulation of the person who was supposed to be her protector in the eyes of the society—her husband.

Having understood her situation clearly, she let Rana unbutton her dress and fondle her breasts, and then burry his face in the deep valley.

She responded by leaning over him to claim his lips with an equally fiery passion.

Having understood the score, Khoobchand also acquiesced—the anger in his eyes receded to leave them empty. Slowly, he looked away from the rear-view mirror to concentrate on the road ahead, which was dark as well as bumpy, ridden with small potholes, all of a sudden.

Some fifteen minutes later, when she lit the stove to warm the food, though her hands went about the job mechanically, her mind was elsewhere. The severity of the outrageousness in the car had descended on her conscience only after she entered the house and began peeling off her uniform. After washing her face and untying her hair to lie loose around her shoulders, outwardly she may have looked calm and composed, but underneath the placidity on her face, there was turmoil; deep turmoil. Her eyes were vacant as they stared at the sizzle of the curries heating up in the two pans placed on the hot plates of the stove.

The distant roar of a car broke her trance. The two beams of light turned the corner and illuminated the dark stretch of the lane some distance away, right across the empty yard outside the window of the kitchen. She saw the car pull in to the side and come to a halt. In a moment its headlights were turned off and the engine killed. But no one alighted. In a couple of seconds, even the inside light, which had briefly revealed Khoobchand's greyish figure behind the wheel, also died down. Silence returned, very dark silence, leaving only a vague outline of the vehicle visible to the eye. Standing still she watched the unsettling stillness of the situation, stoically.

It seemed an eternity before the cabin light came alive again with the sound of a soft click, and the driver's door opened, revealing Khoobchand. Immersed in his thoughts, he walked away from the car to enter the empty yard. Midway, he motioned the remote over his shoulder and without turning around pointed it in the car's direction and flicked the button. With the sound of the electronic beep, the cabin light of the car went out and the vehicle was locked. He did not look up to meet his wife's eyes, gazing at him steadily. Silently, he opened the front door and entered the house. She bent down over the pans and pots to return to her chore listlessly, indifferent to the discernible sound of the leaking tap.

In a while, as she entered the main room with two plates of food in her hands, she found him seated in the darkness by the small table adjacent to the wall. She stopped at the doorway of the kitchen and considered him for a couple of seconds. In the bluish moonlight falling through the small window, he looked like a dark and mysterious statue with his one hand resting on a bottle of liquor in front of him. She tiptoed up to him and placed the two plates on the table. She then returned to the doorway and turned on the light. He did not shift his posture even slightly, though now in the brightness of the light, he did not look as mysterious as before. She walked back to the table and sat down on the other chair facing him. After gazing at him silently for a moment, she pulled her plate towards her and picked up the spoon. He slowly uncorked the bottle and took it to his mouth.

Nine

The blazing tarmac raced back like a silvery surface of a lake, past the giant wheels of the aeroplane. Like a bird retracting its legs into the layers of its feathers, the undercarriage of the giant flying machine too was slowly pulled up into its belly, along with the flaps, leaving only a huge shiny surface underneath. It was a surrealistic visual. The fast receding plane cast a diminishing shadow on the mirror-like tarmac for a while. Soon it got eclipsed by the swirling clouds and became a tiny strip of a shining knife, intermittently reflecting the light of the sun.

With dreamy eyes Saanvri continued to stare at the swathes of clouds floating past the window. Too many things had happened—all too soon and too suddenly. Just like the swarm of clouds beyond the window of the airplane, her mind was in a nebulous state, reflecting on the amorphous nature of the years gone by and what lay ahead. And just as the airplane began to rise into the clear blue sky, high above the long stretch of white carpet underneath, her mind also swam out of the cluttered mass of her debilitating thoughts. With renewed spirit, she resolved to look life straight in the eye and take each day as it came. Having come so far, there was only one way for her now—to move forward.

Each ripple of her naked body oozed sensuality as she snaked up Rana's naked body. Sizzling with ecstasy, he shivered to the punishing movement of Saanvri's trenchant tongue, which had now reached the area around his nipple. It was a dangerous, erogenous zone, quite electrifying. Unforgiving in its greed, it licked around playfully before suddenly mounting a tantalising attack on the small mound. As he seethed with pleasure, her tongue abandoned it and moved away to do the same to the other nipple. But just as Rana began to gasp under his clenched teeth, her tongue moved on further up to his armpits, one after the other searching in the wet growth of hair while her nostrils drinking hungrily at the sexy musk of their fierce love-making a few minutes earlier. Further aroused by his moans, she let her tongue probe behind and inside his earlobes, his neck and then finally, descended the slope of his nose to claim his lips in a fierce assault.

Rana tried to clasp her face in his steely hands, retaliating with equal passion, probing her mouth with his tongue. She quickly grabbed both his arms and took them back where they were before, outstretched over his head, holding the backrest of the bed, without letting go of his mouth with her uninterrupted kisses.

In a while, she withdrew and regarded him like prey. Her eyes gleamed and a bewitching smile of a victor appeared on her lips. With a burst of heat emitting from her nostrils, she sat astride him. Letting go of his hands, she positioned herself on his manhood and then with clenched teeth impaled her already lubricated interiors on his shaft. His hands, now free, went on her inviting breasts with the fury of a rebel. The pounding that then began was unsparing, right to the point when spent and totally satiated she collapsed on his sweaty, still tremulous chest, after a cataclysmic orgasm. But despite its primal appeal, the experience this time had penetrated her flesh and bones to reach the core of her heart. In a state of self-deception she clung to him even more tightly and started kissing his hairy chest much more fondly.

This was the fourth day after their arrival in Bangkok. All the four days had been spent in the hotel, as though they were a honeymooning couple who had not had enough of each other. They had travelled on the same flight but in separate classes—she in the economy and he in the first class—and had judiciously avoided each other at the airports in Mumbai and Bangkok as well as on board. At the Bangkok airport, they had taken separate cabs and had checked in separate rooms, in the same hotel. But once inside the hotel, they had spent most of their private time in Rana's suite.

After the outrageous incident in the back seat of the car, with her husband driving it, Rana had walked into their life with the outlandish confidence and abominable indifference of a feudal lord, who not only treated his slaves as his private property but also objects of his sexual whims and fancies, any time. Suddenly one day, he sent for her and informed her that she was going to visit Bangkok with him, where he was to go as part of a business tour. That's that. She was neither given any choice in the matter, nor any opportunity to offer any opinion. Of course, she was certainly informed that her husband had already been told about it and the matter was under control. She knew now that she was not only a mistress for him, but also his whore-on-call.

Yet, she was falling for him today, in the manner of a barefoot individual trying to ascend a slippery slope on a rainy night. She was an automobile, mired in a muddy pothole. The more its wheel raced to get out, the more it dug itself in. Ironically, as a result of the heavenly consorting they had just experienced, the outpouring of pleasure from each cell of her body had dulled her senses sufficiently to dwell any further on the shadowy aspects of her equation with Rana, and she soon slipped into a snooze, just as he did.

They were awakened by the sound of Rana's cell phone ringing on the table nearby. He made no move to take it. He bent his head and kissed her hair before locking her closer in his arms and falling into a light sleep again. The phone rang again after some time. He again ignored it. When it rang the fourth time, Saanvri, with her head still on his chest, mumbled drowsily in half sleep.

"Take it na, Rana-ji. How many times will you ignore it?"

"Leave it, *na*. I know whose call it is," he said evasively.

Her eyes flung open out of a sudden impulse. She lifted her head and burst into peals of unstoppable laughter before saying, "You know we have become like small school children—like the ones who run away from classes."

All of a sudden, Rana sprung up to sit in the bed and swore loudly: "*Ma ki choot duniya ki*. Ever since we've come here four days ago, we're scurrying into the corners out of fear. *Arre* we've come here to enjoy life…Then enjoy life, *bhenchod*."

Saanvri was completely taken aback by his blunt admission and his sudden outburst. Slowly she sat up while continuing to gaze at him.

He, now, almost pounced at her, "Nothing will happen to your job. I am here to take care of it, aren't I?" He jabbed his finger at his chest angrily before turning it to her pointedly and saying, "You! You have come on a study trip. Your department has sent you for it on my recommendation…that's it. Matter over. Nobody can touch even a hair of your head. And I? I've also come on a business delegation folks." He laughed tauntingly before suddenly saying threateningly, "I don't have to explain to any fucking body, anything. That settles it. Now tell me, what else?" He said challengingly.

Saanvri's face relaxed and she said in a tone of light tease, "Can I ask something, hukum?"

"Go on ask." He waved his finger imperiously, "Ask whatever you want to ask."

"Are we going to do the entire study inside the hotel room only? We haven't gone out of the hotel premises since the last four days!"

For a moment Rana looked lost for words. Then he jumped out of the bed and said in an expansive and generous tone, "Come on, let me show you the Pattaya night life tonight, *yaar*. We'll have our dinner somewhere there."

Saanvri's face lit up, and she extended her hand to him in a theatrical posture. Rana grabbed it and pulled her off the bed in one powerful sweep amid her shriek and laughter.

That night, they went berserk. Caution was bid a goodbye. The self-imposed protocol of having to remain inconspicuous was thrown away once and for all. Both were donned in provocative casuals that even teens would be self-conscious to wear. Then they uncorked the spirits of the bottles, to bolster the spirits of youthfulness, with happy abandon.

In an unknown place, among unknown people, it was not only the permissiveness of the red-light district of the city that had gotten to them, but also an inner urge to unsheathe the life of pretence and return, even if briefly, to the days of free and uncomplicated adolescence. Pubs, pool halls, billiard games, karaoke bars, go-go bars, discos, they missed none. After feasting on all kinds of Thai and other oriental delicacies, when they landed in a strip club, the night was still young for them... truly young.

The gorgeous strippers stepped out of their slinky robes, one by one, their movements matching the high-octane music. They took to pole dancing, with all forms of enticement with every bit of their body. Most spectators, both men and women, unabashedly joined in with a ribald display of appreciation.

Saanvri slipped into an introspective mood and despite his state of arousal, Rana sensed it. He enveloped her in his arms protectively, and kissed her on her cheeks and hair, reassuringly. This touched her deeply and she snuggled into his embrace, kissing him on the neck. But even with her eyes beaming, she continued to remain pensive. Instead of any tension or outrage on her face, there was now a dreamy resolve in her eyes.

What she did not let out to Rana at the strip joint was the seeding of a thought—something that had germinated in her mind in that coarse, sleazy environment—an aspiration to produce something highly creative someday, someting in her cultural context. However, it did not remain entirely unexpressed as they strolled onto a beachfront at her insistence, towards the wee hours of the morning. Suitably high on champagne she let go of any remaining trace of restraint as soon as they got down from the cab at the narrow coastal street.

After walking through the cluster of palm trees, they stepped onto the cool sands of the deserted beach. Swinging to the words and tune of one of the revue numbers, played at the strip club earlier, Saanvri walked ahead of Rana. Occasionally, she subsituted some impromptu Rajasthani words here and there, as she went about humming, singing and swinging to the number. When Rana teased her for her attempt to atrociously murder the song she burst into shrieks of laughter, and like a small school girl ran further ahead throwing off her shoes left and right.

Rana also ran after her. Trying to catch up with her after he stopped to pick up her shoes, she was suddenly nowhere to be seen. As he looked around baffled, he found her reappearing amid a row of tourist shacks.

She stood behind one of the poles that held its roof and was in a teasing mood. She first flashed a leg, naked up to the upper thigh, before revealing herself fully. Then, she broke into a jig around the pole more or less like the dancers at the strip club. But there was more in store.

Having noticed that she had aroused Rana's curiosity, she started peeling off her clothes, one by one, as though she was performing in the club.

Taken aback, Rana screamed in mock rebuke, "*Arre re.* What're you doing?"

"Doing the pole dance, Rana-ji," she continued her enticing act. "Making you happy."

Though not quite able to hide the sexual stirrings within him, a genuinely horrified Rana looked around for any human intrusion. Not bothered about his mock protestations, she went on taking off her clothing with gay abandon, with extreme passionate movements. In no time, she was just in her bra. She had done the full monty.

Feigning anger, Rana pounced at her. Her child-like spirit fully aroused, she gave him a slip and sprang out of his reach. Now squealing with unfettered joy, she ran towards the shoreline while removing her bra in one swift motion and swinging it over her head like a lasso. A scandalised Rana picked up her long silken scarf, which she had tossed aside on the sands along with her other clothes, and ran after her. By the time Rana caught up with her she was already waist deep in the water, jumping and shrieking with joy, diving-in and surfing with the waves advancing towards the shore.

Having noticed him enter the water, she became even more daring and retreated deeper into the sea. Realising the danger in her romp, Rana dived after her and grabbed her from the waist. He pulled her out of the water with a steely grip and thrust her towards the shore. Once in knee-deep water, he covered her as much as possible with the scarf, which he had quickly slung around his trunk in a knot before diving after her.

With her arm still in Rana's grip as they walked towards the shack, she suddenly stopped and beckoned with a winsome smile on her lips and a wistful glint in her eyes.

"*Ai-ji* Rana-ji. Stop for a moment please." There was an intense quiver in her voice.

Rana also stopped and while trying to figure out the expression in her eyes, he teased, "What happened? *Marna chahti hai.* Do you want to die?"

"*Ha-y-e*," She let out a deep sigh and then mewled romantically like a young girl in love, "Absolutely. I sure feel like that."

Rana turned away from her, bursting into an uncontrollable laughter.

She persisted, "Just turn your face this way, Rana-ji." She had a dreamy sombreness in her eyes.

Rana obliged and stared at her searchingly. After a moment's gaze in his eyes, she held his face in her hands and claimed his lips.

It was a wholesome kiss deeper into the mouth, ripe with feeling. As she withdrew slowly, her voice quivered with emotion saying, "You've changed me completely, Rana-ji."

A certain wistfulness returned to her eyes as she continued, "I never drank before—you made me start on that; I never smoked—even that you put me onto; I had decided that I won't ever dance—now I feel like dancing as well; I could never think of being without my children, even for a day—now I am here with you,so far away from them." She took a pause and said weakly, "My persona is no longer my own. My heart is no longer mine. I've lost it to you. I've started loving you."

Immobilised for a moment, Rana's eyes continued to gaze into hers. More deeply now. He noticed her eyes moistening. A strange gleam lurking in them, of honesty and sincerity. She stood still too. The current travelled to his own, moistening them as well. Slowly he bent down to her face, tenderly lifting her chin, he kissed her softly. Then he said, "Shall we go?"

"So soon; a little while more? Please?"

"It'll be morning soon. If somebody saw us?"

"So? We are tourists. Aren't we?"

"But like this?" His eyes went to the flimsy scarf, which hardly covered her.

She considered the situation for a couple of seconds before a mischievous glint appeared in her eyes. She released the scarf and tossed it aside and said, "You mean like this…?"

He grinned at her childish defiance, which was peculiarly endearing at the same time.

"Yes, like this…naked, with nothing on!"

She too considered the situation for two, three seconds without saying anything. It was a bewitching silence, full of portents. Abandoning her pensiveness she met his eyes squarely and said with disarming simplicity, "Rana-ji, I now no longer feel naked in front of you. In fact, not at all. I feel secure in your presence, whichever state I may be." Then she quickly hastened to say, "But only you. It doesn't go for anybody else. Man or woman!"

Rana's grin expanded and he nodded empathetically. However he still teased, "So? That's what I am saying...If somebody else saw you like this now? With nothing on?"

She was stumped for a moment. But her sprightly spirit returned quickly.

"Who says I am not wearing anything?" Suddenly she was at once playfully sensuous, naughty and defiant.

"What do you mean?" He too was mischievously daring.

"I am still wearing this *nathnee*." She pointed at the golden nose stud in her nostril and then tugged at her earrings and the pearl necklace around her neck. "These *jhumkas* in my ears, pearls around my neck and right down to this," she suggestively pointed at the valley between her undulating breasts, leaving Rana also stumped for a moment. Now she brought a mysterious darkness in her eyes and invitingly gave a little swing to her waist while patting at the jewel-crusted waistband worn loosely around her lower torso, "Then I have this *tagdi* around my waist."

Before he could utter anything, she slowly and seductively raised her foot like a statue of Ellora and pointed at her silver toe rings saying, "And, and these *bichchuas* too...how can we forget these?"

She could see that she had been successful in making him feel the way she intended. Now, standing on one foot with her waist bent sideway like a bewitching Ellora mural, she snared him with a deliberately tantalising glimpse of her slightly parted vagina by the artful manoeuvring of her thighs.

Suddenly aroused, Rana raised his eyes and realised there was more in store. Lance-like gazes in her eyes, long and penetrating, instantly excavated those in his own—equally long and penetrating. The lances shone bright for an instant before they went at each other in a fearsome clash. It was a lethal friction, subsuming the two, completely, into an unsparing duel on the wet and rough sands.

He took her the way she desired—with beastly brutality and unrestrained vulgarity. They were both plunderers in sex. Intoxicated by the constant barrage of the filthiest words flung at each other in their hysteric romp, if she was biting and scratching like a bitch on the heat, he too was unrelenting in sucking on her large breasts like a hungry wolf, and his organ pounded her equally retaliating cave with punishing ferocity. Even the pain and lesions that the grains of sands were causing in the process, and the immense saltiness of the oozing sweat and sea water, seemed to add to their ferocious love making.

Subdued and satiated, for a long time they lay at the shoreline itself, calmed to the core after a most earth shattering orgasmic explosion they had ever experienced together. Lulled by the soft flapping of the occasional wave disintegrating around them and the sonorous hum of the light wind, they dozed off for a few minutes. However, soon she woke up with a start, awakened by the slapping of waves much closer to them now. In a panic, she extricated herself from his cover and sprung to her feet.

"*Uthiye*, Rana-ji." Bending down she tried to wake him up.

"*Arre*, what happened? Why the panic?" He got to his knees.

"We should leave, day is about to break," she pointed at the first hint of redness in the sky.

"*Theek hai*...but what's the hurry. It'll still be dark for a good fifteen minutes or so."

"Water is rising...the waves are about to smother us," she seemed worried.

"Since when did you start being fearful of the water? Remember I saved you from drowning yourself?"

"That's not the issue," she said shyly.

Smitten by her post-coital glow, he kissed her softly before speaking. "Then...?"

"I have to save something. Something very beautiful." Even in semidarkness, the sudden redness on her cheeks could not be invisible.

"Save something...? What...?"

"What you gifted me a little while ago...which is inside me, still..."

The suspenseful silence was too endearing for both to disengage from. After what seemed moments of eternity, Rana held her face between his palms kissing her even more tenderly on her slightly parted lips. Then, without displaying even a hint of tension, he asked, "You know what it could lead to...?"

"Not to worry, I've taken care of that." She reached for his face this time and kissed his lips softly as her eyes beamed reassuringly.

"Shall we leave?" He said at long last.

"Yes," she said contentedly.

Then, silently, with their arms around each other's waist and her head resting on his shoulder they walked to the thatched shack.

Half an hour later, sizzling with as much pleasure inside as she felt outside, she savoured the soothing feeling from the jets of water hitting her naked skin under the shower.

On returning to the hotel, she had decided to give herself a good soak in the super-luxury bathroom in Rana's suite. She had longingly filled the pond-shaped sunken tub almost to the brim and had mixed the turquoise water with expensive bath salts and herbs, which every pore of her body yearningly craved, to soothe out the aches and pains encountered during their dalliance at the beach. To add to the aesthetic effect, she had also let loose some petals as well as a few fully bloomed rose flowers on the surface. It was truly going to be the most pampering bath for the two, before retiring to the bed together.

But, after beckoning him to come and join her, just as she had peeled off her undergarments to enter the small pond, a thought hit her. Instead of dipping into the warm water, she sat down at the rim of the pond. Then, she bent down and pulled the plug from the bottom of the tub. Settling back at the rounded rim, she watched with amusement, the scented water gurgling out wastefully. She wanted to savour the precious juices flowing inside her and its temporary fantasy, all of which would have been washed away had she descended into the pond, full of chemically treated fragrant water, to frolic with Rana. After the vessel had emptied, somewhat resignedly she stood up and turned on the overhead shower.

As if to compensate her unfulfilled wish, after a lengthy and unhurried shower, first she lovingly dried herself with a soft Egyptian cotton towel before sinfully dabbing her entire body with the choicest moisturiser. Wrapping herself with another large white Egyptian towel, up to her breasts, she stepped out of the bath and tiptoed to the large mirror at the vanity counter. As she removed her bathing cap to let loose her long and lustrous hair, she looked like a bewitching sex goddess. The gorgeous, luring reflection on the mirror, seemed to ensnare her.

Her eyes looked dreamy and distant as she turned away from the counter. A mischievous expression appeared on her face. She took cat-like steps to the door leading to the short passage to the bedroom. She slowly opened the door, peering into the small passage. Unable to make out anything, she stepped out, walking nimble footedly, before coming to an abrupt halt. She was jolted by Rana's curt voice, slicing through the silence that had filled the room.

"You're unnecessarily making a mountain out of a molehill *yaar*. How can you be compared with that woman?" It was quite apparent that the caller had irritated him.

"Listen Madhavi-ji, you are the *maalkin*, *yaar*; yours has been a family of Rajwadas...You are a queen, behave like a queen for god's sake."

Rana had not noticed Saanvri, as his back had been turned towards the short passage connecting the bathroom, where she had stopped to listen to him. Although what she heard him say was nothing that she had not already known or suspected, yet it had the sharpness of an arrow that pierced through her.

"Yes, yes…it is true…that woman is with me here…but, but, haven't people from Rajwadas been known to keep *golees* before?"

The crude and emotionless guile in the man, she had almost come to love, took Saanvri's breath away. Yet, she continued to listen, too shocked to move. But soon the bullet had to hit her lethally, where it hurt the most—in the heart.

"Listen Madhvi-ji, trust me…This woman's status is not more than that of a *golee* for me…She is only a concubine of mine." He spoke condescendingly about her before pausing to listen to the other person for a moment. But the interjection that came now was most savage of all:

"*Arre yaar*…She is there just to warm my bed from time to time, that's all. Do you understand?" After another pause, he said more forcefully and trifle angrily, "Yes, yes, yes. *Vachan deta hoon mein aapko*, I promise."

The more she listened to him, speaking to his wife on the phone, the more lifeless she felt. Her eyes, which seemed so full of hope and enthusiasm when she had taken the first step out of the bathroom, looked more and more empty. Her hand went to the wall to support her listless body as she slowly retraced her steps back to the bathroom.

A good fifteen minutes later when she re-emerged from the bathroom, she was in complete control of herself and surprisingly radiant.

Rana was not in the bedroom. She could hear his voice attending another call in the sitting room of the suite. Now, as she opened the closet to dress herself, she had already reconciled to the reality. A song rose from her heart and escaped through her lips as she pulled out a dress. She hummed it again and again, swaying her body as she went about dressing herself

Saanvri did not notice Rana as he entered the room and stood silently some distance behind her, while she, leaning closer to the dressing mirror, intently gave final touches to her lipstick. He was awestruck by her appearance in the alluring low-neck gown that she had deliberately chosen to wear for the luncheon they had been invited to by a business associate of his. His hands were in the pockets of his trousers and he wore a stern look. Satisfied with the sexily pronounced lusciousness of her lips, she straightened and turned around breezily, only to nearly collide with him.

"What happened?" a trifle shocked, she asked.

"Just turn around." He sounded mysterious.

Saanvri met his stare with searching amusement. He gave away nothing. A hint of a mocking smile appearing at the corner of her lips as she turned around slowly with an ensnaring jolt to the body. Their eyes met again in the mirror; neither conceded anything. Then, she noticed the movement of his hands, coming out his pockets. The right one held something.

Before she could fathom anything, his hands lifted up and came over her shoulders, placing something around her neck, quickly and expertly; finally clasping it at her nape with remarkable efficiency. As his hands came down to rest at the sides of her slim waist, she gasped and her hands went to her chest. It was a necklace with a big shining diamond encrusted in a large pendant. The shock, which was vivid on her face, lasted at least a couple of seconds. Slowly she closed her mouth, and she had to compose herself. After gazing deeply into his eyes, she turned around.

"No Rana-ji," she declined politely, her eyes turning wooden; no longer sparkling as they seemed so far

"What do you mean?" Rana looked perplexed.

"Something that was originally not for me, cannot become mine now," she said with the calmness of a placid lake

"What are you trying to say?"

A bewitching smile appeared on her lips as she said, "Trying to measure me by the very diamond that you had seen me through once?" Sarcasm in her voice was not indiscernible.

"I didn't quite follow. What're you trying to say?"

"You had bought this diamond for Munni-ji…This diamond cannot be mine now."

Rana looked confused and lost for words. Then, slowly it all came back to him. He remembered the incident.

"So, you had heard everything that day?" His voice sounded very weak.

"When you were gazing at the several images of mine, through this piece of stone that long time ago, even I was able to catch a glimpse of you, Rana-ji," she made a blistering comment with her playful smile. Both stood immobilised, arrested by each other's eyes.

Rana broke the silence. "Munni's matter is over…I can't give it to her now." He said with finality.

"May I say something?"

Rana looked confused as well as somewhat suspicious, wondering what else she had to say. He nodded.

"This is a very expensive diamond piece. It is befitting for people of the Rajwadas," she said with absolute sincerity, without even a hint of sarcasm. "Rani-sa is the only one who can be the proper claimant of this…You should gift it only to her."

"But…" he tried to argue feebly.

A mysterious smile spread across her face and her eyes beamed as she said, "If you do definitely want to offer me something, then I have just one desire."

Rana looked at her with an expression that was at once questioning, yet searching. The dreaminess expanded in her eyes and she walked stealthily towards the window overlooking a vast greenery.

"We, the small people inhabiting the earth, always nurture a dream…to have a glimpse of the inner quarters of the women from the Rajwadas—how they live their private lives." Her voice quivered with longing before she stopped to stand still, peering across moodily.

After a couple of seconds, she turned around and broke the silence pregnant with anticipation, "Just for once, if you can please arrange for me to have a *darshan* of the room where Rani-sa sleeps or spends most of her private moments; that is all I seek."

The shock on Rana's face melted into wonderment at the tribal woman's dare, and yet her earthly innocence. But she was already far ahead of him in the department of guile, as she put it seductively, "Then, if you would also want something else, there itself, perhaps we can."

Rana was spellbound. His face changed colours as he glared at her. She matched his penetrating stare just as defiantly. At last, capitulation came. Rana recomposed himself with a slight nod and said, "We are returning to India tomorrow night. I shall do something after that..."

Saanvri smiled and nodded gratefully.

TEN

It was well into the night. The big pendulum in the clock tower, some distance away, struck twelve times when the main gate opened and an old Fiat was allowed to enter. Like a thief, it slowly and almost soundlessly rolled inside the large compound and came to a halt at a small door along the side wall behind the mansion, instead of the ornate entrance in the main yard. A shadowy figure of a woman, clad in a dark saree, with a pallu drawn over her face, alighted and hurriedly entered the door, which was opened by someone from inside, just in time.

Once the woman stepped inside, an old domestic, well into his mid-seventies, swiftly shut the door behind. Pulling aside her pallu, which was used to cover her face, Saanvri handed over her small medicine bag to the old man, who had already extended his hand to take it. He hinted her to follow him down a dimly lit narrow passage—enough for just two to walk side by side. The labyrinthine passage passed through the service quarters, storerooms, a wine cellar and living quarters of resident domestics, to lead to a staircase used for service purposes.

Hurriedly, yet soft footed they climbed the two floors of dimly lit stairs to emerge into an extra wide carpeted corridor with bedrooms on either side. As she followed him through it, she was struck by the sheer opulence of the place. The old man knocked softly at an ornate door at the end of the corridor. A muffled sound from inside asked him to enter. He slowly turned the handle to open one of the heavy doors halfway and nudged Saanvri to enter.

"So here you are...Is everything fine, Sevaram?" Rana's voice came from a far corner of the room, bathed in darkness.

"Yes, hukum," said Sevaram, swiftly closed the door behind them.

He groaned slightly as he pulled himself up and sat with his back against the bed rest.

"Sorry, Saanvri, I troubled you at this time of the night."

"No trouble, hukum. What am I a nurse for?" She said with all the pretence of a professional.

Sevaram turned on the chandelier in the room and moving efficiently, placed her medicine case on the side table, alongside the large four-poster bed on which Rana lay.

He exchanged a quick meaningful look with Rana before saying respectfully, "I have arranged for Saanvri-ji to rest in the guest room next door till the morning, just in case hukum might need her again in the night."

"Hmm," Rana nodded and exchanged a conspiratorial look with him.

"Hukum, please summon me if you need anything."

"Fine, Sevaram."

As soon as Sevaram exited and pulled the doors after him, like a school girl, Saanvri darted for the bed and flung her arms around Rana, who was trying to get up and step into his slippers. Catching him unawares, her mouth sunk into his with her tongue playing truant. With difficulty he extricated himself and said, "*Arre*, first close the doors from inside, at least."

"Why fear Rana-ji? If anybody dare barge in now, would I not have his head chopped off?" She said imperiously as she lowered herself on an ornamental chair nearby.

"Even so...may be the wind might make its way in. We won't see it, while it will see everything." Rana teased playfully.

Even more playfully she sprung up from the chair and dashed to the door. She bolted the old styled brass latch from inside and whirled round like a danseuse.

"Here you are…It is locked. Now it is only just the two of us…*aap hain aur hum hain*. Neither the outside wind can come in, nor can the wind inside go out," she said flirtatiously.

Beginning to feel aroused, Rana sprung towards her playfully, "I need to fix you first."

Saanvri quickly stretched her arm and stopped him in his track by placing her palm on his chest.

"Please stop…*Hum aapke mehman hain* Rana-ji, an honoured guest. First give me a guided tour…If not of the whole haveli, at least give me a tour of the *antarmahal*. The enormous size of this bedroom calls for it. Doesn't it?"

Fully relishing her child-like playfulness, Rana took hold of her hand and leading her in, he teased, "*Aaiye meharbaan*, let me show you round."

"So this is how royalty live," she said with joyous wonderment as she took her first step after him.

She had an innocent girlish glee and amazement writ on her face. At her insistence, she was shown not just the fixtures, appliances and trappings of luxury in the vast suite and its large bathroom with a pool-like sunken tub, but also the various robes and lotions used by Rana's wife.

No matter how impressed by it all, she could effortlessly transform into a seductress when the moment came. Even her act of stepping out of her saree had the panache of an accomplished sex goddess, and her ministrations on her own body as well as that of Rana's were unapologetic triggers to sensuality.

She was full of surprises that evening. As a naked and highly aroused Rana lifted her in his arms and motioned to the bed, she stopped him just before he could place her on the bed.

"*Thamo, thamo*, Rana-ji. Please stop for a moment."

"*Arre kya hua*; what happened?" He looked flabbergasted and sounded quite irked.

"Just let me get down for a moment, please."

"Whatever for...What is the problem?" He stood unmoved, still holding her naked body in his arms.

"Just put me down, I have a wonderful idea."

After a moment's uncertainty, he put her down on the ground a little upset, "What now?"

She swung like a dancer and twirled on her toes to a divan by the side of a wall. Disregarding the cushions, she pulled out the quilt-like covering adorning it.

"What is it you're doing?" Asked a befuddled and a trifle irritated Rana, his interrupted passion making him restless.

"Arranging for extra pleasure, Rana-ji," she said seductively as she quickly moved back to where he was.

•◆•

The sun was still to rise, but its redness had already turned the eastern sky like a painter's palette on which the first stroke of his brush had been drawn. The furtive movement of an occasional passer-by or a lone cyclist, on the empty street some distance away, the shadowy stillness of the trees and parked vehicles presented a mysterious mosaic.

In the spacious balcony of the top floor of the palatial three-storey building, Madhvi, adorning a light shawl over her nightie, was lovingly watering an array of plants. The pink rays of the emerging sun had spread an angelic hue on her face as well as on the wall, windows and the door behind. Lightly humming a Rajasthani folk song, she was immersed in her activity, when a young maidservant entered with a tray in her hand.

"Rani-sa, your tea."

"Keep it on the table." Madhvi pointed with a nod, "I'll take it in a minute."

In a while, she settled in one of the easy chairs and picked up the cup. It had barely reached her lips when another young maid approached her with a handset.

"Madam, there's a call for you. Something urgent."

Madhvi had a quick sip of her tea and took the phone.

"Hello, yes." Suddenly, her face had contorted in shock. "What... since last night...What the hell?" Her eyes, which had been tender and dreamy only moments ago, had ambers leaping out of them as she spoke with repressed fury, "I'm coming. 'Will leave within few minutes... Don't tell anything to anybody...not a word...okay?"

She snapped the phone shut, and springing up dashed inside the house.

Saanvri stirred in her sleep and slowly opened her eyes. Still in the lingering grips of the dream she had been having, it took her a while to realise that she was not at her place and was not alone. She was still coiled up with Rana on the mattress on the floor, close to the master bed. The satin sheet barely covered their naked bodies, spooned together in the post coital state after another wild romp just before dawn.

Slowly, she slid over him and with her mouth almost rubbing his lips, she whispered, "Rana-ji...*aye* Rana-ji, wouldn't you get up? Its morning already. If Rani-sa returned suddenly?"

Rana, who was in deep sleep, opened his eyes with some effort and stared into her eyes for a good length of time, unable to figure out straight away, where he was. Having gotten back his bearings, he remarked indifferently, "*Arre*, she's not coming anytime soon. She has gone to her parents' place. She won't return before lunch."

"Very clever, Rana-ji...Everything is so well thought out by you."

Rana gently let her off his body and sat up. After a sleepy yawn, he leaned across for a smooch and then asked, "Yap...but I can't understand as to why, after insisting so much on coming here, you chose the floor instead of the bed?"

She put her arms around his neck and once again fondly put a peck on his lips before saying mysteriously, "The ground has altogether a different thing about it," her eyes looked into his eyes mischievously as she continued suggestively. "Once in a while one should experience the thrill of making love on the ground too."

Before he could say anything again, she too sat up and pulled the sheet to her breasts. Once again, she kissed him lightly on the lips and got up. Leaving him naked and bemused, she made a dash for the washroom.

•◆•

As soon as he pulled open the huge floors of the main gate, the doorkeeper's mouth fell open and the twig of the neem he had been chewing upon as an early morning ritual, to clean his teeth, fell out.

The engine roared, and like a white beast the Corolla leapt at him, giving him barely half a second to jump out of the way, but not before the tyres had splashed enough dirty water to drench his naked torso above his dhoti.

Unmindful, the machine stormed along in its fury, splashing water from puddles left behind in the vast courtyard by the late night rain. It came to a halt right in front of the main entrance of the mansion. The driver's door was flung open and he dived out to reach the rear door before the occupant could open it.

At that precise moment, the head of the night security, still in his khaki trousers, hurriedly worn shirt and untied laced boots, made a dash to the entrance and loudly banged the door knob on the metal plate, heralding the staff inside to open it. By now, Madhvi had sprung out of the car and marched to the entrance door.

"Pranam, hukum. Rani-sa." The head of the security immediately bent down to touch her feet.

The entrance door opened revealing an equally shocked female staff, who quickly made way for Madhvi to rush past.

Rana, by now casually attired in a T-shirt and a pair of jogging pants picked up the intercom that rang.

"Yes, what is it?"

"Bado-hukum, Rani-sa has come back!" A panick stricken security-chief whispered in the receiver, mounted on the wall of his small cabin. "Rani-sa has come back..."

"What do you mean by 'Rani-sa has come back'?" shouted a flabbergasted Rana.

"She just came in, huzoor. She's on her way up," he said awkwardly.

"Oh god!" Rana replaced the receiver and turned to Saanvri, who was dressed in a loose top and a pair of jeans, stealthily giving a final touch to her hair with a brush in front of the large vanity mirror. "Saanvri leave all that, you have to run out, at once."

"What happened?" She looked alarmed.

"*Arre*, Madhvi has come back. Rani-sa...She's about to storm up here."

"Don't worry, I'm absolutely ready...will run along right now...I'll hide in the stairwell alongside the corridor, the one going upstairs...Is that okay?" She made a dash for her things.

Meanwhile, a fiery Madhvi came like a tornado, down the long corridor leading to the marital bedroom. Midway, in a crevice-like space, stood a young maidservant with her head bent down reverently. As Madhvi came close, their eyes met and the maid hinted meaningfully by a sideway glance, indicating that the quary was still inside. Madhvi silently acknowledged her assistance and charged towards the bedroom with fiercer paces.

Her hand had hardly gone up to the door that it flung open on its own, revealing Saanvri, who was about to barge out. Both came to an abrupt halt on facing each other. Even with just the threshold and a wall of silence between them, they were eons apart.

Saanvri immediately dropped her eyes in the face of Madhvi's blazing ones, which seemed to grind into hers.

"I have certainly crossed the *chaukhat* (threshold), huzoor," she said very respectfully and then attempted to raise her eyes only slightly to say, "But I have not broken the house honour, hukum." Again she dropped her eyes and lowered her head a little more.

A moment seemed like eternity in its oppressive silence. Once again as Saanvri raised her eyes, she found them impaled by Madhvi's. She dropped them again and said, "You are Rani-sa, huzoor...I am not more than a *golee*. But both of us still happen to be women...I have not broken a woman's obligation to another, hukum. I did not reach up to your bed...remained only on the ground."

Madhvi was rendered speechless. The embers in her eyes turned to molten lava. Saanvri moved and soundlessly squeezing her way around a statue-like Madhvi, walked slowly down the corridor.

That day was not easy on her. The arrogance with which she had left Rana's place had not lasted long. Her inherent goodness as a kind and fair woman had taken her into a state of guilt by the time she had reached home in the auto rickshaw, disregarding the offer to use Rana's car.

The children had gone to school, and Khoobchand was on duty. Dhaniya, who had come over a fortnight earlier, to take care of the children and look after the household while Saanvri was in Bangkok, had not returned to Phool-Birai. She was in the midst of her early morning prayers when Saanvri returned. She had heard the sounds of the front room opening and then shutting from inside and then everything had gone quiet. She was surprised that unlike her habit, Saanvri had not even peeped inside her room to say '*Pa lagoon*, Amma'.

In the semidarkness of her bedroom, without changing, Saanvri sat on a cot by the window, with her back rested against the wall—quiet, listless and empty. When she had expressed to Rana her desire to witness, for once, the inner quarters—the personal bedroom, where he and his wife spent their most private, the most intimate, moments—it was in fact, a wicked attempt to assuage her hurt self-respect. Her ego had been bruised on being referred as a 'golee' by Rana in his telephonic conversation with Madhvi, which she had overheard moments ago in the hotel room in Bangkok. What was thought out at the spur of the moment, as simply an avenging step, had on the contrary started gnawing at her conscience for the worthlessness of the endeavour that had ended up baring her meaner self.

After finishing her puja, Dhaniya walked to the front room with the intent of making some tea. As she moved towards the kitchen, she noticed through the door, which was slightly ajar, the shadowy figure of Saanvri, seated stoically by the window in her bedroom. She intuitively understood the state Saanvri was in, having had a cursory chat with her the previous night, before she had left in the car sent by Rana, 'supposedly' in response to a medical emergency.

Strangely, what was happening in Saanvri's life lately was not unknown to her. Despite the tricky relationship, she was the only one in whom Saanvri confided everything. While making tea she decided that the time had come for her to have a frank chat with her daughter-in-law.

"Here, drink the tea," she said, placing the glass in front of Saanvri. In their private moments they loved sharing tea, which they had in glasses, instead of cups.

Saanvri made no motion to take the glass and remained seated in her pensive state. Dhaniya sat down beside her on the same cot and took a long sip from her glass before saying, "Drink it. It'll help in letting the load off your chest."

Though still silent, Saanvri picked up the glass and took a sip. Both took many a shallow sips, allowing the silence to seep in and be the only mode of communication. Then Dhaniya spoke, as if to herself: "Same story…There's something wrong in the 'soil' itself."

Saanvri's hand holding the glass stopped midway, short of reaching her mouth. She did not say anything for a few seconds, trying to fathom the import of that apparently innocuous remark. Then slowly she turned to look at Dhania questioningly.

Dhania was not looking at her. Her translucent eyes had a distant look in them as they seemed to stare at nothing in particular in front of her.

"...Even you Amma?" softly, almost in a whisper Saanvri ventured at last.

There was no reaction from Dhania at first. After a long pause she nodded, took a sip of her tea and said, "A *banjaran*, that's what I was... Had gone to the Ugadi mela with the rest," she said reminiscing, without looking at Saanvri. "There, he met me. I had lost my way in the large fair and asked him to give me direction, to get back to my people. That's all. That alone cost me dearly."

Saanvri waited. Silence flowed again, amid more unhurried sips. Then after a deep sigh she spoke again: "What is the point now of recalling the whole story—It has happened before to many, will happen again...I was young, young and foolish. Very foolish...He charmed me. I fell under his spell and fought with my tribe to marry him."

She had a defeated smile on her face. "What marriage? Just an exchange of simple flower garlands in a dilapidated little roadside temple...That was it. My people threw me out of the tribe. He also abandoned me after a few months. Left his orderly's job in the hospital and disappeared never to return ever." Her eyes were misty and sad, her face shadowed with bitterness. "But he left something behind."

Saanvri looked at her with questions in her eyes.

"Your husband..." A look of resignation had descended on her face now.

Saanvri's jaw dropped in awe. Impulsively her hand reached out for Dhaniya's free hand and held it in hers.

"You are lucky, *beti*...Even if only for a show now, you have a husband of some sort...Your own children from him." She spoke in a broken voice. Then she smiled and a spark returned to her eyes. "And, you have me—your mother-in-law and mother, both in one…I understand your predicament."

It touched a chord instantly. Saanvri put her glass on the window sill and went to the older woman, surrendering herself at her chest. Tears flooded her eyes and flowed relentlessly.

It was strange how they bonded yet again on this issue; their strong kinship becoming stronger than ever. Saanvri poured out nearly everything she had in her heart from the time she met Rana for the first time, to what had happened that morning at his house. An inconceivable act of emptying oneself to someone who should be the last person to confide in. But Dhaniya was no ordinary woman. She had a rare humanism to accept everything with equanimity. The turmoil and the twists of fate she had experienced in her life had much to contribute toward who she was. It was for quite some time that she had intuitively understood the barrenness of the relationship between her son and Saanvri, without it ever being spelt out.

"Have you ever stared at the vast desert during the day, when for miles it is only sands, blazing sands in front of you? She asked Saanvri and then said. "Yes, you must have, for your small village is at the edge of the great desert anyways."

"Yes, I have. Why do you ask this?" Saanvri was confused.

"You see water at the far distance…You run towards it because you are thirsty, very thirsty. But when you reach it, you find there is no water. Then you see water in another direction, you run to it…Again no water. Just an illusion, a mirage!"

"Yes, I know that only too well."

"There would be nothing but sorrows for you in this," she cut her in a sad voice. "He'll never accept you in public."

Saanvri looked up in shock, "What? Why are you saying this, Amma?"

"Because you are falling in love with him…"

"What?" Saanvri was taken by surprise as she had not mentioned a word to Dhania about how she felt when she was with Rana at the beach in Pattaya.

"How can you say that Amma, I only…" she mumbled.

"I can see that on your face." Dhaniya was forthright. "You may think that he is only a benefactor for you…But is it so? Not quite…You know that," she said challengingly.

Saanvri was stumped. She lowered her eyes and said nothing. Sadness engulfed her.

"But our stories are not quite the same, still." Dhaniya too turned sad.

Saanvri looked up again, expectantly.

"You've been luckier than I."

Questions lurked in Saanvri's eyes.

"You've had your own feet to stand on. You had your own house too, before this thing hit you," she said empathetically and then turned reminiscent. "Not like me. I had nothing going for me. I was all alone and shattered, very shattered. More men came. All cheated me. I almost committed suicide once. Lay myself on a railway track, only to see the train change tracks and pass by, on another line. But that brought yet another man to rescue me and change my life."

Having read the anticipation on Saanvri's face, she said with sparkling eyes. "That man was Khajooria Lal, who gave me my identity, my self-respect and married me. It was Devi's miracle and nothing else that a man who worked in the same hospital as that *harami* Lachhman, and was even a friend of his, was to prove so different, so honourable."

Tears sparkled in Saanvri's eyes as she listened to Dhaniya speak with reverence about her late husband. Tears are such equalisers. Now as the two women held each other, their tears flowed freely, enjoining them further. That singular moment made Saanvri reaffirm her resolve that, whatever may be the circumstances or her feelings, she would not compromise her individuality or self-reliance, ever again.

Eleven

The atmosphere was electric. The entire stage pulsated with energy. The wooden floor, under the feet of two dozen performers, vibrated visibly, as did the side walls of the huge theatre. They were dancing to 5,000-watts of the enthralling music, reproduced by more than a dozen large speakers.

Each wide and well-co-ordinated swirl of the lehengas—the large colourful ones that tribal women wear—sent the spectators, in the huge hall, into raptures of ecstasy. The group of young men and women, all attired in tribal costumes as *nats* and *natis*, danced with abandon to enchant the audience with raw passion. The lead dancer was particularly captivating with her scintillating performance, though just like the others a good part of her face was hidden by the *ghunghat* to tease the spectators.

It was a number that was being presented by the nursing staff of the local health department as a segment for the Annual Day function. On a large sofa, in the front row of the cheering crowd, all by himself, sat Yashpal Sarena, the Health and Welfare Minister. On another sofa, separated by a couple of other sofas, sat Rana with some VIPs.

Midway through the revue, a couple of dancers placed two very tall poles, protruding from two circular platforms on the two extreme sides of the stage, and then tied a rope across them. A female dancer, attired as a Mughal courtesan in a colourful salwar-kameez, with a long scarf covering everything excepting her eyes, stood balancing herself on the rope with an ornamented shaft in her hands. Walking the rope from one pole to another, she executed magnificent acts keeping time to the music that had changed to an Arab folk tune. Her movements had at once the fluidity of an accomplished gymnast as well as the grace of a veteran dancer.

Both Yashpal Sarena and Rana were completely taken in by the dancer. But more surprises were in store. The dancer positioned herself on the platform around one of the poles, while another similarly attired dancer arrived and positioned herself on the other platform. Now, with the music getting more sensuous, both the dancers started peeling off their dresses. First went the salwars, then the figure hugging tops in swift artful motions, revealing them in sheath-like body stockings. Winding their bodies like creepers around the poles, they started slithering up amid sensually captivating, spellbinding acts. And then, all of a sudden, off went the scarves, which had hitherto hidden most of the faces of the two accomplished performers.

Rana's jaw dropped while an audible sigh escaped Yashpal's mouth. One of them was Saanvri, who had been the lead dancer in the earlier acts. Rana was taken by complete surprise because he had no inkling, whatsoever, of Saanvri being a part of the show, that too performing in such a daring seductive way. Surprised as he was with this unexpected revelation, he was also highly impressed with the fascinating fusion of the Indian tribal movements with the Western pole dancing that she had enjoyed in Bangkok. It was indeed a masterly composition. He now realised that Saanvri wanted to surprise him with her creativity and had worked secretly for this day.

On the other hand, Yashpal was visibly aroused by Saanvri's oozing sexuality and her provocative movements. It was an amazing item— artistic and intricate, unhesitatingly sensuous, yet devoid of any vulgarity. He was entranced by Saanvri's whole being and a film of passion slowly descended over his eyes. He seemed to notice no one else but her. In a while, he leaned across to the man sitting on a sofa next to him and whispered something into his ears. The man surreptitiously pointed at Rana. Yashpal nodded slightly and stole a glance at Rana, who noticed the gesture.

The air of excitement and throbbing jubilation among the spectators, who mainly comprised the hospital staff, students, bureaucrats and their families, made Rana more and more self-conscious with their applause. And now having noticed Yashpal's surreptitious stares and greedy looks, he was all the more ill at ease. At the conclusion of the item, when the emcee of the evening excitedly addressed the gathering, the audience sprang to its feet in delirious clapping and whistling.

"This spectacular fusion of the Western pole dance and the *khamb nritya*, the exquisite dance form, grown in our own soil, was presented by the nursing staff of our local Health Department, under the direction of the senior nurse, Shrimati Saanvri Devi, who has recently returned from her foreign tour, where she had gone on a study exchange. She was also the principal performer in the item. And now..."

Midway through the announcement, Rana got up from his seat and, gesturing his apologies to the guests, especially to Yashpal from afar, he gingerly walked towards the exit. But just as he reached it, he turned to the small door on the side of the stage and after throwing a cursory glance behind him, he quickly opened it and hurriedly climbed up the four steps to the side of the stage. However, much as he wished, he did not succeed in dodging Yashpal's eyes, which followed him throughout.

Rana caught hold of Saanvri in the space beside the wings, chatting with some other girl. She was still dressed in the same costume in which she had danced. Her face lit up on seeing Rana. But noticing the frown on his face, she excused herself from the other girl who scampered towards the green rooms. She walked up to him with an expression of concern.

"What happened, Rana-ji? Any problem?"

"*Yaar*, you should have at least cautioned me that you were also going to perform like this," he murmured in a hurt voice, acutely conscious that another item was about to begin, a few feet away on the stage.

"Wanted to give you a surprise." She beamed and then teased him. "Why, didn't you like it?"

Just as Rana wanted to rebut, he noticed two girls pass through another wing. They threw discreet glances at them, before exchanging meaningful looks with each other and moving on.

Rana mumbled in an exasperated tone, "That's not the point. Try and understand, a man looks like a fool," he said, sounding deflated. "The minister was also sitting there. It is easier, if one knows in advance."

"So-o-r-r-y," she said, a little hurt. "I thought you'd be happy."

"I'm happy, very happy," he cut her short. "But even so..."

"If you're happy, then give me a *pappi,* quickly," she said quick-wittedly. With mischief dancing in her eyes, she tried to sneak a kiss.

"*Arre*, what're you doing...have you gone mad?" Embarrassed, he dodged to restrain her and said, "The entire department's people are here. The minister is also seated there."

Just then, someone beckoned her from the other end of the stage.

"Saanvri, your item is in three minutes," said a male stage-hand. He had a knowing smile on his face, visible even in the semi-darkness of the wing. Saanvri looked a little embarrassed as she nodded at him.

"I need to go."

"Fine," Rana also needed to rescue himself quickly. He dashed towards the steps to the exit.

Rana rushed through the corridor. He wanted to slip away unnoticed before the programme ended. But suddenly he was face to face with a portly man who almost blocked his path.

"Rana-ji, you can't leave just yet, sir."

"*Yaar*, Bhandari-sahab, I really have something important to attend to. Please try to understand."

"No way, sir, how can we let you leave without sharing a little refreshment with the artists? They have worked so hard for this day."

"But, you know me, I..."

"No hukum, it won't be nice," he cut him short. "They are all from your constituency. You are the MLA from here. Moreover, the minister is still here. You must stay, at least for a few more minutes."

The man had played the lethal card. Despite his strong aversion for Yashpal Sarena, Rana had to surrender. The license for building a new luxury hospital to be constructed by his company was yet to be issued by his adversary's ministry. He had to comply.

The small hospitality area, adjacent to the assembly hall, was teaming with people. VIP guests, artists and organising committee members were congregated, chatting over cups of tea and coffee and other refreshments. Yashpal Sarena was plonked on a three-seater sofa, all by himself. His hangers-on—mostly male bureaucrats and businessmen alike—were leaning over and trying to humour him, though no one had the courage to occupy the empty seat next to him.

Yashpal noticed Rana some distance away, also engaged in a muted discussion with a few of his own men. His eyes lit up as he pushed the two men in front of him aside to wave at Rana. He patted at the empty space on the sofa next to his, beckoning him to come and join him. As Rana made his way through the cluster of people, Yashpal waved his hand to disperse the hangers-on who were surrounding him.

True to his brash character, he came to the point almost straight away. As soon as Rana sat down on the sofa, he leaned over the hand rest and craning his neck to him, spoke suggestively, "*Arre*, what a terrific function you arranged, Rana-ji. No praise is enough."

His tone was at once licentious and patronising. There was no trace of any deference towards Rana's royal antecedents. This deliberate frivolity did not escape Rana's attention.

"It's nice that you liked it. Thank you, Sarena-ji," he said reservedly.

"But Rana-ji, you are a true *johri*, indeed," Yashpal continued, not letting him off. "What a talent you have discovered in that lady. What's her name? Yes, yes, Saanvri...Saanvri Devi. She is a huge talent sahab, truly a huge talent," he chuckled.

"Yes...yes, yes...she is, she is." He was vividly ill at ease, knowing well what was playing on Yashpal's mind. He added a little squeamishly, "She puts in a lot of hard work."

"Absolutely sahab, absolutely...it is so evident," Yashpal concurred forthwith and then said, tongue in cheek, "With your blessings, one gets a chance to blossom too, isn't it?"

Rana's face went red, but he said nothing. All of a sudden, the silence became oppressive. Despite the chatter all around, time seemed to have frozen for Rana.

But Yashpal was not done yet. Once again, he leaned across and whispered in Rana's ear, almost secretively, "I hear, she is...I mean this lady is, very close to you?"

Rana was beginning to feel incensed but he had to control himself and not show anything on his face as he spoke, "Yes, her husband is a driver at our place, so we run into each other sometimes."

"Oh yes...of course, of course!" he remarked sharply. Disregarding Rana's vivid discomfort, he pulled even closer and shamelessly whispered in his ear, "Why not send her to me too. Such a talented lady she is. Let me also experience her talent a little bit... hmm?"

Suddenly, the earth stopped spinning. Rana sat like a stone for a good many seconds, neither flinching, nor uttering anything. The man was outrageously brazen in wielding his ministerial power to deliberately wound Rana's self-esteem. In the olden days, Rana could have had his head for this insolence. But things were different now. It was a blatant disdain of a minion who had suddenly risen to power. There was a moment of awkward silence and then Rana cleared his throat and merely said, "*Hoon.*"

Yashpal was quick with his dismissal. Pointing at Rana's associates, he said summarily: "They, your people over there, are waiting for you I think...*chalien aap*."

"*Ji*." Too stunned to say anything further, Rana got up and, after a moment's uncertainty and without as much giving a sideway glance to Yashpal, walked towards his companions. He felt a ton of weight bear down on him.

A smirk appeared on Yashpal's lips, and his eyes squinted like a wolf as he followed him with his eyes.

•◆•

The brief encounter with Yashpal Sarena had shaken Rana deeply. Weakened by his business compulsions, he felt he had been castrated of his power to retaliate. For many days, an unquenched fury kept him edgy. However, gradually, the volcanic flames swirling inside him subsided due to the priorities of day-to-day engagements.

But his torment was not to end anytime soon. The license for a twelve storey luxury hospital had been stuck at the ministry for a painfully long period despite the usual greasing of palms. For the first time, he thought of making a call himself, not to the minister but his PA, for a gentle nudge. His head was buried in papers when the intercom rang.

"Yes, Gupta," he spoke brusquely.

"Yashpal Sarena-ji's PA is on the line, sir. You wanted to speak with him?" Gupta's voice crackled.

"Okay, I'll take it."

Rana replaced the receiver of the intercom and picked up the other phone.

"*Arre bhai*, what's up, Singh-sahab?" he said in a tone of familiarity, and then without waiting for the other person to respond, he continued. "That license was to reach us. It's been over a week, it has not arrived."

"It's done sir, it's done. Mantri-ji has already signed it today," he spoke very respectfully and reassuringly, "Tomorrow the license will be on your table, sir."

"Thank you."

But before Rana could replace the receiver, Singh cleared his throat and said quickly, albeit hesitantly, "Well…sir…Mantri-ji was mentioning," he lowered his voice and said secretively, "about some talented person you had to send him. He asked me to remind you, sir."

"Yes, yes…I'll see what I can do. I'll do something," he put down the receiver slowly, and almost in a reflex slammed his fist on the desk; he was gripped by disconcerting thoughts—disconcerting and infuriating.

A few days after moving into a new house, arranged by Rana, Sannvri and her family were having a dinner together in the small front room. This was so different from the time when just two or at the most three people would crouch around a small table in the bedroom. A happy bonhomie was evident between the parents and the two children as they ate the food cooked by Dhaniya who, having already eaten, rested on the cot nearby.

Suddenly, Saanvri sprang out of her chair and made a dash towards the bathroom with her hand clasped over her mouth. She barely flung open the door when she threw up, right on the floor. Dhaniya, who was taking a drag from her small hand-held hookah, sat up with a jolt, witnessing the commotion. She saw Saanvri retching and gagging miserably. But nothing came out despite her groan ricocheting in the empty confines of the small bathroom.

An all-knowing expression surfaced on Dhaniya's face. As she turned her face towards Khoobchand, they exchanged a fearful glance with each other. Despite not a word being spoken, that brief moment was enough to ask and answer many things.

When Saanvri straightened and turned around to move to the sink, she found Khoobchand standing at the doorway. He had come by quietly and was staring at her silently. She shifted her eyes and went to the small basin outside the door and began rinsing her mouth. On straightening again, she found him still staring at her. She held his stare for a while, but neither said anything. Yet, enough had been exchanged in that silence. In a moment she moved away, leaving him gazing at the empty space she had left behind.

•◆•

Two days later, at the hospital where she worked, Saanvri was seated in front of a middle-aged lady doctor in her cabin. She waited with bated breath while the doctor opened the envelope containing the one page report that her assistant had handed over.

"Everything is fine," she remarked with a smile, but unable to figure out the gloominess on Saanvri's face, she leaned forward and quizzed, "It's happy news, why are you sitting with a long face?"

A defeated smile appeared on Saanvri's face. How was she to explain to the doctor, the complexity of the situation? After returning from Bangkok, her menstruation had arrived on the stipulated date, saving her from any worry. It was only after the libidinal encounter at Rana's haveli, which she had thought had happened within the safety zone, that the trouble began. Having reached the second month in that unaltered state she was now panicky, especially after the nausea some days ago.

The doctor got up from her seat, saying, "Not to worry, everything is normal and healthy. But…" she came up to Saanvri and affectionately patted on her head, "no more after this. This is your third baby… Hereafter, it can trigger health issues."

A pathetic smile spread across Saanvri's face.

Once out the doctor's cabin, she wanted desperately to be alone. But the corridor was full of people as if it were a railway station. Benches were full with patients, with their relatives sprawled on the floor. She knew there would be no refuge in her ward either. There was only an empty telephone booth in the corridor. That seemed a godsend sanctuary for her at that point of time. Her eyes brimmed with tears.

For a moment, she just threw herself back to the tiny corner between a side wall and the closed door. She artfully put her dupatta over her head to create a kind of a veil and blocked her eyes from any intruder's view. She picked up the receiver and, without dialling any number, just let herself go. No one could see her tears flowing silently; uninterrupted tears. Once emptied of tears, she dialled Rana's number in earnest.

"Hello," Rana answered his cell while travelling in his car.

"Hel-lo," her voice trembled. She cleared her throat and attempted again in a quivering voice, "I, Saanvri."

"Yes, Saanvri...Good that you called, I was thinking of calling you to talk about something. I had to tell you something." He went on without asking why she had called.

"I too had to say something, Rana-ji." Her voice seemed to be breaking.

"You meet me at the Fateh Sagar flat, in an hour," he said hurriedly and disconnected.

The doorbell was answered by Rana's driver. He mumbled a 'pranam' and, with his head bent, stood aside after pulling the door open to let her in. She walked in and went up to the sofas in the middle of the sitting room. The driver shut the door after her, and instead of approaching her and saying anything, disappeared into the kitchen. The large room suddenly looked very empty. She dropped her bag on the settee and slowly and a little self-consciously sat on it.

In a moment, the driver returned with a glass of water held on a small tray. She took the glass and drank a little. While putting it back on the tray, she spoke, "Hukum...is he inside?"

"There he is..." The driver pointed at the space behind her and left the room.

She turned around and saw him now, like a dark cut-out, standing by the wide window, behind her. She had not noticed him because he had neither greeted her on entering nor made any sound. In his stillness against the perfect daylight outside the window, he looked like a black sentinel, peering at the placid waters of the grand Fateh Sagar Lake and the vast span of green alongside it.

She rose slowly and tried to take in the scene, continuing to stare at Rana from behind. The morgue-like silence disconcerted her. But why was she thinking of death when she had come here to talk about a new life? The thought uplifted her. A smile appeared on her face and brought translucence to her eyes. She moved. The measured paces she took to reach him had the shy sway of a newly-wed. With tranquillity and tenderness sweeping her face, she gently placed her head on his back. Her face, with her eyes closed and a tiny smile on her lips, oozed contentment and love.

He remained still. Then his hand rose, holding a glass with some drink. He took a sip, looking stiff and steely. But then an invective escaped his clenched teeth and he lashed out like a wounded animal.

"*Bhenchod*...not even two *kaudi* worth in stature, and he dares to show eyes? *Saala*...son of a bastard."

A shocked Saanvri pulled back. Rana swirled around and bounded across to the other side of the room, shouting obscenities to let go of his bottled frustration.

"You don't want to give the license, don't give, you bloody pimp. I'll be ruined, so what? I have suffered losses before, I'll suffer them again, *saale*."

Saanvri turned around with a jolt. Listening to his outpouring as he sprang out, her heart went to him. Overtaken by a tremendous sense of concern, she tried to go up to him. But before she could reach him, he turned around again and now stormed back, incensed by his own helplessness. She struggled to keep pace in an effort to hold him in her reassuring embrace. Fired by the spurts of his uncontrolled fury, he continued to spring back and forth, mouthing fresh curses.

"We lost our kingdoms, our palaces, fleets of vehicles, retinues of staff. We've lost a lot. We are not going to break down and collapse, *saale*." He paused for a couple of seconds, spent in his contempt for the whole democratic set up that had robbed the likes of him of their status and princely possessions.

Saanvri froze in her place, struck by the utter disdain spewed out by him—a member of the erstwhile royalty—against those who, till recently, were their subjects, but had now seized the reins of power to rule them instead. Unwittingly, what she witnessed was not merely the outrage of one class against the other, but the simmering anger, distrust and hatred between the two men.

"*Saala*, deceptively snatches away the ministry from me, and then tries to threaten me, *harami*."

After a moment's hesitation, she again attempted to go and hug him. But he again twirled around, this time even more forcefully, swearing aloud at an unknown entity, as though there was someone standing in front of him.

"Rob me, rob me of whatever you want, *maderchod*…rob me… come, on rob me. But I'm not going to accept your trade-off *bhenchod*… a filthy trade-off…*saala*."

Driven by his fury, he turned again and was now face to face with Saanvri. He stopped abruptly. Their eyes locked, they froze in their places. Time stopped for a few moments. She read fear and hopelessness in his eyes. She felt as helpless, and that triggered a genuine concern for him. He said nothing, but she understood everything.

"Yashpal Sarena is bothering you, isn't it?" she said. She already had an inkling, having noticed his deliberate and cheap antics at the time of handing her the trophy at the awards ceremony. After her dance recital at the JJDA function, he pretended to have accidentally caressed her hand.

Rana did not utter anything. He nodded, looking defeated.

"Wants to sleep with me, does he?" she asked, boring her eyes into his. "Isn't it so?"

Rana lowered his eyes.

"Isn't it?"

Rana lashed out at her, “Yes, yes, yes. What do I do, tell me what do I do?”

Saanvri’s mouth fell open. She said nothing for a few seconds. The impenetrable silence was breached only by his heavy breathing, as if he had been sprinting uphill. At last she spoke, “I shall go to him. Tell him, I am ready!”

Rana slowly descended into the chair near him, his face stupefied, his body statue-like.

Saanvri’s eyes had the calmness of the dead. She moved up to him and went down on her knees. She held his hand between hers and said dispassionately, yet meaningfully, “Shall I say something Rana-ji?” her eyes had the sparkle of a winner.

He looked up, nonplussed. She continued, “There is unique pleasure in reeling in filth. You lose the fear of getting your body dirtied, once and for all.”

Rana lowered his eyes. Neither did he ask her the reason for her wanting to talk to him, nor did she feel the need to reveal to him what had been eating her up. Once again, and more clearly than ever before, she knew where she stood.

TWELVE

The taxi entered the campus through a majestic gate manned by security personnel clad in combat fatigues. The cabby followed the instructions, and after travelling through the narrow drive, amid lush green lawns and the undulating landscape, he reached another set of gates. They opened automatically to reveal a smaller lawn and the porch in front, of what looked like a newly built building.

The lobby of the building had the aura of a luxury apartment of the high and mighty, with plush sofas and a plasma TV in the waiting area. As she found her way to the lift, across the empty hall, an attendant appeared from nowhere. He informed her that due to a grid failure the lifts were not working. A mechanic was on the way. She had the option of either climbing up the stairs all the way to the seventh floor or wait at the lobby till the problem was rectified.

She chose to take the steps of the circular staircase, which looked quite inviting at first, with the carpet lining it all the way up. But what she had embarked upon, somewhat enthusiastically, was soon to turn tiring and a little dizzying. When she finally reached the door of the apartment, she was completely exhausted and ready to collapse on the floor. Her hand trembled as she tried to fit the key in the ornamental keyhole on the door. With every bit of the residual energy left in her body, she turned it and the door opened almost on its own to reveal a hall beyond a small passage.

Breathing heavily, she made her way through the passage to the solitary furniture in the huge sitting room—a chaise lounge—and collapsed on it. Though she was intrigued by the fact that there was no one inside, right then she was beyond caring and let her hands drop the bags she was carrying. Feeling a little drowsy, she barely closed her eyes when she heard someone beckon her in a loud and inviting tone, "Ahh! Saanvri Devi has arrived."

Startled, she opened her eyes and found Yashpal Sarena walking down a staircase from the floor above.

Still panting heavily, Saanvri sprang up again. Yashpal breezily flitted up to her and grabbed her hands, even before she could raise them fully in a fold to greet him.

"*Arre*, what is this? Your hands are cold and you are out of breath?" He wrapped one of his arms protectively around her and still holding her hands with the other, he helped her to the chaise lounge again, saying with concern, "Come on, sit, sit."

But in the process, he let his hand move over her breasts, while half leaning over her as he helped her recline. He said mischievously, "Oh ho! The lift must not be working again. Power goes quite often here. But it was working when I arrived." He seemed slightly apologetic but turned playful just as quickly, "But, *dekkho ji*, after all, for coming up in life, one has to climb up the steps, isn't it *ji?* Then only you get the real pleasure. Look at your own case right now *ji*, the way you're out of breath, your chest heaving up and down. It's so lethal *ji*. And my hand here…" He hinted at his hand pressed over her breasts, "Such a current is passing through it, that it refuses to come unstuck."

A flash of anger flickered in the deep placidity of her eyes. Without letting him read anything, she regarded him like a quary—one of many she had silently vowed to devour and use, when she had first witnessed the utter selfishness in Rana—the man she had started loving unawares—who was nothing but a user. She decided to act the script now.

Rising to the occasion, Saanvri responded equally fervently. Continuing to hold the clasp of his hand pressed over her breasts and without letting go of his gaze, she said with unmitigated suggestiveness in her voice, "Absolutely, hukum. I had understood this current well enough at the competition function itself, when at the time of handing over the award to me, your hand had, shall I say, accidentally, caressed mine?"

"*Ha-a-y-e, kya baat hai.*" A look of lustiness swam across his eyes as he continued, "*Ghanee baat hai thare mein*, Saanvri Devi, *ghanee baat hai.* You're really something else."

Infused with sudden energy, he sprang up. With a tug of his hand he pulled her to her feet while beckoning, "Get up, *yaar*. At least, have a proper look at the place where you will practice your art."

Saanvri moved around in the empty space of the hall and said, "It is indeed a very fine place for dance practice." She turned to Yashpal and said sincerely, "Very kind of you, hukum. Our artists will never be able to thank you enough for this favour from you."

"I am known for encouraging artists to come up in life," he boasted. "That is why I have offered my sister's apartment for this purpose. Here," he waved his hand in a big sweep, "in this empty hall, do all your rehearsals. And if you want to rest, then there are full arrangements upstairs. Come on let me show you."

He grabbed her hand and led her towards the staircase. As she followed him, she asked, "Hukum, what do I do with the key for this place? I better give it to you, isn't it?"

"*Ajee*, let the key remain with you. After all, you'll be visiting here quite often, *aana jaana laga hee rahega.* I shall take it from you when I need it."

Saanvri walked up to the broad window of the expensively done up master bedroom and pulled the curtains to reveal an enticing view of the city.

"Your town looks so beautiful from here, Mantri-ji," she exclaimed.

Yashpal walked up to her and held her from behind. His arms wrapped up under her breasts, giving a noticeable lift to the mounds, he stole a glance at the valley between them and remarked lustily, "The scene is breathtaking even here, Saanvri Devi. You are looking no less than any *apsara* in this saree and blouse." She could feel his heavy breath warming the skin at her nape. He continued, "*Haye*, it is cruel, I tell you, absolutely cruel."

She wanted to say something but just then she felt a shaft coursing her backside. She was appalled. The man was not merely lecherous, he was an animal. Coarse and shameless with his lust. But she had no choice. In her quest for worldliness, she had opted for it—willingly. The fire that had flashed in her eyes receded slowly and now what shone, instead, was an avenging gleam. Deciding to put him out of his misery, she turned around slowly and, drilling his eyes with a mysterious gaze, she asked, "Where is your bathroom, Mantri-ji?"

Yashpal pointed in its direction, "There...Shall I take you there?" He was salivating.

"I shall call you...if I need help." She matched his eyes with equal fervour.

Once the door to the bathroom shut behind her, Yashpal turned to the window. His face already flushed with anticipation, he closed the curtains. He turned around and scanned the room with a quick glance before going to the bed and turning on the bedside lamp. Just as he straightened and turned to look at the bathroom door, his jaw dropped.

Almost with the practiced ease of a super model in a fashion show, Saanvri, clad only in her slinky panties and a brassiere, appeared at the doorway and took a few paces towards him. For a moment, she stopped with her long bare legs, slightly crossed over each other, like a statue grafted in the ground, and considered him with a come-hither smile. Then, disregarding his mouth, which was stupidly agape, slowly she unhooked her bra and slid off the strap of the brassiere from one of her shoulders, and then another. Once again, resuming her enticing walk up to him, she stopped dangerously close to him and whispered coyly, "Mantri-ji, I suspect files do not move at all in your ministry...People must be waiting endlessly for you to sign their papers...Now look at this...I am already here, risen to the occasion, and you are just standing with your mouth open."

As if a lever had been pressed, Yashpal's mouth clamped shut. But as Saanvri inched further towards him and her fingers nimbly unbuttoned his shirt and unzipped his trousers, his mouth came agape once again, partly out of wonderment at this woman's daredevilry and partly because of the sensuous strokes of her fingers. While his face changed expressions several times, hers only bore the impassivity of a surgeon on an operation table, her fingers going about the task with masterly efficiency. Without changing her expression, she brought her mouth within brushing distance of his and whispered almost conspiratorially, "Your mouth has opened up again, Mantri-ji. You can shut it."

Yashpal's mouth promptly clamped up again even as she continued, "Now, whatever had to come down has already come down, and whatever had to rise up has also risen." His face suddenly jerked as if he had touched an electric current, obviously due to a mischievous ministration to his organ by her. Again with a straight face she whispered, "The bed is cold Mantri-ji. It needs to be warmed up. Shall we move to it?"

Despite everything happening on its own, just the way he had desired, Yashpal was not himself. Perhaps for an insecure man, the validity of his masculinity was to have some control over his circumstances. In innumerable sexual encounters before, he always remained the 'master' and the woman a 'supplicant', an object of his pleasure. Saanvri had effortlessly and unashamedly snatched that away from him. For the first time in his life, there seemed to be a role reversal. Even when she went down on him, it was not as if he could manipulate her for his pleasure; a playful tease, she was controlling every move, even the extent of his arousal.

What Saanvri did was a manifestation of her silent resolve to treat the men of the world as mere objects of gratification hereon, after having been reduced to a pawn to be traded. And in this new paradigm, she was determined never to let the respondent forget who called the shots. In this new-found adventure, she had chosen Yashpal to be her first prey, but he was not going to be the last, she was certain. She had, however, mixed feelings about Rana, for reasons that had germinated lately.

Hence, after the copulation, when Yashpal slipped out of bed to go to the washroom, it was she who triumphantly sat up against the headrest and pulled the sheet up to her naked breasts. She lit a cigarette, indifferent to what her benefactor might think about it. The long release of the smoke after the first puff was an expression of the freedom she had granted herself from the moralistic clutter that had been infesting her mind for too long. When Yashpal reappeared at the doorway of the washroom in front of her, she teased him with the flourish of a victor, "*Arre*, just come this side, a little closer Mantri-ji," she chided him mildly. "What is this? Enjoyed me thoroughly and now quickly getting dressed? This is not fair at all."

Clad only in his underpants and the shirt, with its buttons still open, like an obedient child Yashpal walked up to her on the side of the bed. Tugging on his shirt, she nudged him.

"Sit, sit, sit down here, *na*." She patted the bed. Yashpal obliged. She dared him further. "Come a little closer. The distances between us have already been erased now, then, why this gulf?" She pointed at the space between them teasingly.

Yashpal slid closer. She took another drag of her cigarette and slowly released the smoke on his face, almost in a caress, sending him into strange throes of ecstasy. As she watched him react to the fumes, she teased him further with a sexual suggestiveness, "You've just given me so much of your stuff with so much heart, in return take something from me also."

Yashpal went into a kind of sensual tremulousness and said, "*Arre saali*, you are really some magician. Even the way you emit this damn smoke, you shake everything inside a man."

While continuing to hold the cigarette in one hand, Saanvri wore a come-hither expression to her face and put her arms around his neck. For a moment, she watched him with fascination without doing anything. Only a tiny smile appeared at the corner of her mouth. Her fulsome lips reignited something in his loins. Knowing pretty well the effect she was having on him, she put a peck on his lips and then whispered coyly, "How will I address you, hukum? Can't say 'Mantri-ji' always. Calling you by name won't be nice either."

"Address me any which way you like."

Cosying up she said enticingly, "Shall I call you 'Daddy'... 'Daddy-ji'?"

"Daddy? What kind of an address is that?" He seemed affronted.

"Can't call you 'sajan' in public, now can I? 'Uncle' sounds so old fashioned, and 'Mantri-ji' would sound very official," she teased him further. "'Daddy-ji' has something new about it. It also has a tinge of love in it and indicates some closeness."

Yashpal was nonplussed, unable to say anything he looked ill-at-ease. She teased him further, "Publicly, even you are going to address me as *beti* only, so what difference does it make? Our relationship is going to remain what it is, isn't it?"

"Oh, call me whatever you feel like," he said in a tone of surrender after a moment of hesitation.

Saanvri kissed him passionately and said naughtily, "Thank you, Daddy-ji."

The vast span of green by the side of one of the main roads of Civil Lines was abuzz with activity, early that morning. A group of dancers, male and female, were in the midst of performing the dress-rehearsal of their folk number on the lawns of a yellow colonial building, housing the offices of the Rajasthan Kala Academy. Beyond the long shadow of the two-storeyed building, spread across almost half the lawn, the artists were engaged in their activities under the warmth of the first rays of the sun. Some distance away, another group of performers, seated in a circle, enthusiastically rehearsed their dialogues.

Soon, there was a break for refreshments. Buffet tables had been arranged close to the building. The mouth-watering smell of freshly made savouries and hot jalebis had magnetic magical effect on all. Artists, assistants, members of the organising staff, made a beeline to the buffet tables. Goaded by one or two attendants, Saanvri, who had been keeping to herself, also picked up a plate. But her eyes were continuously scanning the congregation, searching for someone who hadn't arrived.

She took a little chutney on her plate and moved towards the bowl containing *bhajiyas* some distance away, when she noticed a tall, aristocratic grey-haired lady, clad in a silk saree. She was not there before.

One of the office boys came around discreetly and said something in her ears. Saanvri, immediately, crossed through the knot of people around the tables and went up to the tall lady, who was about to pick up something to eat. Saanvri addressed the lady with great respect:

"Namaskar Sulakshana madam, I am Saanvri. I had been to your house to pick up the key for the flat at the Royal Heights," her voice quivered a bit as the lady remained engaged in what she was doing. "Mantri-ji, your brother had ordered me to do so."

Now as the lady straightened, Saanvri said in an even weaker voice, "You were not home at the time."

The lady lifted up her dark glasses and regarded Saanvri with a long look. Saanvri's cool and well-composed demeanour instantly disintegrated in the face of her penetrating gaze. She lowered her eyes, as if it was the only defence available to her. Little did she realise at the time that this very person would become her nemesis someday. Without the slightest shift in her stern stare, Sulakshana spoke with a caustic edge to her voice:

"Saa-n-v-r-i…hmm…What one had heard was not wrong after all. Yes, there is youth…There is intoxicating beauty…There is attitude too." She brought down the glasses to her eyes and continued slightly sarcastically, "The attitude is a little bit on the higher side. So much attitude is not a good idea."

"Madam," Saanvri mewled, distinctly ill-at-ease.

Sulakshna again pulled up her glasses over her head and said with an acid touch, "If a key opens the doors, it is also a key that closes the doors. Don't you ever forget this, girl."

Completely shaken, Saanvri stuttered apologetically, "Madam. I was bringing back the key to you…but Mantri-ji ."

"No, no. It doesn't matter. You keep the key with you for now," Sulakshna cut her off and then said with a little more sharpness in her voice, "You'll need it again and again. I have another key for myself."

Saanvri, unable to say anything, merely shook her head. Sulakshana said dismissively, "Your plate is empty…Go and fetch something. You must be tired." and she abruptly turned and walked away, leaving a very confused and much shaken Saanvri, stupidly standing by herself with the empty plate in her hands.

The 'love-nest' at the Royal Heights soon turned into an addiction for Yashpal. More and more gadgets and luxury contraptions were installed in the penthouse. Quite often, even during the day, sometimes in between official meetings and sometimes even in the midst of heated debates in the Assembly, he would surreptitiously disappear to recharge his batteries. His trusted staff always had a perfect tale to tell anybody whose nose itched for news.

One such day, Yashpal and Saanvri sat relaxing in the large Jacuzzi tub. Jets of water hit their bodies from different directions and the bubbles covering them sent them in raptures of ecstasy.

"First the oil massage from your magical fingers, then this firing of the bubbles…*bhai*…it's really something else! All the knots tightening inside have eased out from the body." Yashpal said.

Saanvri raised a leg above the surface of water and placed her foot on Yashpal's chest, tantalisingly rubbing it with her toe. As he wriggled with waves of pleasure, she teased him in a lusty voice.

"The more knots get untangled, the more one enjoys in knotting up with each other on the bed, isn't it Daddy-ji?"

"*Arre tu*...you're going to kill me with your silver tongue," Yashpal muttered in a voice dripping with lust.

"Why are you accusing me, hukum? As it is I am going to leave soon," she put on a complaining tone.

Yashpal sprang up to sit and grabbed both her arms saying, "*Arre*, but why are you going, you cruel thing? Turned me into an addict and now you talk about going...and that too for six months?"

"Not as if I am going for good? If it was not important, I would have never thought of leaving." She was immediately reassuring with a 'put-on' concern. Then she again teased, "And you are not going to be here either. You too have three foreign tours in the next four months."

"Yes...that way, you're right!"

"But will you be able to handle the matter of my continuous absence from work? In the last three months, I have been to Jodhpur only in bits, only a couple of days at a time, and that too just to pick up the cheques. If some sort of *raada* comes about, then?"

He forthwith pressed his lips on her neck and her breasts before saying, "*Arre*, how would there be a *raada*? Urban Development and Power—both the ministries are with me. And, then as it is you've put so much current in me. Wouldn't I give them a bite they'll remember.?" He gave her a series of quick sting-like mock bites as he spoke.

In a flash of passion, as he dug his teeth on her breast, she yelped in mock protest. "*Arre*, it'll leave the marks, Daddy-ji. How many people will I answer to, then?"

THIRTEEN

The backyard of the small house was bathed in the first rays of the January sun. The atmosphere was blissfully calm as a lazy afternoon in the outskirts of a new suburb usually is. A cow tied to a *khoonta* in a corner of the *aangan* was quietly doing its *jugalee*, munching over the remnants of regurgitated food. Close by, a servant boy in his late twenties was tightening the strips of a *newad* cot. Some distance away, seated on a jute cot, Saanvri's fourteen-year-old daughter, Basanti, was busy doing her homework. Seated alongside on the same cot, her grandmother Dhania was knitting a sweater. In a while, she stretched herself and took a big yawn. Then she announced, to nobody in particular:

"My eyes are tired. I'm going in. Will lie down for some time."

No sooner had she dawdled inside that Basanti lowered her book and addressed the boy in a hushed tone.

"Lachchu, what're you doing?"

"Tightening up." He pointed at the job in hand.

Basanti put down her book and gave him a long 'come-hither' look, before silently getting up and walking up to the other end of the *aangan* where there was a barn with bundles of fodder. Lachchu stopped his work to follow her with his eyes. She stopped for a moment to turn around and gave him another long meaningful look before disappearing behind the bundles of fodder. Lachchu tried to get back to work at first. But in no time he stopped and looked around for any possible intrusion.

Then he sprang up, dashed towards the barn and swiftly disappeared behind the bundles.

Inside the house, Dhania turned on her side, trying to catch some sleep. But it deserted her. Though moments ago her eyes were heavily laden, her mind now strayed to Saanvri, who was to arrive the next day. Those thoughts had been robbing her peace lately. She turned over to the other side, hoping to catch some sleep, but to no avail. In futility she opened her eyes and sat up on the cot. She strained her ears to catch some noise from outside, but it was unusually quiet. Something seemed to disturb her. She got up and walked towards the *aangan*. Finding neither Basanti nor Lachchu at their places, she was immediately suspicious. As she looked around her eyes went to the barn, where she noticed a slight movement. The bundles seemed to shake slightly. She grabbed the long bamboo stick resting on the wall nearby and dashed towards the barn, screaming in rage, "Lachchu, Lachchu…Where are you *naaspeete*?"

Within moments, an exasperated Lachchu, jumped out of the barn, hurriedly fixing his clothes at the same time. But before he could utter anything, he felt the whack of the stick on him, and then another, amidst Dhania's choicest curses.

"*Arre kutte…harami ki aulad*."

But, before another strike could hit him, he jumped over the low outer wall of the *aangan* and fled, while Dhania continued cursing him.

"You only found this house to violate with your dirty deeds? You had to spoil only my granddaughter with your filthy game?"

Just then a much shaken Basanti sneaked out and hurriedly made way towards the door to go inside the house, without risking even a side glance at Dhania, for the fear of her wrath.

"*Arre*, you burnt face, you'll ruin your life. It is better that you go and kill yourself." Dhania turned towards her now, howling as she spoke. Basanti stood frozen at her place for a moment and then quietly sneaked away.

Just then, the back door flung open and Khoobchand entered in a huff, obviously having heard the commotion. Looking lost, he asked, "*Arre*, who are you killing, Amma? And why, was that Lachchu running like that? He collided with me outside and when I asked what had happened, he said nothing…Just ran away."

Dhania got up haughtily and reprimanded him.

"When the man of a house starts depending on his wife's earnings for his livelihood, this is what you get to see " Shaking with rage she said beseechingly. "Protect her if you can, otherwise your daughter's life will also be ruined, for all time."

Both stood like statues for a good length of time, with their eyes pinned on each other.

The next day, after a bath, as Dhania spread her wet clothes on the line across the window of the bedroom upstairs, she noticed a commotion in the narrow lane outside. Rowdy children were following a gleaming big car. It was a rare sight in a lane where an occasional Maruti 800 or a banger of a Fiat were the only vehicles traversing its potholed path. It was only when she saw the Hyundi Sonata pulling in outside their house and Saanvri getting out of it that she realised that her daughter-in-law had travelled very far indeed.

Saanvri had barely emerged from the rear seat of the car when her son Neelesh darted out of the front door of the house and promptly touched her feet. With a spring in his steps he moved to the boot, which had already been opened by the driver. Lifting up his mother's large suitcase and the shoulder bag, he moved inside. Saanvri thanked the driver and followed her son inside. The driver boarded the car and drove away after reversing the car with difficulty, amid the noisy children clustering around the vehicle.

Like always, as soon as Saanvri entered the house, she went straight to where Dhania was and touched her feet. Dhania, however, did not give any hint of what was eating her. After Saanvri went into her room, Dhania went into the kitchen to fetch a glass of water, biding her time to speak to her. By the time she entered Saanvri's room with the glass of water, her suitcase had already been raided by Basanti and Neelesh.

Saanvri withdrew a bundle wrapped in newspapers from her bag and offered it to Dhania.

"Take it, Amma."

"What is it?" Dhania was confused.

"There is some money in it," she said in a subdued tone, in order not to let it out to her children. "Keep it in the safe." She took the glass in the other hand.

Dhania hesitated for a moment before turning to the door, saying, "You put it yourself *bahu*, it is open. The key is inside."

"Amma, please," she pleaded plaintively as Dhania moved towards the doorway. Her tone stopped Dhania. She turned back and noticed the earnest plea in her eyes. She took the bundle from her and moved to the steel cabinet. Saanvri reached for the wall switch and turned on the fan, saying to nobody in particular.

"It's becoming quite hot. We must have an A/C installed, isn't it?"

At that point Neelesh looked up at his mother with an expression of anticipation, who was quick to reassure him.

"I'll get you your bike also *beta*. Just wait a little while more," she then turned to her mother-in-law who was locking the safe. "Before that we should have our own car standing at the door, so that all of us can enjoy its comfort. Don't you think Amma?"

Dhania closed the cabinet and met Saanvri's eyes with a hard look, partly in reproach and partly in empathy, before saying with a touch of panic in her voice.

"*Beti* is growing up...If she slips once, we'll never have her back!"

The reprimand hit Saanvri like a thunderbolt. She froze in her place with the glass of water still in her hand. She understood immediately why Dhania was so aloof.

"I'll be downstairs." said Dhania and left.

Her eyes stony and gloomy, like an indicted person, Saanvri turned her face to her daughter, who tried to look away from her.

Later that night, the mother and daughter talked for a long time. Having learnt everything from Dhania of what had happened the previous day, she preferred to come out clean with Basanti. She opened up not only about the circumstances that had taken her where she had landed in her personal life, but also about her inherent fallibility to temptations and the lack of maturity in emotional matters, all of which had brought her to a dark tunnel from where she could not see ahead. An impenetrable sombre silence descended, broken only by Saanvri's remorseful plea, "Your mother was indeed unfortunate. But, at least, you try and improve your luck. You follow what I mean, my *lado*, don't you?"

Basanti walked into her mother's embrace saying, "Sorry, Ma!" Saanvri locked her in her arms and lovingly caressed her back. Silent tears flooded their eyes.

•◆•

The following morning after bath, alone in her room, as she stood in front of the mirror, she found a woman staring at her whom she did not recognise. Who was this woman, she wondered? A mother, a whore, a girl in love, a self-serving wench, what? Slowly she sat down on the stool, so did the woman facing her. The audacious stoniness of the woman's eyes grilled her own, burning them behind the enlarging drops of water, which then broke loose to soon trigger in her, spasms of laughter—a laughter of remorse, of defeat and shame, and a strange resolve.

But Saanvri's resolve about her own sanity and self-respect was like flowing water. As always, once with Rana, there was no holding back. Two days later, at their usual love nest as she stood naked in front of him, he—seated at the edge of the bed, also without a stitch on his body—buried his face in her breasts and growled lustily:

"Addiction; that's what you're—an addiction! Not a day has passed that my body has not ached to crush you in my arms. But you…" he muttered with clenched teeth, "Completely uncaring you are! Didn't even bother to know how I was."

"You're so cruel, hukum." She retorted in a voice steeped in passion. "Putting the blame without knowing the pain of a hungry river. This body is aflame with desire. You have to now extinguish the fire that's already burning within my body.

Suddenly, Rana threw their entangled bodies on the bed. Hissing with raw sexuality, he smothered her with kisses and love bites. A while later, deeply satiated by the fierce love making after a long gap, both receded into a state of tranquil calmness. But was it tranquillity or something else fluttering inside them?

Reclining on the headboard, Rana took a pensive drag on his cigarette. She lay across his stomach with her arms clasped around his trunk. Her eyes, dreamy in the post-coital languidness, with the sheet barely covering their naked bodies. He exhaled and planted a kiss on her hair.

"You are looking quite fulsome these days. Face and the body are both radiating."

"I don't look good, is it?" she teased.

"What're you saying?" He grabbed her hair and turning her face towards him, he muttered with clenched teeth. "Many times I feel, I should leave my seed inside you. I'll face whatever happens after that."

Saanvri went silent for a moment, before saying ponderingly, "A seed has already been laid Rana-ji and has been grounded too."

"What do you mean?"

"That…that I am pregnant."

"What?" He was completely shocked.

She held his eyes in a steady gaze, not letting go even for half a moment before saying with utter calmness. "That I am carrying a child in my womb!"

Rana remained nonplussed for a while. He merely stared into her eyes, as though trying to make out what she had said. Then he coolly put down her head and extricated himself from her arms. He slid away from underneath her body and pulled up his underpants. He rushed towards the wall some distance away. Suddenly at the window, he swirled around with great fury and lashed out at her. "You wretched, low-level woman," he fumed, "In one stroke, one stroke only, you showed your character."

Saanvri was astounded. She sat up facing him and demanded. "What is it you are saying?"

Flying into rage, Rana charged at her and slapped her stingingly across the face. "Did I send you for this, you deceiver, that at the first opportunity you carry his seed inside you?" He was already frothing in the mouth.

Saanvri was crestfallen. It was a stunned silence—stunned and oppressive. Then she collected herself and said as calmly as possible, "What are you saying? It is not his…not Yashpal's".

It unclamped another bout of rage in him.

"What are you trying to say," he screamed, "If it is not his, whose it is?"

Saanvri stepped down from the bed while trying to wrap her naked body with the sheet. She then, took a defiant posture by putting one of her hands on her waist and asking him coolly, "You do the calculation yourself Rana-ji. I have been with him, only since last three months. For my pregnancy, it is the fifth month commencing."

Rana's eyes were bloodshot. He swore at her, "*Saali raand*, trying to chuck someone else's dirt on me, you wretched woman."

"Don't shout, Rana-ji," she screamed, "I also know how to shout… and if I start shouting, all tongues would stop wagging at once."

Rana was speechless. She spoke in a normal, unemotional voice. "I've already made my booking in the hospital. You will get to know the rough date of the pregnancy automatically."

Then raising her voice a little bit, she said with a touch of bitterness, "But you better listen to this," she continued in a hurtful voice, "My husband no longer has enough courage to even touch me. Whatever had been going on before these last three months, had been only with you."

As though in a spell, both stood still in their places. Rana was the first one to break out from the long silent stillness.

"Why didn't you tell me earlier, if it was so?" he said in similar, unemotional voice as hers.

"That day, I had come to do precisely that," she met his eyes and then continued sombrely. "As soon as I came to know about it at the hospital, first and foremost I called you and came to meet you, in this very apartment. But before I could say anything, you mentioned your problems."

Rana collapsed into the chair near him. He looked a broken man, unable to say anything. After a while he stuttered and said almost in a whisper, "What do we do now?"

Suddenly she was grim. After a moment, she nodded with determination and said, "You don't have to do anything. Whatever has to be done, has to be done by me now." Her moist eyes shone with a strange brightness—the brightness of a resolution. "After today, I won't meet you. If I do at all, it would only be when you come at my door personally to express remorse and seek forgiveness."

With this she silently got up and went into the washroom and closed the door after her. Like a condemned criminal Rana lowered his head.

The washroom transformed into a sanctuary for Saanvri. All of a sudden she felt lonely, utterly lonely. The choking feeling in her throat gave way and the translucent film that had been blinding her as she had marched to the washroom, broke loose. She cupped her face with her hands to muffle the sound, and leaning over the sink let herself go. Almost burying her face deep into the sink, she howled in and uncontrollable release.

Rana was not in the bedroom when she emerged from the washroom. She got into her clothes hurriedly, dreading every second she was there. Already fully dressed, Rana stood like a sentinel near the sofas in the sitting room. She had to go near him to pick up her handbag, which lay on the large settee. Though it was a split-second exchange as her eyes rose to meet his, the redness in hers did not go unnoticed by him. Without a word, as she walked away from him, the silence was both impenetrable and impermeable. Swiftly yet soft footedly she crossed the large sitting room to reach the door. A hushed click was all he heard as she exited and pulled the door after her. He stood amazed at how it took only a moment to alter things irreparably.

Saanvri had nowhere else to go except her own house. And that was the last place she wanted to go to in the mental state that she was in. For a long time, she rode about in a rickshaw aimlessly, all over the town. It was well after two hours and quite dark when she instructed the driver to drop her at her door.

She found Neelesh and Basanti seated across the table near the window in her room, immersed in their studies. The sight brought a slight smile to her face. She went up to them, quietly stroked their heads and then left. Soundlessly, she pushed open the door to her mother-in-law's room and peeped inside. She found her seated in front of her idols, praying with her eyes closed. Softly she pulled back the door and decided to postpone the unburdening of all that was gurgling inside her for another time. Strangely, she found company at the most unlikely of places.

Coming out, she found Khoobchand in the corner of the veranda behind the house. He was plonked on a discarded old settee with a bottle and a glass of drink on a stool in front of him. Their eyes met and in a silent exchange they read each other like a book.

Saanvri stood for a few moments before going for his liquor-filled glass. Without another glance at him, she brought the glass to her lips and took a large swig, which tore through her gullet like a knife in its stiffness. She stumbled on her feet and tears flashed in her eyes. But she steadied herself and went for another gulp, even larger this time. Still without uttering a word and without her eyes even fleetingly straying on him, she kept the empty glass on the table. She stood quietly for a couple of moments and then left. A thick silence was all there was, to tell the story, if there were any to be told.

After a while, as Khoobchand proceeded to fill his glass again, a pathetic smile came to his face. His senses had not been dulled enough by his drunkenness to not notice how, even in her brief spell of vulnerability, the unspoken equilibrium, which had been established between them, remained unaltered when she opted not to sit down beside him on the settee—the equilibrium in which he was the supplicant, and she the provider

•◆•

A couple of days later, looking visibly pregnant in a loose salwar-kurta, Saanvri alighted from an auto rickshaw in the porch of an old colonial-type building, which bore a large signboard on one of its walls: DIRECTORATE OF HEALTH & MEDICAL SERVICES (Rajasthan Govt.). She paid the driver and confidently climbed the few steps to the front veranda, which had a small table with a register on it and an empty chair. She waited for a while but when nobody came to attend to her, she entered her name in the register and went inside.

Strangely, even the PA to the director was not in his cubicle. The peon also behaved indifferently and with the practiced arrogance of an office boy in a higher office, directed her to sit at the bench outside and wait. After some five minutes she turned restless and without even bothering to look at the peon, marched up to the director's door and knocked on it.

As soon as she heard a voice say 'come in', she opened the door and entered, ignoring the peon, who rushed towards her in consternation, but she was already inside.

"Yes?" demanded the man seated behind the large desk, in a safari suit, with a highly authoritative disposition.

She crossed the immense space of the spacious office, a trifle imperiously, to reach the chairs in front of the desk.

Saanvri Paliwal! I had an appointment."

The peon withdrew from the door. The man threw her a cursory glance and after pointing at the chairs in front of him, a little indifferently, dug his eyes into the file he had been going through. Saanvri noticed a deliberate evasiveness but quietly took a seat. After a while the silence became awkward and oppressive. Uncomfortable with the treatment meted out to her, she opened her bag and absentmindedly withdrew a packet of cigarettes and put one in her mouth. Just as she was about to light it, she heard him speak.

"Didn't you see outside? 'Smoking not allowed'. It's a public place," he growled.

Unable to react in any way, she stopped. She knew he was a very senior officer, and she could get into trouble if she did not comply. But partly out of her newfound confidence in the wake of her affair with Yashpal and partly out of newly germinated irreverence and anger against men in general, and men of authority in particular, she not only recovered from the snub but also thought of giving back. With the cigarette still between her lips, she pointed at the ashtray on the table.

"Then, what is this ash tray on the table for?" She spoke in slight defiance. "And how is it a public place when only two of us are here right now?"

"It is a public office. That's why it's a public place," he said curtly.

"Sorry!" She put back the packet in the bag.

"Tell me," the man said reservedly.

"*Ji?*" she was confused at what he had said.

"Tell me, what can I do for you?"

Saanvri opened her bag again and withdrew a couple of sheets of typed paper, which she extended towards him along with the envelope.

"I had put in this application for the maternity leave. You rejected it."

"I know, I know. I am aware of it." Suddenly he flared up curtly, "What do you think it is? It's a government job...not for sitting at home." He waited for a moment and then barked, "Want a leave for four months...What do you think, I am a fool?"

A stunned Saanvri sat back in her chair, leaving the papers on the desk. Then she asked in a cool and composed tone, "How many months has it been since you have taken up charges here, Bose babu?"

He looked at her blankly.

She continued, "Three months, right?"

He didn't say anything, only gazed at her, intrigued at her intrepid comment. But Saanvri suddenly became a different person. All her bolted anger after the showdown with Rana came to the fore as she now spoke with a menacing tinge to her voice:

"Roll your beddings, then." Incensed, she waved a finger at him threateningly. "Three days...in only three days, I'll have you thrown away to such a godforsaken place that neither will your children get a school to go to, nor will your wife have a parlour to visit or even sweet water to drink. Not only that, I'll have that enquiry reopened, which you were facing in connection with your false qualifications. I'll make you run from pillar to post." She abused him and mocked him with blazing eyes. "*Sale*."

He was stunned by the utter audacity of her brazen threat to the most senior officer of the department. He sat motionless at his place, gaping at her with his mouth open, when she once again pointed her finger at him and said venomously:

"This is a promise. I'm leaving now." She got up and picked up her papers and swung around angrily to leave. She had hardly taken a couple of steps towards the door that he jumped out of his spell and called after her.

"*Ai*...*aa*...listen, Madam. Please sit, please sit." Saanvri turned around and without moving gave him a searching look. He nodded towards the chair with an appealing face. Saanvri returned to the chair and sat down. He extended his hand and said:

"Give me the papers." As Saanvri handed them back he continued, "I'll see what can be done."

Saanvri eased herself in the chair and opened her bag again and took out the packet of cigarettes. In a relaxed pace she put a cigarette in her mouth and picked up the lighter. And then she changed her mind. Putting it back in her bag she addressed him, "Actually my lighter is not quite working, would you please lend me your lighter for a moment?"

He gave her a long submissive look as his hand went to the drawer in the table to bring out his lighter. He extended it to her. She took it and gave it an admiring glance. Then unhurriedly she flicked it open and lit the cigarette. As he took the lighter and put it back in the drawer she stretched herself a little, took a long drag from the cigarette, followed by a leisurely exhale of a thick cloud of smoke.

Fourteen

The whirr of the camera had taken her mind back through the pages of her life's book of the past three years—ever since she left Jodhpur after the birth of her third child…a daughter.

Except the occasional contact with Yashpal Sarena, who had continued to be her benefactor, to her advantage, she had generally severed most of her past relationships outside her family; her visits to Rajasthan had also become infrequent. Although the dream she had of pursuing the tinsel world had proven to be difficult, she had plodded on without giving up.

The rude jolt she experienced from her sudden breakup with Rana had thrown Saanvri in a topsy-turvy terrain of ephemeral emotions, especially after the birth of her second daughter. Only she knew who had actually fathered her. The snub from Rana had in time been internalised by her, and had turned her into a bit of an adventurist, sending her hurtling towards a trajectory of reckless affairs.

It began with one of the instrumentalists, a tabla player in her dance group, Kishan, who motivated her to take up singing, for she had a very mellifluous voice. She began with Rajasthani ballads and devotional songs. Sharing of musical notes extended into sharing of beds, not just with Kishan but others like the video director, in time. The journey had ultimately brought her to Mumbai to try her luck in films and TV as well. But, if not outright a mirage, Bollywood had not been very responsive to her efforts. Despite being a minor celebrity in the sphere of devotional videos in Rajasthan, she had at best reached a status of a chorus girl and a group dancer in 'B' grade movies.

She was jolted out of her reverie by a female voice shouting her name on the loudspeaker. It was the choreographer who had been summoning her, but lost in her thoughts Saanvri had missed it. The portly woman in her mid-forties, who was known for her crassness while addressing the junior dancers and technicians when infuriated, screamed on the P.A. system:

"*Oye* superstar, are you sucking someone's prick in your thoughts that you can't hear me? Move to the bridge, otherwise I'll have a real one shoved up your ass."

Saanvri sprang to her feet as if she had touched a naked electric wire. The flush of anger she felt gave way to utter embarrassment as she looked around and found hostile faces staring back at her. She knew that she could not take on the woman who, despite her bad mouth, was adored by all the dancers, starlets, technicians and even many senior female stars for the quality of work she produced and for the many careers she had crafted. She meekly made her way to the bridge.

A stanza of a modern song was being choreographed over the wooden bridge across an artificial canal in a corner of the manicured park. A group of six boys in a row moved from one side of the bridge to serenade a group of six girls—one of whom was Saanvri—who breezed in from the other side. Saanvri was one of the supporting dancers and not in the lead.

For no fault of hers the shot went wrong again and again and was being retaken.

Suddenly, between the takes there was some kind of stir in one corner. The visiting spectators and even some technicians stood up and started staring in that direction from where, surrounded by commandos and bouncers, Yashpal was being led in. The production manager respectfully offered a seat to Yashpal some distance away from where the director of the movie was seated. Disturbed by the commotion, a visibly irritated director asked his assistant, "What the hell is going on? Who is that man?"

"Sinha-saheb was mentioning some minister from Rajasthan who was supposed to come. Maybe it is him," the assistant speculated.

"What nonsense is this? We have so much work left to do." The director frowned.

Just then, to his great astonishment, Saanvri broke off from her group, which was waiting to be called for the shot, and sprinted towards Yashpal, shouting gleefully, "Daddy-ji."

Everybody was flabbergasted as they watched Saanvri throw her arms around Yashpal to lock him in a passionate embrace and plant a kiss on his cheek. He reacted coyly and reservedly while people exchanged dumbfounded looks.

No sooner had the minister taken a seat that the producer, Mr Sinha, came into the sets and gave explicit instructions that no one was to hassle Saanvri. His Rajasthani financier had informed him of her close connection to the visiting minister, without whose blessings no money would get funnelled.

Unsurprisingly therefore, the spot boy who carried tea at her orders brought it in an expensive cup and saucer instead of the regular glass and approached the vanity van with great trepidation. A mean looking gun-mounted bouncer, with a no-nonsense expression, stood outside its doors.

Yashpal plonked on the sofa, took a sip of the tea and addressed Saanvri, seated close by on a chair, who had lit a cigarette as soon as the spot boy closed the door behind him.

"What is all this...small roles, insignificant videos. Leave all this. You've tried enough in these two, two and a half years. Nothing is going to happen in this *Bambai*. Come back and live there with respect and in comfort. Whenever you want to be in Jodhpur, go to Jodhpur; whenever you prefer Jaipur, stay in Jaipur. Family will also be with you, everybody will be happy. Once in a while, you can tend to your duties in the hospital also—these bastards pass sarcastic comments on my face these days that 'Saanvri-ji comes only once a month to pick up her cheque'."

Exhaling a cloud of smoke, Saanvri said wistfully, "But Daddy-ji, I wanted to acquire some position in life, first. It's been such a tireless and disappointing situation."

He put down the cup and said, "Leave this, coming to and fro from Mumbai. I'll fix something for you there itself."

"What will you fix?" she asked half-heartedly.

"Leave that to me." He responded and stretching his hand towards her, he said, "Now come over here for a minute."

He had barely pulled her when she willingly flung herself into his arms. Like a hungry animal, he at once lustily buried his face on her chest beneath the blouse covering her breasts.

•◆•

Less than a month later, Saanvri was back in Jaipur again and happily ensconced in the penthouse at Royal Heights. As Saanvri answered the doorbell a beaming Yashpal entered. After closing the door behind him, he dramatically turned around and withdrew an envelope from the inner pocket of his Nehru jacket. He held it high in his hand and as he took steps to move to the sofa, he announced triumphantly, "The order has arrived…Orders for Saanvri-ji's appointment has arrived."

Saanvri leapt out in joy. Trying to snatch it from his raised hand, she screamed, "Has it come? Show me *na*? Please give it to me."

Yashpal bent down a little and putting on a reverent posture, announced, "Our compliments may please be accepted by Saanvri Devi for being appointed as the Chairperson of the Rajasthan Lok-Nritya Anusandhan Samiti."

"Let me see, let me see…" Saanvri managed to snatch the letter from his hand and opened it. As she read it, Yashpal continued boastfully:

"In two weeks' time you'll have your own car too, just as you wanted...with a red beacon to adorn it on the top."

"Red beacon too?" Saanvri jumped up in excitement, "Give me, give me, Daddy-ji, you better give me a kiss on my lips for this."

Both of them were locked in a deep, passionate kiss before he withdrew and asked mysteriously, "Now tell me...what you would do for me in return for this?"

"Everything belongs to you. Ask, whatever you want to..."

Without uttering a word, Yashpal gazed at her, admiring her like a piece of art displayed in an exhibition. Then slowly a kind of lustiness began to melt into his eyes as he said, "*Yaar*, you know that dance you do around the pole. People keep talking about it *yaar*." His eyes turned greedy and plaintive at the same time. "I have these very important friends. They are really very important to me. All are party fellows. They help me a lot every now and then." He paused for a couple of seconds before continuing slightly secretively. "They want to see your dance, but not in public, in private, here somewhere."

Saanvri seemed to crash-land on earth as she uttered, "As in...?"

"Meaning we'll put up things in this penthouse itself," he went on, lost in his own thoughts.

"Ya, you can put it up here itself, I can see that. But what else?" she asked suspiciously.

"What else?" He seemed confused.

"Yes, what else? Who else do I have to sleep with? Or do I have to sleep with all of them?" she demanded with eyes as cold as flint.

Now it was Yashpal's turn to get a similar jolt like her. Turning stern all of a sudden, he screamed like a fiend, "What do you think I am? I'll ask you to sleep with them? What do you think? You think I am a pimp?" His eyes were afire as he shrieked, "I am not Rana. I am Yashpal...Yashpal...Yashpal Sarena!" He was frothing as he barked, "I enjoy tremendous respect in the society. My party worships me. I'll ask you to sleep with all others? I'll ask my main keep to sleep with others?"

Suddenly, there was silence. A long, impenetrable silence. None spoke, none moved. Saanvri gazed into his eyes with utter disbelief. He lowered his eyes. Slowly she turned and stealthily walked up to the window at the other end of the room, her eyes brimming with tears. Without blinking she peered through the open window at the city spanning far and wide. The tears in her eyes refracted the image, making it misshaped, out of focus, as though it were a segment of a surrealistic film.

Yashpal stared at her back in awe for some time before he too walked up to her. For a couple of seconds, he stood quietly behind her. Then he put his arms around her. Her eyes gave way to her tears, which of course he did not see.

Saanvri knew that there was no escaping from this one-way street; the street she had inadvertently entered, the day she had agreed to entertain Yashpal Sarena at Rana's behest. She also knew that it was the jungle where the most dangerous predators thrived, and the best course to remain unscathed was to befriend and turn them into benefactors without taking recourse to or seeking any refuge in the finer values of life. Once you had entered this world, you had no option but to embrace it. Its rules were coarse and ruthless with no room for scruples of any kind. She also knew that the wrath that could befall a dissenter or a challenger, in this cloak-and-dagger world, was often beyond the comprehension of common man and a complete ruination at the hands of the league was all too common.

The choice was only one and simple—*Play the game.*

The entire look of the place had been changed. It did not appear to be the hall of a penthouse, rather it looked like a small and cosy, though expensively done up, night club. Four rectangular tables had been joined to create an oblong rostrum in the middle of the hall. Discreet lighting had been provided under acrylic sheets to present an illuminating surface. Two of the tables, placed at some distance from each other, had two shiny poles emerging from them, fixed firmly to the ground. There were festoons and decorations hanging on the walls and fixtures.

More than half a dozen politicians—all in their late fifties or sixties—were perched on revolving high stools, arranged around the rostrum. Some others, in semi-formals, subservient to the leaders hung around, humouring them or refilling their emptying glasses with expensive alcohol every now and then, brought in by waiters from the makeshift bar arranged in the alcove underneath the staircase. In another corner near the entrance to the washroom stood a high-quality music system. This was managed by one of the invitees, who was also a small-time disc-jockey.

The patrons were all pretty drunk, swaying to the music with their glasses in their hands. Unburdened of any pretence of culture, position or protocol, the old fogies were in their element as sexual predators. Every now and then, someone would lecherously throw himself over a scantily dressed Saanvri, performing a lewd number on the rostrum.

She too let herself go. Having made peace with her situation, she had innovatively worked out a highly seductive number, an energetic fusion between a most basic Western piece and a Rajasthani folk song-and-dance sequence, with a surfeit of libidinal movements. But even while portraying herself as easy and available in her act, she was tactful and sufficiently self-preserving. Every time any of her patrons got into a spirited participation, she would teasingly leap from one pole to another to further whet his appetite, yet escape his animalistic pawing. In her act of striding through the air, if an accidental glimpse of her privates materialised, the men behaved like adolescents, instead of respectable politicians that they were in the eyes of the world.

But even in that free play of permissiveness and amorality, she did not miss out on the display of her assertiveness, not being a plaything anymore but a player as well. At a poignant point in the song, highly suggestive in its intonations, she alluringly stretched her bare leg and put it on Yashpal's chest, sending him aflame with her outrageously sexual movements. The tease was followed with others with equally coarse manifestations.

But vulgarity, like vermin, has a tendency to gorge and grow upon itself, if left unchecked. And, when laced with alcohol, it regurgitates, not only filthiest invectives but also bottled up frustrations. By the time the party had wound up, the invitees were not only wretchedly repulsive individually, but also abusively offensive to each other. With practiced tact, the minders who had wisely kept themselves within the confines of sobriety, escorted each to their respective vehicles. Only Yashpal trudged up the steps to the master bedroom and was left under the quilt on the large bed, in the heavily inebriated state that he was in. Even in his pathetic condition he had not forgone his right to claim her, though in vain.

Later on, in the dead of the night, Saanvri sat resting against the headboard, with the quilt covering her nudity up to her breasts, silently smoking a cigarette. Her eyes, despite the emptiness, had a trace of wetness in them and were fixed at nothing in particular as she slowly took drags from the cigarette and then released a pall of smoke, slowly. With her other hand, she brought a glass to her lips to have a liberal sip of whiskey.

Frozen in her loneliness, as she seemed to drown her demons in the sips of whiskey and drags of smoke, Saanvri did not appear affected by Yashpal's mutterings of profanity, under the same quilt. If anything there was an expanding glow of piousness on her face and a glimmer of equanimity in her eyes, each time she took a sip or exhaled a plume of smoke after a drag.

She was a fish that had discovered its pond—a pond of gloss, glitter and glamourous stakes at the high tables and high beds of society.

Two days later, as she walked to the swimming pool of the five-star hotel where she was a guest, she resolved that life need not feel so burdensome. Attired in a two-piece bikini, she peeled off her bathing gown to reveal her awe inspiring sexiness. She dropped the gown on the reclining chair to move to the rim of the pool, inducing gasps among onlookers with every step she took. She stood still for a bewitching moment and then took a dive at the deep end of the pool.

After swimming the full length, she returned to the deep end with underwater strokes. From a chance sideway glance, she noticed a man come and position himself at the rim of the pool in the middle. As she took another length underwater, she became more conscious of him. He was planted at the same spot, his lean image trembling in the unsteady water. On her return, she chose to swim back with her head above water. It was then that she gasped in surprise—it was Rana who stood there, looking absolutely dapper in a designer T-shirt underneath a light jacket, cotton trousers and a pair of reflective sunglasses adorning his eyes. She waved at him gleefully.

A few minutes later, wrapped in her white bathing gown, Saanvri lolled back on the recliner. Rana, meanwhile, made himself comfortable on the poolside chair. A waiter approached and placed two glasses of orange juice and left. Saanvri picked up a glass and took a slow sip.

Rana pushed up his glares to the top of his forehead and remarked with a tinge of sarcasm: "What an aura does our Saanvri Devi have now, folks! A suite in the five star hotel for residence, a penthouse for rehearsals and occasional stay, government's vehicle to travel around…Saanvri-ji's entire world is on a new trajectory."

Saanvri looked a bit surprised and asked, "You had gone to Royal Heights, is it?"

"Of course, I had gone. After all, one wants to see the place you work from," he said quick-wittedly, with an extra dose of sarcasm. "That's where I learnt that your official residence is in this hotel." He clapped with mirth. "Bravo, bravo! This is called going up…rising high!"

Saanvri coolly took another sip, before responding, "Wasn't it you who had sent me?"

"Of course, I had sent you. But not for forgetting the past altogether," he retaliated bitterly and then snapped in a hurting tone, "Not to lose yourself in the new one, completely!"

Saanvri did not respond. Rana took a sip of his drink quietly and then replaced the glass on the table before challenging her curtly.

"You always had big things to say about your feelings for me…What is it that you have discovered in that old man that you've forgotten everything." His face contorted and then he said savagely, "Don't you forget that your position is not more than the slippers on his feet."

As if she expected the conversation to take this turn, Saanvri neither looked at him nor showed any emotion. After a moment of awkward silence, she calmly picked up her glass and leisurely took another sip before saying, "A slipper doesn't identify a foot before arriving in this world Rana-ji." She replaced the glass on the table and then turned to look at him squarely in the eyes and said coolly, "It submits itself to the foot that fits it perfectly!"

Quietly getting up, she dropped her gown on the recliner and said, "I'll just have another dip." As an astounded Rana looked up at her, she mumbled dismissively, "Sorry!"

Rana was agape as he watched her walk away, smugly, towards the pool without even once looking back at him. As he adjusted back his shades, Saanvri's agile figure, taking a dive into the water, reflected on its dark glasses, which were sufficiently opaque not to let out to anybody the affront that he felt. He reached into the inner pocket of his casual jacket and withdrew an envelope, which he placed on the recliner. On second thought, he pushed it underneath her large towel to ensure that it did not fly away. He straightened and after throwing a fleeting glance at Saanvri, walked away.

A few minutes later, Saanvri with water still dripping from her body, discarded the gown on the recliner and picked up the towel to dry herself. She noticed the envelope. Curious, she picked it up even before drying her body. It had an invitation card. She read it and the accompanying letter. She turned introspective for a few moments and then put it down. Preoccupied, she began to dry herself.

The night was deep and mysterious and rather still. Rana was in a dark mood. He had hit the bottle and had been drinking since sundown. His wife had tried to persuade him to come to the dining table, but he had declined. He was grumpy since the time he had returned from Jaipur. It was well past three in the morning, and he had not moved away from the bar except for an occasional visit to the washroom.

Although fearful of his response the servant entreated: "Shall I serve the dinner, hukum?"

Rana took another swig and slowly turned around to look behind at the far end of the large room. The man appeared like a black cut-out against the light in the passage behind him. The sitting room was dimly lit.

"*Abbe*, how many times have I told you, don't bother me again and again with your ghost-like appearance. Go, scamper off. I shall come, when I shall come!"

The servant withdrew. With his glass in his hand, Rana alighted from the bar stool and swaying on his feet moved to the large paintings of his predecessors adorning a wall. He stood in front of the one of them that was his father's. He looked up at it with a fiendish gaze for a few seconds as if sizing up an adversary, before mumbling:

"You kept many *golees*, didn't you?" His tone which at first was accusative changed to a plaint solicitation. "Tell me, did you also fall in love with any of them?" He was about to say something further when he was interrupted by the ringing of his cell phone. Vividly angry he cursed aloud, "*Bhenchode*, what the hell."

He tried to ignore it, hoping it would stop, but then gave in due to its persistent ringing and swaying on his feet walked to the bar counter where it had been placed. He picked it up and brought it close to his eyes, which he squinted to identify the caller.

"Oh ho...Glory of Rajasthan...Life of the ministers and the icon of the *Khamb-Nritya* world, Shrimati Saanvri Devi is calling me." Then he spoke aloud as if beckoning a cluster of people, "*Arre bhai*, turn on all the lamps, light up the whole place." After this little hilarity, as if he was enjoying his own humorous invocation, he turned to the phone again and asked dramatically with a tinge of sadness and sarcasm, "Tell me Madam, how come you remembered me?"

His hurt did not go unnoticed by Saanvri, who was leaning over the high railing around the broad balcony of her bedroom at the Royal Heights in Jaipur—a glass of whiskey in one hand and the cell phone in another.

"You know the whiskey is a wretched thing Rana-ji. One may be miles apart but it can bring back memories and suddenly connect two people," she slurred. Then she took a pause and continued, slurring even more, "There your tongue is swaying a little unsteadily, here mine is also swaying a little unsteadily."

Rana laughed throatily before saying with a tinge of defeat and loss.

"*Arre*, the whole world itself is swaying unsteadily, Saanvri." He took a long sigh and then asked, "So, what is it that you called for?"

Saanvri took another swig of her whiskey and said, "You had left the card for your daughter's wedding for me...I wanted to submit that your invitation is a command for me. I shall be honoured to present myself at the event." She too took a ponderous sigh and asked, "Anything else, hukum?"

Rana once again burst into peals of laughter, a distinctly self-deprecating one.

"Anything else, hukum!" He laughed again and continued, "Hukum? *Arre* Saanvri Devi, there was only one more request, you see."

"No request, Rana-ji, just order me," this time her voice was not only steady but was also as calm and reverential as it used to be when their relationship was still at puberty.

"They say the CDs of your devotional songs are getting very popular everywhere...Women in the family were keen to have an item from your team at the time of the reception."

Saanvri burst into a peel of laughter, which even brought small tears to her eyes. A startled Rana interjected, "What happened? Why the laughter?"

She responded with another burst of small, though sad, laughter before saying, "At least some other aspect of Saanvri came into being discussed." Then she turned solemn and said, "Rana-ji thank you very, very much. It will be my good fortune to perform the item on this auspicious occasion!"

"I shall wait for you."

"Your request is my pleasure, Bade-hukum!" She switched off the phone.

Rana also disconnected the call and with his face brightening up a bit, took another large swig of his drink.

Saanvri suddenly felt a surge of loneliness shoot through her. With the cell phone and the glass of whiskey still held in her hands, she peered at the vast blackness above the interminable city lights from her balcony. Listless, she went down on her knees and rested her forehead on its glass wall. Gradually her eyes, which had been gazing through the transparency of the wall, began to smart with silent tears distorting her vision. She shut her eyelids gently and let the tears flow. She sat quietly for a while. A moment later, she turned around and sat up. A slight smile swam across her face as she emptied her glass. Then she got up.

She dragged herself through the door connecting to her bedroom. She felt a light shiver because of the cold air of the A/C. She moved to the bed and poured some more whiskey in her tumbler from the bottle still sitting on the side-table along. Tossing off her slippers carelessly, she slid under the thin quilt, and half reclining against the headboard, she took a large gulp of her drink. A distant look settled in her eyes as she gazed straight ahead at the painting hung on the wall opposite her. It was a picture of a lighthouse on a choppy dark sea. The frame of the painting seemed a bit skewed to her. No matter how much she turned her head from one side to another, the painting looked crooked. It disturbed her. Wondering if she was tipsy, she got up to check it from close.

As she fiddled with the painting, off came one of the hooks supporting it. Now it was hanging precariously from just one end. In her effort to re-fix it on the hook, she noticed a narrow duct in the wall. Some thin cables could be seen coming out from it, and they were attached to the painting through a hole in its frame. Curious, she slid off the clips at the sides of the frame, which held the cover in place. The cables, she noticed, were inserted into a very small gadget, which had been cleverly affixed exactly where the lighthouse in the picture was. Because of the brightness of the supposed light source, a naked eye from even a small distance in the front would never have suspected anything wrong. Saanvri now discovered to her great horror that it was the lens of a miniature camera, skilfully wedged in the groove behind.

As she pulled on the cable duct, the slight pressure on it made the cover come off, revealing a small chamber with a recording chip in the wall. She stood stupefied and shocked for a few minutes. Then she started re-fixing it all. She managed to get the loose hook in place and gingerly put up the frame. It was still a little askew, but she had so much more to think about. She went back to the bed and collapsed on it with misty eyes and a wounded heart.

Fifteen

A ball struck with a great force, travelled across the length of the billiard table but missed the hole. Sulakshana Chawdhary, dressed in a casual trouser and a loose jumper, straightened and began chalking her cue while saying.

"You are right. It is deception!"

A shiver passed through Saanvri's body as she considered the stern visage of the older woman, who seemed nonchalant even while confirming her fear. On discovering the recording gear and mulling over all options, Saanvri had decided to broach the matter with Sulakshna first, since the apartment was in her name. But she was in for a surprise when Sulakshana readily admitted that the gear had been installed at her behest. Saanvri's comment, "But this is deception!" which escaped her lips in mild shock had received another surprising response.

Having tended to the cue, Sulakshana looked up at Saanvri, who stood by the table. Without letting go of her eyes, Sulakshana coolly walked up to her and stood very close. With a penetrating gaze she said calmly, "Look woman, in this society affected by politics, polluted by politics and repressed by politics, you can get by in life if you have at least one of the three things: *dal* (party), *bal* (power), *ya chhal* (deception). If not all the three together. By that I mean either by having a big group of people or a party to support you, or by the power of money and muscle at your command, or by practicing sheer deception."

Saanvri gazed at her, speechless at Sulakshana's audacity in not only admitting the breach of privacy without batting an eyelid but also justifying it so brazenly. Neither spoke a word for a couple of moments. They stood still, face to face. Sulakshana finally broke the spell.

"I have to get to the polo ground." She walked ahead of her and then suddenly stopped to say, "Why not come with me. Just give me a few minutes to change." With that she was gone, without even giving Saanvri a chance to respond.

Within a few days, Saanvri's proximity to Sulakshana grew to the extent that they shared the same gym and spa and even went out for an occasional coffee or a meal together. Despite her fox-like intuitiveness, Sulakshana had mistakenly presumed Saanvri wanted to be in her tutelage, willing to be mentored to obtain benefits of high society.

Whenever she had a chance Sulakshana passed on words of wisdom, culled through years of experience to Saanvri, who listened to her most attentively.

"...All this 'truth' and 'integrity' things that you talk about, mean nothing...neither any solution to anything, nor do they bring any benefits," she would claim. "Civilised society accepts you for what you appear and not how refined your thoughts are. What are you attired in is more important than the depth of your belief," she advised.

One day, while returning from the inaugural function of a boutique, where Sulakshana as the chief guest had taken Saanvri along, they had stopped for a cup of coffee. Sulakshana was attired in an expensive chiffon saree, but so was Saanvri, as instructed by the former.

As usual, Sulakshana was in the midst of another advisory spiel. After a sip as she put down her cup, she said with a steely edge, "It is important for a woman to be a '*bala*' rather than '*abla*'...a possessor of destructive power, who can rain trouble on people instead of being a hapless doll."

Saanvri continued to stare at her with fascination. She realised Sulakshana was not only at her confident best, but she displayed an unusual charm and a unique sexiness. Sulakshana said with an easy smile, bordering on wickedness, "Whenever I suspect the need, I immediately turn a *'bala'*."

Acknowledging it with a tiny smile, now Saanvri also took a sip of her coffee and again looked up at Sulakshana whose eyes were studying her.

"I've known it for a pretty long time, that my brother has a problem, as we colloquially say, *naade ka dheela hai*...He has a big weakness for sex." A condescending spark flashed in her eyes before a hint of a winsome smile appeared at the corner of her lips while she continued, "And when a man is found to be *'naade ka dheela'*, it becomes incumbent upon you to be careful." Her face suddenly turned grim and she said with a kind of moral solemnity. "That is the reason the recording was taking place." She paused for a couple of seconds and then spoke in a voice that was not only cold but menacingly so, "It bodes well for him, bodes well for me and *chhori* it bodes well even for you."

Saanvri's eyes, which had held the other woman's gaze unflinchingly, dropped momentarily, only to find Sulakshana's eyes now dancing with a bit of a playful gleam.

"In English they call it the 'balancing act'." She concluded. Sulakshana took yet another sip and said, "Let me tell you another thing of great value." Her eyes beamed with a mysterious gleam as she spoke. "The two of us have a lot of this *bal*, the power that I am talking about."

As Saanvri's eyes widened with curiosity, a cryptic smile appeared on Sulakshana's lips and she said, "You have the *bal* of sex, the *bal* of a young woman sizzling with sensuality and the promise of carnality." She paused for a moment to take stock of the reaction on Saanvri's face, which surely was of that of utter fascination. Then with a confident poise she said, "And I possess the *bal* of experience, of having known from close the world I am talking about." Noticing the curious eagerness on Saanvri's face, she continued tantalizingly, "If these two *bal* were to work together then, you bet, the result is going to be unimaginable."

She took a considered pause, pregnant with tense anticipation and watched it trickle into Saanvri. Then she spelt it—the master stroke, "But, but...I remain at the front and you follow."

Saanvri seemed confused, which was instantly dispelled by Sulakshana, her translucent eyes turning into an icy gaze, as she said, "There should never be any slip up on this, or else, as I said...the *bal* and *bala*, both are right here—in front of you."

Saanvri felt a chilly shiver run down her spine. There was an unmistakable threat in the last bit of her playful comment. She sat speechless for a good length of time, absorbing the import of whatever Sulakshana said, nodding a couple of times in assent before dropping her head.

It is strange how a simple statement can send a chill up your spine to last for many days. Saanvri was in and out of bad dreams that night. Even during the next few days the nightmares had not ceased. She was not been able to decide as to what steps to take despite knowing that she had inadvertently entered a very dangerous phase in her life by confiding in Sulakshana.

Her white Ambassador, with the red beacon flashing on top and the words 'Adhyaksh RLNAS' above the number plate, drove through the circular driveway to come to a halt in the porch of the ministry building. Her heart missed a beat.

Earlier that morning Sulakshana's menacing words had come revisiting her: "...There should never be any slip up on this, or else." She imagined herself as a hapless fly in a spider's web. The blinding tears in her eyes made her determine that 'tears' it would be, hereafter, to rid her of the tears tormenting her. But she was not entirely sure whether it was advisable to open up to Yashpal yet. Finally, when the chauffer opened the door for her to alight she decided that there was no going back.

Walking through the stream of people with a couple of files under her arm to make her visit look officious, she still felt hesitant and tried of figuring how to go about it. It was only after the door had shut and the elevator started ascending that the scheme came together.

By the time she reached the minister's floor, she was a transformed person. Imperious and confident, as if she were another minister of equivalent stature, she didn't knock or wait. She simply barged into the PA's office and announced her arrival: "I had an appointment with Mantri-ji…had called him half an hour ago."

"Yes, yes. Please come in, sit. I shall inform him right away." The poor chap rattled while hurriedly standing up to acknowledge her, having a fairly good idea of her equation with the boss. Having had no prior knowledge of her arrival, he hesitantly mumbled something quite inaudible to Yaspal into the receiver while she hovered near him.

"Lok Nritya Anusandhan Samiti's adhyaksha has arrived."

Yashpal seemed lost as he retorted, "What is that, speak clearly man."

"Sir, Madam has come…the chairperson of the Folk Dances Research Committee that you set up. She says she spoke to you," he mumbled on.

"Oh yes, yes. Let her come, let her come." Yashpal was suddenly effusive, having realised that his PA was referring to Saanvri. Then turning secretive, he said softly, "And listen, Don't disturb us for some time."

Once again, even before the PA could usher her, she barged in.

No sooner had the door closed behind her than she asked, "Is there any camera installed in here?"

"Of course. What do you think?" Yashpal sounded amused.

"Turn it off please, quick." She sounded both a little alarmed and matter-of-fact

"But why, what happened?" Yashpal was surprised.

"You turn it off first."

Yashpal reached for the switch under his desk, "Here, I've done it. Turned off the switch."

"There's only one camera…Or are there more?"

Yashpal turned off yet another switch and said, "The other two cameras are also switched off. Now tell me what's all this about?" He was curious. He could see, Saanvri meant business.

Now a mischievous smile appeared on Saanvri's face, and she teasingly began to strip herself of her clothes.

As if he were touched by a live electric wire, a shocked Yashpal jumped out of his chair and blurted, "What the hell are you doing? Not here." Yashpal protested in shock.

Saanvri could not care less. She went on stripping with the flourish of a striptease artist. A completely surprised Yashpal fell back on his seat again. In no time, she was completely nude but for her undergarments. While Yashpal panted with anxiety, Saanvri coolly mounted his large desk. Then she unhooked her bra and dropped it on the table. As Yashpal's mouth fell open in utter disbelief, she sprawled over the table, facing him with her naked breasts. Then rising on her elbow, she beckoned, demurely, "Now turn on the cameras."

"Have you gone mad or something?" he screamed.

"No hukum, I'm merely asking you to do the very thing that you enjoy getting done secretly," she said with a streak of playfulness on her face. "Go on, do it openly. Get the act recorded in the broad daylight, in the office itself."

Yashpal was more than shocked now. He barked, "*Arre*, what nonsense are you talking about? Get dressed and tell me clearly what you want to say." He looked livid.

She pouted instead, and sounding hurt she dared him, "Why do you have to get the boudoir games recorded on a CD, slyly like a thief? Do it openly, right here in the office, on this very table. After all, what we do is also a kind of work, isn't it?"

Yashpal sprang up from his chair and thundered, "CDs? Which

CDs, what CDs? Put on your clothes...put on your clothes first, and then tell me everything..."

"Go and check in the bedroom of the penthouse. You'll get to know for yourself, which CDs and what CDs."

His mouth agape, Yashpal staggered and then said with great urgency and in a no-nonsense manner, "Put on your clothes, put on your clothes. We shall leave right now. I need to see this."

In little over an hour, Yashpal Sarena stormed into Sulakshana Chawdhary's bungalow. Taking no heed of the welcoming pranam of the maid, he strode through the long expanse of the expensively done up sitting room. At the other end of the hall, he barged through the half-open door connecting to the dining room. He almost collided with Sulakshana's adolescent daughter who was at that very moment making a hurried exit, ignoring her mother's exhortation.

"Akshara, finish your lunch first, I am telling you."

"I can't, I can't. I've to reach the library at once...Sorry Mom." Akshara rattled evasively without even looking back at her mother before coming to a sudden halt as Yashpal appeared in the doorway.

"Sorry Mama-ji."

Yashpal, whose face was unmistakably flushed with anger, feigned normalcy, "No problem, my child. I too had to talk about a few things with your mother in private."

Akshara zipped out of the room without paying any attention to him. Yashpal closed the door after her and now as he turned to face Sulakshana, his face had turned red again.

Getting up from her chair at the head of the table, she addressed him in surprise while her hands still held the pear that she was peeling for Akshara.

"Bhai-sa...You here at this time? What happened?"

Yashpal charged up to her and pushed her down into the chair in one quick forceful motion.

"First, you sit down." Before she could react, he gave her a tight slap across the face and he continued with bloodshot eyes, "Now listen to me nice and proper. Don't think that I am a stupid fool like *Jijja*. I'll cut you into pieces myself, if you try to play smart with me, even slightly. I am Yashpal, Yashpal Sarena! I shall forget that you are my sister."

But Sulakshana, though shocked, was quick to stand up and shout back, "What has happened to you? What manners are these…" she screamed, "to barge in this way? And what wrong have I done?"

"Nor will you succeed in doing me any wrong." He roared. "It's me, isn't it, who made it easy for you to advance in politics?" He raised his finger and threateningly pointing it at her, he continued, "I'll have you wiped out so completely that nobody would even get a wind of it. Then try and show as many CDs about me as you like."

Sulakshana's mouth fell open. Her eyes burnt with rage. "Your CDs? Which CDs? What kind of CDs?" she enquired.

"*Arre*, CDs of Royal Heights."

"CDs of Royal Heights?"

"Yes, yes, yes…and its bedroom. Who got the recording done of it?"

"Did you see yourself, or is it something you heard?"

"*Arre*, I've seen with my own eyes. I'm coming straight from there, after seeing them." His eyes were blazing.

"You've come here after seeing them?" Sulakshana repeated his words in utter confusion before asking again, "Where did you see them…I mean who showed them to you?"

"Saanvri did." He glared.

Sulakshana was lost for words. While keeping an unruffled visage, her mind raced wondering how much more he had been told. After a couple of seconds she ventured again, "Saanvri showed them to you… what did she say…who got them recorded?"

"That is exactly what she wanted to know. She thought it was I who got them done."

"Ahh...and so you assumed it was me. What if she herself got the recording done?"

"She herself got the recording done?" Thrown off-balance he repeated what she said, sounding very confused.

"Then?" Sulakshana glared challengingly.

"Then!" Yashpal repeated weakly.

"Yes, yes...Then?" She dared him.

For a moment he gawked at her foolishly, with his mouth open. Then suddenly he snapped and gritting his teeth said, "Where will the bitch be right now?"

"You come upstairs. We shall talk calmly in my room," she told him. "There are servants here." She grabbed his hand to lead him out.

Sixteen

The ostentatious stage was not less than that of a Bollywood set. A regular film choreographer had been engaged to design the number, which was fashioned in the tradition of a Kathputli item with Rajasthani folk songs. The large banquet hall in Jodhpur's posh locality was full of men, women and children, guests from the side of bride and groom, most draped in formal regalia of long lost royalty.

When the curtain finally rolled up in the old Ramlila style, a group of half a dozen women, acting as puppets on strings, sat up slowly from their prostrated positions—their veils rising up to partly reveal their anguished faces—the sight turning captivating and remaining so till the end. Of course, Saanvri was the most bewitching of them all, not only because she was the principal character, but also because of her expressions, her singing and the fluidity of her motions—all at once beguiling and entrancing.

The majority of guests were captivated with the enticing movements of her curvaceous body, generously pronounced in the tribal outfit. Others, especially the women, were enraptured by her expressions of pain and anguish of that of a persecuted soul, in a beautifully synchronised rendition of the folk song. The music and the verse of the ballad conveyed the raw deal the earth had been meted out due to the perpetual exploitation and betrayal by the very people she had implicitly trusted in—like an innocent girl—and the songs were the sharing of her grief with her lord and lover, Natha-ji. Conveyed artistically through the act of puppets, it meant to present a certain helplessness, suggesting destinies were in the hands of the forces, unbeknown and unforeseen.

At the end of the programme, in the dressing room, while Saanvri was removing her anklets in an atmosphere of high spirits, amidst bouts of laughter with her co-dancers, the fun and frolic was interrupted by Rana's wife Madhvi. She entered with an envelope in hand followed by her trusted aide, Kamli, holding a large bag. She addressed Saanvri imperiously, "Here you are Saanvri...There is Rs 50,000...Twenty-five for you, twenty for your group and the rest, five thousand, as baksheesh."

Saanvri was crestfallen. "Bak-sheesh?" she stammered

"Yes, yes baksheesh...Your tip," Madhvi responded sprightly. "You sang outstandingly well and danced so gracefully." With this she shoved the envelope in Saanvri's hands, who was too confused to react. Then Madhvi picked up two bottles from the bag carried by Kamli. Putting them on the floor near Saanvri, she said, "And here, these are two bottles. They would be enough for all of you, won't they?"

"Bottles?" Saanvri still seemed dazed.

"Yes, yes...Whiskey bottles, imported whiskey. Will they be enough, or shall I send more?" Madhvi spoke patronisingly.

Saanvri was speechless and unable to react. Madhvi knew that she had managed to hit her at the intended spot—her dignity. But she deliberately played naive and once again spoke patronisingly, "And do take food before you go...all of you...There are wonderful delicacies to eat."

Stupefied, Saanvri merely stared at Madhvi for brazenly rubbing in the class difference between them. She knew that Madhvi was attempting to get even with her for the slight she had caused by fornicating with her husband in her bedroom. For a few moments, she felt herself to be cut off from the scene she was caught up in, till she heard Madhvi say dismissively with a touch of a swagger. "I must leave now. Very important people are expected to arrive. I have to attend to them." Swiftly turning to Kamli, she said, "Let's go Kamli."

Kamli also turned around imperiously and followed her mistress, equally haughtily. Long after they had left, with tears in her eyes and a wounded expression, Saanvri continued to stare at the vacant space where the trenchant woman stood.

Saanvri was never instantly reactive to onslaughts on her self-esteem. But that day was different. She felt uneasy till a catharsis of sorts took place. She had agreed to entertain the guests at the wedding with a specially designed show as a tribute to the beautiful days of her affair with Rana and that too because he had made the plea in an emotionally vulnerable moment. As she shared the drink and dinner in the company of her other troupe members, her mind reeled from the after-effect of Madhvi's slight, and it kept running in her head like the loop of a film-reel with greater intensity with each peg of whiskey.

Some two hours later, a private party was in high spirits in a large room next to the banquet hall where the dance had been performed earlier. A select gathering of high-profile guests, mingled with each other. Some were seated in groups on ornate sofas, arranged in three or four clusters, and some were hanging about here and there, chatting over their drinks in small units of three to four. Uniformed waiters served drinks and snacks with remarkable adroitness. Occasionally, an uproarious laughter over someone's gauche behaviour broke out to the delight of equally shallow mates.

Suddenly, the main door flung open and hit the wall with a loud bang. All eyes instantly swung to it to witness a shadowy human form standing at the doorway, unidentifiable because of the flood of light in the corridor outside. As the form moved forward to come under the lights in the room, the bewildered guests witnessed a very drunk Saanvri, clapping clumsily and walking unsteadily, while bellowing aloud, "Bravo Rana-ji."

She clapped again, "Bravo! What a great marriage ceremony you organised, the whole of Rajasthan will remember…It was so enjoyable." She stopped for a moment and swaying on her feet, she searched for Rana, who stood in a far corner of the hall cloistered among his close family. His daughter, the groom, his wife and his daughter's in-laws, all frozen in their place, shocked out of their wits by this unexpected intrusion. On noticing him, she addressed him even more loudly, "What decorations, what food, what drinks." She clapped again and stumbled towards a round table nearby and picked up someone's unattended half-filled glass, while a young couple, the sole occupants of the table, gawked at her in disbelief. She took a large swig of the drink and said again, "It really satiated the spirits. People will remember this wedding for a very long time to come."

She emptied the glass of whiskey, in another gulp and laughed throatily as she deposited it back, threateningly close to the dazed young couple. Then, before anybody could react in any way, unsteadily she crossed through the crowd to make way to Rana. Not concerned about his befuddled relatives, especially his daughter and the son-in-law, she grabbed the collar of his designer long coat and pulling her face close to his, she said loudly, in a tone that was partly emotional and partly threatening, "But don't you forget, Rana-ji…that you have another daughter too."

She immediately turned her eyes to Rana's son-in-law and his parents, to watch the spectacle of their jaws dropping in shock, only to turn around and address the rest of the gathering, "How does it matter if she is not born from a wedded wife, she is still your daughter." Turning back to Rana again, she tugged at his collar to say, "Your own blood flows in her too. Her marriage should also be held with the same pomp and show."

At this point a fuming Madhvi tried to slide away, but Saanvri quickly moved sideways to block her path while continuing her loud proclamation, "Sumptuous feasts, sumptuous music, pulsating songs, and feet thumping dances…Everything should be top grade."

As Madhvi tried to avoid meeting her eyes, Saanvri turned a bit brazen. "And each of the singers and dancers should also be given the baksheesh beside their fees…Also, bottles of liquor, to each one, the imported ones, like here. What do you say Rani-sa?"

Everyone was tongue-tied, unable to move or do anything except gawk at her in disbelief. There was a stunned silence. Saanvri slowly glanced around herself as everybody lowered their eyes. She picked up another unattended glass from a nearby table and once again treated herself to a languid, long swig before wiping the spilled whiskey from her mouth with the back of her arm, staring back at the lowered heads around her.

For a moment, she stood stoically silent as if awed by what she saw. Then she laughed, first slowly and in short spurts, then letting herself go into a full laughter, before remarking mockingly, "Why this silence all around suddenly. Get the DNA test done if you like."

No one responded. Everyone stood with their heads lowered. She burst into even a freer, longer laughter this time before saying condescendingly, "Come on, Saanvri, let's leave…If any of them passes out, you'll get the blame for it."

Abruptly she turned around and humming the *mukhda* of her Natha-ji song in jest, she coolly walked out of the room, pulling the door forcefully shut, with a loud bang, behind her.

What Saanvri did not know at the time was that by slamming that door, she had inadvertently slammed several other doors—the loud report of that slamming had travelled far and wide. But there had been a grave miscalculation on her part. In her intoxicated state of the mind, she had felt like an avenging angel against the exploitative and pitifully degenerative feudal class. But instead of being able to send her detractors scurrying for cover, in one fall sweep she had pushed them into a conspiratorial huddle, instead.

Unsurprisingly, after the impulsive catharsis, while she had a very deep and restful sleep that night, fear and anxiety gripped her as soon as she woke up in the morning. Though not a *golee* or a mistress in the strictest sense, but having surreptitiously traversed through their nauseous corridors, she had unwittingly witnessed the 'scheming' and 'conniving' behind the closed doors of the 'royal', male-chauvinistic feudal society.

Now that the effect of the alcohol had worn off, the dread of a collaborative wrath gripped her. Her immediate concern was chiefly the security of her children. She knew the futility of seeking any help or support from Khoobchand. She chose not to confide in her children, lest something spilled out and she needed the counsel of her mother-in-law, Dhania. So, next day, she made an excuse of going on a couple of days' official tour for RLNAS and took the bus from the outskirts of the town to Phool-Birai.

After her retirement from the hospital in the city, Dhania had settled back in her village, Phool-Birai, where her small *kachcha* house had since been converted into a pretty three-room cottage, encroaching upon the free land around it. There was also a vegetable patch where she grew plants and vegetables, which gave her not only a steady supply of food, but also made it look quaint and beautiful with some flowers or other on the bloom, through the year.

She treated her plants and flowers in her little nursery like her children, and hence after spending a few days with her grandchildren, she was always in a hurry to get back to her place in the village. Saanvri and her children loved the cottage no less and looked forward to their holidays with Dhania.

In the late afternoon, when Dhania got down from the cycle rickshaw outside her house, the first thing she noticed was the continuous flow of water in the water channel along the outer walls, spilling into the underground sewage pipe the village municipality had recently put in.

Fearing that the tap may have remained open, she rushed to the rear, which was on a slightly raised ground. To her great astonishment, she found Saanvri standing near the tap, holding a narrow pipe used for watering the flowerbeds and the rows of vegetables and plants. Lost in her thoughts, she was oblivious of the water falling into a small cement tank connected to the water channel along the house, instead of the flowerbeds.

Her small suitcase was placed near the steps at the rear entrance. In an instant Dhania understood everything.

Half an hour later, as they shared tea in the bedroom, snugly under a light quilt, Dhania finally asked, "Tell me what has gone wrong…"

As if a switch had been flicked, tears welled up in Saanvri's eyes as soon as the question was asked. But that did not surprise Dhania. What made her heart leap out was the expression of deep fear that followed, as soon as the tears had flown out.

Tears! They have a strange way with humans. More often than not they make words non-essential, especially, when there is an existing bond between the two individuals. Dhania swiftly took the mug out of Saanvri's hand and placed it along with hers, on the stool nearby. Then she slid across and locked Saanvri in her embrace, patting her at the back as if she were a child.

Earlier, when Dhania had pulled her out of her reverie, taking the water pipe out from her hand, Saanvri had merely volunteered that a sudden urge to meet her mother-in-law had brought her unannounced. Dhania had asked no questions and welcomed her with a broad smile and a kiss on her forehead. Even later, while walking back into the house, neither had spoken much. Dhania had prodded Saanvri to take a small nap in her bed while she made some tea. It was only now that the two had finally got down to catching up. It was worrisome for Dhania without even being told anything.

The more Dhania caressed her back, the more Saanvri shuddered in her arms, till she had emptied herself. Finally, she narrated the whole story. Exhausted by the end of it she turned to Dhania and asked, "What do I do, Amma? I brought all important documents for you to put away in a safe place."

"You did the right thing by bringing the stuff here. First, I'll put them at a safe place as they are now your only security, then I'll come to Jodhpur with you. Can't leave you alone at this time."

But little did Saanvri know that she had already burnt her bridges in Jaipur as well as in Jodhpur. The elite of Jodhpur may ordinarily be complaining against each other, but the moment there was an aggression from beyond the fold, the entire decadent clan banded together. Some of the former royals and the elites who had witnessed Saanvri's outburst at the marriage celebration had gone into a huddle and had vowed to 'put the woman in her place', who in their view was merely the scum of society.

•✦•

Within the next few days, Saanvri had been served suspension orders from the Health Department for continued absence from duty. Likewise, in Jaipur, a ministry circular had been issued regarding de-registration of the RLNAS, on account of crunch. Her official car had also been withdrawn without so much a courtesy call. Rattled by the sudden developments, she chose to do the obvious thing she could to save herself from the misery. She took the train to Jaipur.

Although she was quite sure of the outcome, from the station she first decided to call the Le Meridian hotel, where she used to be booked in the name of RLNAS. As expected she was informed by the reception that the booking against RLNAS had been cancelled.

From the station, she took a rickshaw straight to the house of a dancer friend, whom she had already spoken to from Jodhpur. After some rest, she tried Yashpal Sarena's direct line, as well as his personal cell. Both went unanswered. Even going through his PA did not help—she was not put through, on some pretext or the other. The following day, she chose the only remaining option—visiting Yashpal in the office, unannounced. Even after waiting for more than half a day, she returned disappointed. He never came to the office—or so she was told.

She understood the score. She was still at her friend's place when she learnt that the Assembly Session was on. Assuming that Rana would be in town, she thought of giving it a try, partly out of desperation and partly out of the stirrings of her heart, which had not quite purged. After chasing him for the whole day and even managing to corner him near his car, she could not talk to him. When she returned to Jodhpur, fraught with uncertainty, more was in store. She was told that Khoobchand had been sacked from his job as a driver at Rana's household. Now there was panic.

Meanwhile, Sulakshana was still not finished with Saanvri. The fact that Saanvri had chased Yashpal even at his office, had created a different kind of panic in her. Then there was also the deceitful avenger in her who had not been put to sleep yet.

•◆•

The imposing new mall in Jaipur gleamed in its glassy splendour. Surrounded by important guests, VIP dignitaries, staff of the corporate group owning the establishment and the press, as soon as Yashpal Sarena cut the ribbon, a battery of cameras went off, and the congregation applauded excitedly. Just then, his new personal cell held by his secretary, rang. Drowned beneath the din of clapping and the photographers clamouring for more shots, his secretary struggled to understand what the caller was saying. Then, all of a sudden, his expression turned compliant and servile. He squeezed his way through the milling crowd to get to his boss and whispered something in his ear. Yashpal immediately took hold of the cell and called out to the organiser lurking behind him.

"*Arre* Parikh-ji, Parikh-ji…Where is your, that…that?"

"That? What hukum?" Parikh looked nonplussed.

"*Arre*, that, that…what do they say… *Arre* bathroom, *yaar*," he retorted impatiently.

"Come with me. This way, sir." Parikh said suppressing his smile.

They zipped through a narrow space, followed by Yashpal's bemused armed security men. At the door to the washroom, he suddenly stopped and told them sternly, "Don't let anybody in."

The security men took position at the door with their AK47s while he attended the phone.

Plonked on the toilet seat cover, a shocked Yashpal barked into the cell phone, "One crore! Have you gone mad? Do you have a retarded brain or something?"

Perched on an ornate sofa-settee in her house, Sulakshana threw a fleeting glance at Ramlal, seated in the sofa-chair nearby, and spoke into her cell phone with all the theatrics she could muster.

"Why are you saying all this to me, Bhai-sa? What can I do? Even I lost my marbles, on hearing this."

"Fucking bloody whore's daughter," he muttered with gritted teeth. "She's becoming that daring? Won't spare the fucking bitch... Shall ruin her completely. Where the hell is the bitch, dig her out from wherever she is hiding?"

"She was in Jodhpur till two days ago...I believe she created a lot of ruckus there too, in Rana's daughter's wedding."

"*Raand saali*...What did I not do for her."

"I had told you."

"Okay, okay," He cut her off and asked, "Tell me what I ought to do now."

A silence followed that seemed longer than mere two or three seconds. He roared, "What happened...will you say something or not?"

"Will you follow what I say?"

"*Arre*, say what you have to say," he snapped.

"Pay her off for now...if she does a volte-face after that, we shall have time with us to handle her," Sulakshana said with guile in her voice.

"Hmm..." Yashpal responded after a deep exhale and a brief silence. Then sounding much calmer, he said, "You'll be able to handle it properly?"

"Yes, I'll be able to."

"Who would you send it with...Will go yourself?"

"I have the right person for it."

"Who?"

"Ramlal." She exchanged a meaningful look with Ramlal.

Yashpal slumped back ponderously, "Ramlal…Ramlal?" Then he said agreeably, "Yes yes, it's fine. He has handled jobs for me before. He is a clever fellow. Can be trusted."

"Yes hukum!"

"Okay, then, handle it quickly…I shall arrange for the money. But see to it that this woman doesn't come in front of me again," he said bitterly.

"Bado-hukum."

Yashpal turned off the phone and got up wearily. Then he pressed the lever to flush and got out.

As Sulakshana switched off her own cell phone, she found Ramlal's eyes searching hers. Meeting his gaze squarely she said, "It has been arranged. But listen," her eyes turned cold and piercing before she completed, "I shall give you twenty-five lakh. You'll deliver twenty lakh to her and keep five with you. And your tongue! Your tongue should not utter a single word anywhere." She had a threateningly no-nonsense look in her eyes.

"Have I ever uttered anything in response to what you have told me to do?" Ramlal retorted.

Two days later when Saanvri received a call on her cell phone, she did not suspect anything. Instead, she was amused that Yashpal should ask someone to come and see her. Yet, from the window of the room upstairs when she saw the tall and broad-chested man, attired like a party worker, alight from the LMV and walk to the front of her door, a sudden sensation of disquiet made way into her.

It was all short and simple after that. As she opened the door, Ramlal only threw a noncommittal glance at her and without a word of greeting raised his hand forward in a gesture to push her aside. Though slightly affronted, Saanvri moved sideways to let him in. There was a menacing air about him as he nonchalantly moved in and without any offer to take a seat, sat down on the settee in the sitting room and placed the briefcase that he was carrying with him, on the small centre table. Without moving from her place, she was still considering him when he looked up with a fiendish stare and gestured her to sit on the sofa near him. Amused she found herself obliging and sat down. Coolly, he opened the briefcase and turning it towards her, said, "Its ten lakhs." He patted at the wads of currency notes inside it.

A chill went through her body and she asked, "Ten lakhs…for what?"

"For your family! Mantri-ji has sent them."

"But why…When did I ask for it?"

"You didn't ask for it, but we are giving it to you," he said flatly and then with a tinge of threat in his tone he continued. "And you'll have to take them."

"I'll have to take them. What is all this? What kind of a pressure is this?" Saanvri sounded irritated and going for her cell phone she said, "I'll talk to hukum."

Now he coolly withdrew his gun and placed it on the table near the briefcase before speaking: "His number has changed. Now keep it." Then he raised his finger and pointing it threateningly at her he said, "From now on, neither will you call him, nor will you try to meet him or open your mouth even slightly."

With a slight shudder she held his eyes, which now had an unmistaken glare in them. After a couple of seconds, he put his hand on the notes and asked in a soft though challenging growl, "Now tell me, will you take these notes, or…" he lifted his hand from the notes and put it on the gun.

There was a stunned silence as Saanvri searched into his eyes, which were cold and menacing. Shaken by them, she nodded a few times and mumbled, "Leave the money here."

Ramlal shut the briefcase, picked up his gun and got up. She sat frozen in her place with her head down, her eyes not registering anything. After a couple of seconds when she raised her head, he was already gone.

Seventeen

It was an unusually long queue. People had lined up from early morning. By eight, the queue had extended from the outer veranda, of the British era single-story bungalow, into the lawn. It ran through the long driveway, all the way up to the outer gate. Extra staff had been summoned to tend to the men, women and children moving forward slowly in a serpentine queue. Even so, most of the staff members were at their wits end, serving rounds of water and even tea at times, as well as listening to the tales of woe of an occasional visitor waiting in line.

Ever since the incumbent CM had embarked upon holding a 'Janta Darbar' to meet the commoners at his residence to directly address their problems, the ritual had followed without fail from eight each morning, except when he was out of town. But today, since the queue was exceptionally long, the secretarial staff was not allowing anyone to engage with the CM in unnecessary chat.

In their midst was a burqa-clad woman. When her turn came, she hastily passed on a small piece of paper in the CM's hand. He glanced through it and looked visibly surprised. It was a handwritten note in Hindi saying: *I fear for my life. Please grant me a couple of minutes in private.*

On a reflex he looked up at the woman's face but could not quite read the expression in her eyes behind the slits of the veil. He passed the note to his aide and moved on after folding his hands.

The CM returned to his residence in another ten minutes. But as she walked listlessly with the dispersing crowd, an aide approached her and led her to a side door in the veranda.

She was ushered into a large reception room which had several sets of settees and chairs lined along the two facing walls, each with small coffee tables between them. They were covered in *khadi* material as were the cushions. The CM, Ghanshyam Das was seated on a settee talking to someone on his cell.

On seeing the lady enter he got up and gesturd her to sit in the chair opposite him. She sat down feeling slightly intimidated. He too switched off the phone and sat down. Taking a quick glance at his watch he said, "Tell me."

The woman now lifted up her veil. It was Saanvri.

The CM looked at her with a touch of uncertainty before asking, "You are, you are… Saanvri Devi?"

"Yes, Yes sir," she said nervously and a little self-consciously.

"What happened…This note that you have given…What is this?"

Tears flashed in Saanvri's eyes. Trying to cover them with her handkerchief, she said, "Its true, hukum. I am afraid that…that…I fear for my life."

"Fear for your life? From whom?"

"Between a minister of yours and me…there has been a…" she hesitated and then more tears spilled out.

Ghanshyam, though a little alarmed by the situation, kept a stoic face and said reassuringly, "Look, don't fear anything. Speak freely. You see, only when we have the complete picture that we can help you in this matter."

Sensing empathy, she broke down further. Ghanshyam Das looked perplexed but let her get control over herself. Struggling with her tears, she opened her purse and took out a CD. Placing it on the coffee table in front of him, she said, "This, this CD has it all that…that has been going on between him and me."

Gripped by revulsion, Ghanshyam stared at her in shocked outrage. When her tears subsided a bit, he asked softly, "Who is the minister? Who are you talking about?" Not getting any response, he spoke curtly, "Tell me."

"*Ji*…Yashpal…Sarena-ji," she blurted out.

Ghanshyam's jaw dropped on hearing this and he stared blankly at her. She looked pathetic, as if she were a thief of some sort. After a couple of seconds his expression changed. Composing himself, he asked, "Yashpal…Sarena-ji! You mean our 'Energy and Urban Development Minister'?"

Saanvri lowered her head and nodded silently. As if involuntarily his hand moved to the handset of the intercom placed on a side table. Still continuing to stare at her bent head, he picked it up and softly spoke to the voice which answered.

"Send Mrs Srinivasan, quickly." He turned around to replace the receiver at its place. He seemed to ponder for a moment or two before straightening and addressing Saanvri, "Narrate the whole thing fearlessly to the lady who I've just called for. She is my special secretary. A completely dependable officer. Everything that you tell her will remain absolutely confidential and necessary action will be taken. Shall I keep this CD with me?"

Saanvri dried her eyes and said, "But sir, I have to say something else too."

"Tell me."

"Sir…" she hesitated.

"Yes, what?"

"Sir, if somehow something happens to me, I would like all important evidences in my possession to reach you."

"Look, you don't worry about all that. We are here to take care of things. Nothing will happen to you."

Tears again flashed in her eyes and she said. "Sir, they are very dangerous people. Hence I feel you should at least hear me out."

Ghanshyam considered her empathetically for a few seconds, before saying, "Tell me."

"Only this sir, that if anything happens to me, I would have left all the evidences that you might need, with an extremely trusted person."

"Who are you talking about…Who?"

"*Ji*, Amma, my mother-in-law…she is like my second mother, sir."

"And your husband, children?"

All of a sudden she kind of shrank into herself and her face turned hard. Looking down slowly she said, "I don't trust my husband with any of this, sir. My children are small, still at school." Tears flashed in her eyes and her voice cracked: "That's why I am worried, sir.

Just then a lady in her late forties entered the room. Ghanshyam Das addressed Saanvri, "Alright, you narrate all that you told me to Mrs Srinivasan here. We'll all take care of the rest. Also leave your address and contact details with her." Now turning to Mrs Srinivasan he said, "You take her with you and understand everything in detail, Mrs Srinivasan."

"Yes, sir," she put her hand on Saanvri's shoulder and said, "Please come…come with me."

A little while later still in the same clothes Ghanshyam Das was seated at the edge of the bed in the master bedroom, fiddling with a remote control. What came up on the television monitor, left him agape.

Right then the door was flung open by his wife, an attractive middle-aged lady, with a dressing gown over a flimsy nightie.

"What has happened to you? You haven't had breakfast yet. Aren't you going to the Sachivalaya today?"

"Sh-sh-sh. Hold, hold on a minute. Close the door," he said, shushing his wife.

Now her eyes went to the TV screen and she was completely taken aback by what she saw. "*Arre, yeh kya?* What is this?" she demanded. "Since when have you started watching this sort of stuff?"

"I said shut the door and keep quiet," he cut her off curtly without letting go of his eyes from the monitor.

By the time his horrified wife went to the door to shut it, he had dialled a number on his cell phone. When a voice answered from the other side, he said with an unadulterated glee in his voice, "How are you, Pushpendra Dwivedi-sahab?"

He listened to the voice responding to him from the other side for a few seconds and then said teasingly, "*Bhai*, I thought that since I've been holding on, for that meeting for so long, why not I ring you myself. Will you please call my secretary? He'll fix the appointment, I have told him already…*Ji, ji*…Namaskar."

Ghanshyam ended the call and turning to his wife with his arms spread wide, he said mischievously, "Come, let me take you in my arms, *yaar*."

EIGHTEEN

The atmosphere was electric. Unprecedented security had been put in place. There were three tiers of checks being conducted. Even the channel head and the chief editor had to surrender to thorough frisking after passing through the metal-detector gate, each time.

Security men in civilian clothes, kept a hawk-eye on every personnel, every machine, every computer screen and every button pressed or touched and were strategically placed inside the News Room—like shadows, they followed the slightest movement of each cameramen, his assistants and the floor manager, discreetly in the studio.

Though none of the personnel gossiped as such, there was an alarming buzz among the staff in the console room. An array of monitors were live in the two rows above the glass partition, connecting the studio floor, where the news anchor was already reading the news from the teleprompter in front of him. The only discernible voice was of that of a senior producer seated among the four or five technicians in front of the console instructing his assistants, the floor manager, as well as the 'on-line' editor. The monitors were connected to different cameras already positioned outside the location—the party office, the road leading to the campus and the hand held cameras with the reporters.

The news producer, a balding man in his mid-forties, wearing a head piece comprising of head phones and a mini microphone, spoke out the instructions. "Cut to three..."

The scene on the broadcast monitor in front of him switched from a mugshot of the news anchor, to a long shot of a broad road, packed with people surging from both sides to peep inside the arriving vehicles. The uniformed police personnel struggled to push them back in order to clear the way for the barely crawling cars.

One after other, the bumper-to-bumper cars, SUVs and jeeps delivered the members of the Working Committee of the party at the huge iron gate of an old two-storeyed colonial building, which served as the party headquarter. Two rows of elbow-to-elbow policemen had formed a cordon to facilitate the alighting invitees, swiftly ferrying them through the partially open iron gates.

The visual of this frenzied activity and the cacophony of the attendant sound was accompanied by the bawling voice-over of the news anchor:

It is barely nine in the morning that the vehicles of the Working Committee members have started arriving...

At this point the news producer spoke the instruction, "Cut to studio."

On the broadcast monitor, the scene switched back the anchor:

The media has not been allowed to go inside the committee room, however outside, as you can see...

The visual on the broadcast monitor changed to a wider high-angle shot of the outer compound of the party office. Many TV cameras and reporters were lined up outside the main entrance of the building, struggling to capture the reaction of the Working Committee members alighting from their cars before entering the building. The visuals on the monitor also kept on alternating ground level shots of their other freelance feed suppliers. Some of the reporters were trying to squeeze their microphones through the available space between the bodies, begging for sound bites. All along the news anchor's voice continued over the melange of visuals:

Looking at all the buzz and the body language of the arriving members of the Working Committee as they walk across the compound to get inside the committee room, one gets a fairly clear idea that Ghanshyam Das-ji's stars are likely to be eclipsed today...and it is quite possible in this game of chess, which Yashpal Sarena and his friends have been playing for a long time, they may succeed this time...

The large rectangular committee room with wall-to-wall white sheets spread over broad mattresses was almost full. Seniors were seated by the main wall, aided by large cushions behind them. The space in front was occupied by the juniors, with old-fashioned *gao-takias* to occasionally lean upon; their eyes trained on the seniors.

Large framed photographs of the leading lights of the party hung not only at the main wall behind the seniors, but also on the side walls. Also stuck above the portraits on the main wall was a banner whih read: *All India Lok-Tantrik Party*

The faces of most were drawn and solemn, indicating clearly that some serious confabulation had been on, which perhaps had just concluded. The ominous silence was broken by a sad and weary voice of a man in his late seventies, the president of the Provincial Party: "So, what do we do then?"

Many voices arose immediately, "Pass the resolution, sir, pass the resolution."

"Who will propose the resolution?" asked the president in a voice full of remorse.

"I'll, sir, I'll propose the resolution," a pot-bellied man in his mid-forties flashed his hand, speaking aloud and impatiently at the same time. "I propose that, considering the extremely difficult circumstance the state is passing through, the Working Committee replaces Shri Ghanshyam Das-ji and with immediate effect selects Honourable Yashpal Sarena-ji as the leader of the legislative party of the AILP, in the Vidhan Sabha."

The glum faces of Ghanshyam Das-ji and Rana seemed to go a shade darker, while faces of many of the juniors as well as two or three of the seniors gleamed with a new sheen. After a couple of seconds' silence, the president removed his glasses and took a surveying look at all the people assembled in front of him before asking in a defeated voice, "Who will second the resolution?"

Many hands sprung up instantly, along with a rising clamour. "I'll do it; I'll do it..."

Just then, an old and very senior looking member in the back row, who had been looking at a text message on his mobile, suddenly raised his hand and spoke out aloud, "Sir, sir...Adhyaksh-ji, there is some very important news! Please have the TV switched on..."

A flabbergasted president looked offended as he responded in a tone of irritation, "*Arre bhai* the meeting is still on..."

"Sir, there is some dangerous news pertaining to the meeting...A SMS has come just now..."

A harassed president looked around. "What do we all feel?"

"Alright sir, let's check it for a minute...after all such a senior member is requesting it!" rang a few voices, unenthusiastically

"Sir, this can have great impact on the meeting..."

"Fine then..." said the president, sounding deflated. He then searched for the remote control inside the low writing desk in front of him before pointing it at the TV.

Even as the members began to crane their necks to look at the monitor waiting for the visual to appear, the voice of a male reporter came out loud and clear. It was followed by the shot of a dance by Saanvri, on one half of the screen and a mugshot of Yashpal on the other.

It is believed that this intimacy between Shri Yashpal Sarena and Saanvri Devi has been going on for last many years...

Now the visual on the large plasma screen cut to a slightly high-angle shot of an indeterminate bedroom with a king-sized bed on which a man and a woman, completely in the nude, were engaged in a vigorous sexual activity. A small semi-transparent spherical filter appeared shielding their private parts but not quite succeeding due to the inadequate alignment of the vigorous activity.

Most members were in sheer shock. Yashpal's face looked drained as he sat crestfallen. On the other hand Rana, though equally shocked and seized by a sudden involuntary fear, began to feel more relaxed slowly, with a sly victorious smile appearing on his face even as he stole a glance in Yashpal's direction. However the CM continued to sit pensively without displaying any emotion on his stoic face, his eyes fixed to the screen.

After total silence for a couple of minutes when all the members seemed to have frozen in their places, a man in his mid-forties, seated close to Yashpal, ventured softly, "It proves nothing." He slowly turned his face to look at the members at both his sides as if to draw support and continued, "Can't recognise either of them. They could be anybody."

But almost at once he wished that he had not spoken at all. For, in the throes of passion the man engaged in the sexual act, suddenly, lifted the body of the female, already entwined with his own, and turning around sideways dropped her across the bed, while continuing to pound on her. In the process, the faces of both of them came in full view—they were Saanvri and Yashpal. The ludicrous spectacle on the screen had an amusing aspect too as the spherical opaque filters danced about to shield their private parts.

Even as the members sat stupefied with their eyes dug into the screen, the voice of the anchor rambled on:

The source from where Channel Seven *has obtained this CD claims to have many more besides this one, showing a few more MLAs enjoying boudoir games with Saanvri Devi. Among them is another influential member of the ruling party, who is supposed to hail from a former royal family. There has been speculation that this person may have fathered Saanvri Devi's last child...*

The smug smile that had settled on Rana's face a while ago instantly vanished, and as if in protest his mouth made ridiculous motions of opening and shutting a few times. Many stole sideway glances at his thoroughly embarrassed face, while the voice-over of the anchor continued on the visuals:

We have also learnt that soon many more CDs and documents may appear in the public domain as evidence of all these allegations…

"*Band karen, band karen,*" shouted an outraged voice of an elderly woman from a corner of the hall. This broke the spell that had left the attendees like statues. "Watching porno shows…Is that going to be the order of the day?"

Forthwith the president's hand, which lay inert on the desk so far, jumped up to grab the remote again and pointing it at the monitor, put it off. He looked as much revolted as the woman as he put down the remote and after wearily glancing across at the members, mumbled, "Now?"

"There is definitely a conspiracy, sir. How can we be sure that the pictures are not morphed?" shouted another man seated beside Yashpal who sat unmoved, his eyes fixed on the mattress.

"Whatever it be, we cannot go ahead with the house resolution in this situation sir," another senior member seated not far from the CM spoke aloud in a derisive tone.

"What do we all say?" The president looked around searchingly.

"Will have to postpone it for now sir…Please postpone it," rang many voices.

There was pin-drop silence all of a sudden. Rana, who sat ashen faced, stole a look at Yashpal, who did the same before they dropped their faces again.

The silence was broken by yet another member in his mid-fifties, who addressed the president, "But sir, should we not see what else the channels may be saying? After all the matter of party's honour is involved."

When the monitor was turned on again the anchor was found saying:

Immediately after this transmission, our correspondent Ramesh Maurya took the reaction of the leader of the opposition, Shri Jindal…

The visual cut to a shot of a smart looking mid-fifties man, clad in crisp white kurta and jeans, who was getting into his car as he held its half open door while venting at the camera in utter disgust:

Shame—shame—shame…This government should resign forthwith. Morally speaking, this Chief Minister has no right to remain in the chair even for a second. But you can see for yourself. They have no shame whatsoever… They have pawned it a long time ago…

With this he sat inside, slamming the door shut after him. The driver took off with the car. The reporter turned to the camera to continue his report.

After the shameless incident of a few MLAs watching the pornographic clippings on their mobile phones during the house proceedings, this sex scandal has created an unprecedented sensation. There has been a slew of sarcastic posts on the twitter that it is only a minor matter of a northern state trying to challenge one of its southern counterparts to prove that even in the matter of sex scandal our MLAs are not behind….

"Let us record that the meeting is being called off by the chair, under special circumstances of an emergency!" said the president loudly above the eruption of a mild din.

"We second it, we second it…" echoed many voices.

But Yashpal and Rana were not the only ones who had been jolted out of their wits at what had happened in the committee room. Even Ghanshyam Das was taken by surprise as the visuals displayed on the screen were not the ones he had witnessed privately. Though the visual broadcasted on the TV did ultimately show Yashpal's face clearly, it did not so much show Saanvri's. It had left room for conjecture. He felt cheated. Even though the visual was not entirely unimpeachable to fix his immediate problem, someone was playing games! But who?

Ghanshyam Das felt a chill in his bones even when the immediate fall guy was his sworn enemy, Yashpal, and to a lesser extent the irksome Rana. He was besieged by a particularly tricky situation, almost a whirlpool of conflicting thoughts and emotions. He could neither betray the trace of glee on being rescued from the imminent fall of the government nor the nagging sense of fear in the pit of his stomach.

Ghanshyam Das sank into one of the visitors' sofa, in his room in the party office. Asking his staff to forbid anyone from entering, he ordered a large cold coffee for himself. Once a few sips had halted the fall of his sugar level, he set about thinking systematically as to who else, other than Pushpendra Dwivedi, he might have mentioned about the CD. He was sure that he had not let his caution slip down even slightly. He stopped rolling the cold glass on his forehead and got up, utterly relaxed. But suddenly a thought hit him—Somebody was trying to blackmail someone else! But who?

At the same time, a paralysing fear had gripped both Yashpal and Rana, who had already experienced the first jolt from the pincers of the invisible blackmailer. Bitten by the unbridled shock their tormentor had subjected them to, both sought a personal sanctuary, and that is what they secured by locking the doors of the rooms they were inside right now. Both were in an acute state of turmoil, manifested in their movements of suddenly sinking into a sofa or a chair and suddenly rising and pacing angrily inside the rooms they were in.

Both realised that there was no escape from giving in to the demands of the invisible messenger. Negotiation was the only possibility.

Earlier, they had been approached, respectively, by a friend of a friend, to consider a business proposition of great value. It had turned out to be an offer on how to deal with some vital information, and whether to let them out in the public domain or not. It had been revealed that the information was of carnal nature with dangerous ramifications. When asked for some proof, the voice had calmly informed that a visual sample would be presented at a significant moment. What had just been circulated over the TV was such a 'sample', sending shivers down their spines.

Initially, both had suspected Saanvri as the main player behind the scene—while Yashpal had been gullible to the manipulations of his sister, to Rana it seemed so because of what happened at his daughter's marriage celebration.

Unaware of any of these speculations, Saanvri herself was anxious for her and her family's security when she heard of the TV coverage that was being repeatedly presented on many channels, with attendant spins from the anchors. Ironically, she had not had a chance to see the clips herself.

There was only one person who was able to think with clarity and that was CM Ghanshyam Das. He had acted with great alacrity by posting plain-clothed round-the-clock security for Saanvri. Having taken necessary precautions, he now waited patiently for the pieces to fall in place.

Nineteen

The fact that the TV commentator had given a direct hint about Rana also being a part of the scandal with Saanvri, and since both Rana and Yashpal had gathered through their moles that the source of their torment was perhaps one and the same, the two enemies found themselves creeping towards the same page. But the walls of mutual suspicion and utter contempt for each other were never going to be easy to breach. Yet the need for survival being such, they had little choice but to give it a try.

The advancing sharp beams of the three vehicles made the night look eerie, as they traversed through the heavily potholed dirt path in the middle of acres and acres of fields, which spread like a dark carpet around them. The caravan of the two police jeeps and the SUV between them soon reached a plateau, more like a patch of an island in the middle of a sea of fields.

The vehicles came to a halt some three hundred feet from the rim of the island. Two tall and sturdy men, wrapped in white sheets above their trousers, woollen jumpers and a *bukkal* to cover their faces, emerged from behind the lights and walked down the slope with one hand hidden in the folds. Obviously, each clutched a weapon ready to be fired. Two security guards, in similarly hooded jumpers, alighted from the vehicle in front, to meet them midway. When they were close enough they stopped. Spurts of white vapour escaping from their mouths indicated that words were being exchanged between them.

One of the guards turned around to nod at the guard sitting beside the driver in the SUV; he got down clutching his AK47 under the sheet wrapped around him and opened the back door. A tall man, also donning an off-white *loi*—a light woollen sheet—above his jeans and a full monkey cap covering his face, alighted. As soon they started moving forward, two more guards swiftly alighted from the jeep at the back of the caravan and joined them.

They were led to the incline, where some distance away, near an open hearth, with fire raging underneath a huge iron pan containing some dark liquid, sat Yashpal on a rustic mattress. Small herds of similarly attired men also sat close by. Nearby, a *kolhoo*, a sugarcane crusher operated with a couple of oxen being driven round and round in a grove by a bull-minder, to churn out the juice from the bundles of sugarcane being continually shoved into the contraption from another aide. The resultant juice was ferried through wide steel ducts to pour into the iron pan to be boiled and stirred. The aroma of the boiling syrup wafted up as they walked towards Yashpal, who immediately got to his feet and took a couple of steps forward to greet them.

"*Padharo* Rana-ji *padharo*...Very kind of you that you came!"

He grabbed Rana's hand and pumped it, before putting his arms around him in an embrace. Pointing at a place by a *gao-takia*, the big cylindrical pillow, alongside his own, he gestured him to sit down. "Sit here, sit here hukum...You're our royal guest tonight Rana-ji!"

As Rana began to remove his shoes, Yashpal addressed one of the young ones who had stood up to greet Rana, "*Arre chhora* move, take Rana-ji's shoes..."

Immediately, the young man bent down and helped Rana ease out of his shoes. Another one offered water from a pitcher and a hand towel for him to wash and dry his hands before he sat down.

Once Rana settled down and removed his baklava, Yashpal exhorted another man: "*Arre* bring it, bring the *gud*. The first produce of the season should be inaugurated with Rana-ji tasting it."

In a clean brass saucer two large lumps of hot and dark-grey jaggery, freshly extracted from the boiling syrup, were brought along with a small spoon and proffered to Rana. As he took the saucer, Yashpal continued, "And for me, bring only in the *dona* and no spoon."

Rana watched him with fascination as he leaned back on the *gao-takia* behind him. There was no trace of worry or anxiety on his face. Rana, who throughout his travel to the place had been subsumed with the worries about the threats staring at him, was amazed at this rustic man's resilience in the face of adversity.

A small bowl, fashioned out of a couple of large dried peepal leaves, was brought to him with similar lumps of jaggery. Yashpal took it hungrily and said heartily, "Rana-ji, I am an ordinary farmer. This *matti* is my strength." He pointed at the ground around him with a sense of pride and then continued, "Therefore whenever there is a grave problem of any sort, I quickly get back to my soil. This *matti* and its smell gives me the capacity to think straight. And today the reason was all the more special. Our *gud* from the first crop of the season was going to be ready, and I had to be here as per tradition." He laughed, carefully picked up a bit of the hot jaggery with his fingers and immediately began to blow on it to cool it before taking a bite.

Rana, who had picked up a piece in his spoon, stopped in his tracks and stared at Yashpal curiously as he endeavoured to cool the lump held in his fingers. When Yashpal turned and noticed Rana staring at him with amusement, he stopped and said disarmingly, "Rana-ji, I am a villager. The pleasure I get in eating with my bare fingers, straight from the elementary *dona*, will never be matched by using a plate and a spoon."

"Get me a *dona* also. I won't be too bad with my fingers either, I promise," said Rana with a broad smile on his lips. Both burst into a laughter.

Still licking their fingers, savouring the aftertaste of the heavenly jaggery, as they leaned back on the *gao-takias* and stretched their feet, Yashpal beckoned the attendant to bring water and towels for them to wash.

"We have a saying, Rana-ji—if you share *gud* from the first crop of the season with somebody, then that person becomes your buddy. You always stand by him like he will with you." Yashpal said in a lighter vein.

Rana exchanged a long look with Yashpal, before responding with the expected solemnity of the moment, "I understand Sarena-ji; you can count on me completely."

Both of them were acutely aware that they stood at the precipice of a deep and dangerous gorge, full of rotting carcasses. The inevitability of the hell, if they did not move together, melted the differences between them, in no time. Sipping the freshly extracted sugarcane juice directly from *kulhads*—the baked mud glasses—they shared their thoughts about confronting the grave threat to their social position and their diligently carved out political future—by the hydra-headed scandals unleashed at them by forces still shrouded in mystery.

"Time has changed, Rana-ji. In my youth, life was so uncomplicated. You fancied someone, fine. No big deal. In these very fields, among the sugarcane shoots, god knows how many women I have taken. Just throw a sheet on a bit of a clearing and get on with it. Married, unmarried, whatever—how did it matter? What mattered was that you took care of the woman if the need arose. Otherwise chill. You're happy, she's happy; move on." Yashpal remarked cynically.

He stopped for a moment and looking at Rana said, "And wasn't it the same for the royals too, Rana-ji? If you took a *golee* to the bed, you took the *golee* to the bed! Simple. *Gola* did not make any issue about it, because you took care of them both, and their children. May be they were your children too. Cool. Everybody happy."

Mesmerised, Rana listened to this man of the soil go on in jest about his twisted sense of morality. He knew that the man was capable of singing a different tune, without batting an eyelid, at a forum of a different kind. He remembered the hosannas he had sung at the Jodhpur Junior Doctors Association's function, few years ago—in praise of Indian women in general and the natives of the villages in particular, putting them on the pedestal of goddesses for their high virtues and integrity.

More was in store for Rana as Yashpal started pontificating about his weird sense of justice to chastise the culprit who may have, willingly or unwillingly, brought them both to the edge of a disaster. Without any trace of remorse he spelt out that even if they both had fornicated with the same person, retribution had to be unflinching.

"Rana-ji, in our villages, we know only one treatment to the malaise... twist the fucking neck and bury the body in the fields, whoever it may be."

Rana was speechless. Eyes locked, they sat silently for good three or four seconds. Rana slowly dropped his own but Yashpal continued to look at him for another few seconds with a film of empathy appearing in his eyes. Then, as if he had read the other person's mind he said, "Even my heart says that she couldn't be it, for having known her from close, but the point is that nothing can be risked. She is too vulnerable for our own security...I hope you understand, Rana-ji?"

"What do you propose to do?" asked Rana looking defeated and barely raising his face.

"I don't know. I don't know anything just now, Rana-ji...But what I do know is that the interest of both of us would be in acting jointly, though not openly!"

"And, the steps that you think we ought to take would be?"

"First of all, we'll have to determine as to who the invisible entity behind the demand is, and whether our woman has any connection with the entity. Then, we'll have to somehow neutralise that entity, at least for the time being..."

"What do you mean?"

"I mean, negotiate and meet the demand for the present before a final strategy can be worked out."

"And if the woman has no connection with the entity?"

"She'll have to be sorted out regardless. As I said, 'too vulnerable'..."

Rana lowered his head. His eyes turned sad. After a ponderous silence he looked at Yashpal again and mumbled, "How'll you handle it all? Will you be able to do so, directly?

"No, I can't come in the open. Nor can you...It's the job of a specialist. Tough negotiations will have to be handled."

"Who then?"

"I have someone in mind...Trustworthy in terms of handling the task, though not otherwise!"

"Meaning...?"

"Meaning, too greedy! Bound to cheat me when it comes to money. But that happens...All are same. Here at least, I'll have a good control."

"Anybody I know?"

"No, you don't. She's my own sister!"

Rana's mouth fell. A smirk appeared on Yashpal's face and his eyes shone with a kind of blistering brightness, a reflection of the suddenly leaping flames of the furnace boiling the sugarcane juice. He mumbled, "What do you say?"

Rana nodded in agreement.

The first task of tackling the tormentor having been successfully handled with swift negotiations, late one night, a few days later, they met in a mid-town corporate office—at the conference room of Yashpal's office in a posh up-market building, where his own private businesses were centred. The gloomy atmosphere of the large conference room was heightened by the dim lights and the oppressive silence that seemed to hang between the three occupants.

Sulakshana was seated at the edge of the long and barren conference table. Yashpal was seated obliquely, opposite her on the other side. Rana paced up and down in the empty area of the rectangular room, pensively. Obviously they had been waiting for something important. In a few seconds, a cell phone placed near Sulakshana began to buzz.

"Hmm…Fine! Yes, I'll tell you in a minute." She turned off the cell and put it down. Then she addressed the two men, "He is here…"

Rana stopped pacing. With a tense face, he slowly turned around to look at Sulakshana and then Yashpal, expectantly. The three exchanged silent and meaningful looks. After a pause, Yashpal spoke in a low and gloomy voice, "Shall we call him in, Rana-ji?"

"Yes, call him," Rana had a despairing edge to his voice.

Yashpal signalled Sulakshana, who nodded in acknowledgement and again picked up her cell phone. She spoke in it in a low guttural voice, "Come in…"

A few seconds later, Ramlal entered the room after a soft knock on the closed door. He walked to the opposite side of the long conference table, sombrely. With his hands crossed over his chest and his chin lowered, he stood submissively.

Sulakshana got up and picked a large black leather bag, which was on the ground near her feet. She put the bag on the table and unzipped it slowly. She picked up some wads of notes to show Ramlal. Yashpal addressed him with a growl, "There are two crores there. Everything should be handled very efficiently, not even the slightest slip up should happen…"

"Hukum!" Ramlal nodded deferentially.

Sulakshana pushed the bag towards him. He zipped it back without checking the notes and then picked it up. He stood in attention to bow to all, saying 'hukum' each time, and then left. Sulakshana waited till he exited the room and pulled the door shut after him. She then withdrew a large manila envelope from her own bag and extended it to Rana.

"Rana-ji, for Khoobchand."

Rana walked to the table and as he picked up the envelope, he asked. "How much is it?"

"Ten lakhs...as you had said."

"Hmm..." Rana mumbled.

Sitting morose in the driver's seat, Khoobchand took a swig from the small bottle in his hand. His eyes were red and a film of grief swam across them. He did not notice Rana approach the car, parked in a dark spot on the deserted road—not until he had already opened the back door to slip inside. Khoobchand lowered the bottle and tried to hide it in the side pocket of the door on his side. For well over a minute there was total stillness. Neither could utter a word or move. Then Rana stretched forward and passing on the manila envelope said, "Here take this. There are ten lakhs in there. The man who'll come for her will bring more. Make sure she accompanies him..."

"Hukum," Khoobchand mumbled squeamishly.

"Don't worry at all. They'll definitely bring her back before morning. Everything has been settled..."

"Yes malik!"

"Come on, start the car."

"*Ji...*" He turned on the ignition.

Almost as if on a secret mission, the car slid off slowly.

Twenty

Sniffing around here and there, a small dog strayed to where Khoobchand lay, snoring deeply, with the tripped-over bottle of whiskey in his hand; its contents spilled out. The dog wagged its tail playfully, and then driven by an investigative instinct it raised its front feet and placed them on Khoobchand's chest, sniffing at the source of the sonorous breathing.

At once, a violent burst of air exhaled from Khoobchand's tickled nostrils. It threw the frightened dog back on the ground till it sensed the danger had passed and its object of interest had resettled in its original state, though not as musical as before. And then the savouries left unattended by Khoobchand attracted its attention and it quickly engaged itself in polishing the stuff.

•◆•

It was another day when Saanvri's older children had not gone to school on the advice of their grandmother. After disappearing for the night, Khoobchand had returned heavily drunk in the morning and without speaking a word to any other member of the household, had gone inside the bedroom and passed out. He had not woken up to have any food. Now, having finished their lunch, the children had joined their grandmother in the *baithak* to watch the TV. Ever since Saanvri's disappearance a few days ago, all they watched was news.

Their eyes were glued to the news story relayed on the small colour television. A female anchor was commenting on a collage of alternating visuals comprising still photographs and video bits of Saanvri and Yashpal, showing her performing a dance on stage and him addressing a huge crowd, and so on.

Exclusive breaking news has just been received in our studio...On the orders of the Party High Command, state's Chief Minister, Shri Ghanshyam Das has handed over the matter of the abduction of Saanvri Devi to the CBI. Also the Energy and Urban Development Minister, Shri Yashpal Sarena has been relieved from his post till the time the investigation by the agency is completed. It is understood that the CBI authorities were about to interrogate Shri Sarena, who had to be admitted in the hospital due to a heart condition. The CBI has also begun its investigations around the possibility that Saanvri Devi has been murdered...

The eyes of the three children were instantly flushed with tears on hearing this. An avenging gleam flashed in Dhania's eyes and her frail hands tightened into fists, even as she hid them by withdrawing them into the folds of her saree.

The anchor continued with her commentary:

In the meantime, the meeting of the State Working Committee of the AILP has once again been postponed. It is believed that this meeting will now...

At this point Dhania turned off the TV.

A silence descended in the room. Looking at the expressions on the faces of the children, she took all the three in a wide sweep of her arms and kissed each one of them, while murmuring, "Everything will be fine, everything will be fine...CBI will definitely find her." But her voice cracked as she spoke further, "I have faith, full faith in Natha-ji!"

Then, turning quiet and withdrawn, she got up from the divan and walked to the other door opening into the small corridor that led to the backyard. In the yard, she stood aided by the pillar uncertainly for a few moments. Her eyes went to the bucket under the tap that was partially filled with water. She filled the plastic mug that was placed nearby and involuntarily started sprinkling the water in the *aangan*.

Neelesh and Basanti followed her into the yard

"Dadi, what is the matter?" Neelesh asked hesitantly.

She stopped for a moment and answered him calmly, "Hasn't it turned very hot? I am cooling the floor a little bit."

Looking quite perplexed, the children went back into the house.

But the physical action of sprinkling the water, relaxed Dhania, and she felt better. She decided not to go back to her village Phool-Birai just yet, as planned. She knew that the CBI fellows were bound to come sniffing around to their place too, and she did not want to miss out on them when they did. At least, not now when she had a thing or two to share with them, which could not be revealed even to her grandchildren.

Twenty-One

The moustachioed stout man carefully covered a good part of his face in the muffler-type cotton scarf before creeping out of the nondescript house in the lane of ill-repute in old Bikaner. Except the dim light of a distant lamppost the deserted lane seemed quite dark. But he still had to be careful about anybody getting a wind of him being there. After large pegs of whiskey and good one hour's vulgar frolicking with a large-breasted woman, he was in a celebratory mood as he swiftly made his way to the solitary auto-rickshaw in which he had come. It was a pity that he had not noted the number of the auto-rickshaw.

"Let's go. Back to the lodge," he instructed the driver as he sat inside.

"*Ji* hukum," mumbled the driver and drove off.

Just as the auto neared an overbridge, it started sputtering. The driver pulled it to the side at the mouth of the bridge that they were about to ride. "There appears to be some dirt in the pipe. I'll just check," he mumbled again and got down from the seat to walk to the back of the vehicle, without even bothering to hear what his passenger might have to say.

Despite being fairly drunk, the man was intrigued with the change in the driver's voice. Within seconds, a man materialised from the shadows and slipped in beside him, into the auto. Before he could react, his head was covered by a black bag by another man who also had jumped in from the other side. He could feel the barrel of a gun that had been shoved to his temple.

After crossing the bridge and riding hardly a kilometre, the auto turned into even a narrower alley, where a car already waited. The quary was transferred to the car in the state he was in and the car drove off into the dense night.

•◆•

The walls of the small rectangular room, not more than 10'x8' in size, seemed to close in. A lamp suspended from the ceiling, directly over a wooden table, placed in the centre, left an eerie darkness at most of the area around it because of the shade that covered the high-power bulb. There were two wooden chairs on either side of the table, one of which was occupied by the stout moustachioed man, who was perspiring. Another man dressed in a plain off-white shirt and a pair of jeans stepped forward from the shadows and placed an empty glass on the table and then proceeded to fill it with water from a jug. He had an officious air about it as he did so.

"Is it enough? Or you want some more?" he said as he pushed the half-filled glass towards the stout moustachioed man. Because of the low-hanging lamp shade, most of his face was hidden in the shadows, his features indiscernible yet noticeable for its slow and menacing movements. His white shirt glowed unnaturally because of the direct focus of the light and heightened the eerie feeling. All of this made him quite mysterious as he spoke in his guttural voice with the authoritativeness of a police officer. Sweat shone on the face of the nervous looking moustachioed man as he mumbled, "No, no sir…"

"No no, take some Pheru Ram…It's been seven hours since you have had anything. You must be quite thirsty, surely. And then the whole night is ahead. One has to have a lot of conversation."

The grimness of the threat was not lost on Pheru Ram. He said squeamishly, "Okay sir, give me some more, sir…"

The officer filled the glass and said reassuringly, "Go on, drink it, drink it. When one is in tension, the throat dries up faster."

Pheru Ram gulped down the water. But as he slowly, brought down the glass to the table, the haunted look on his face reappeared.

Now, the officer also slowly sat down on the empty chair opposite him, without letting go of his gaze on Pheru Ram, who was too frightened to even blink. He addressed him in a very soft and friendly tone: "You are badly caught up in the net, Pheru Ram. Ramlal has betrayed you. What else could he have done?"

Unknown to Pheru Ram, the conversation between him and the officer was being discreetly recorded elsewhere. Behind one of the dark side walls, people were at work. A specially laminated surface hid a discreet one-way viewing facility. Seated in front of a portable recorder, a technician wearing headphones recorded the interrogation through a clandestine infra-red camera attached into the wall. Another officer, also donning headphones, watched the whole thing on a monitor, as the officer in the interrogation room continued with his investigation.

"Saanvri herself had complained to the CM about him. She had told him that Ramlal had threatened to shoot her dead."

Tapping his fingers playfully on the surface of the table, he leaned forward a trifle menacingly and said in a slightly conspiratorial tone, "But in the real sense, the noose around your neck has been put by Dhania Devi."

Pheru Ram looked up in utter shock.

"Yes yes, Dhania Devi, Saanvri's mother-in-law. The wad of notes you had passed on to Khoobchand at the time of fetching Saanvri had not gone unnoticed by her, who you mistook to be asleep in the *baithak*. Two slaps was all it took for Khoobchand to spill the whole thing out. You know pretty well, don't you, how these local thana people take care of their guests?"

Pheru Ram's eyes dilated in fear. But the officer was unsparing as he continued. "Now look my friend, if you're not going to state the truth on your own to reveal everything, these senior ones are not going to let you go. They'll have a polygraph test done on you. You'll come round automatically to spill it out. But there is a big difference in saying it then and saying it now."

He held Pheru Ram's frightened eyes with his piercing gaze.

"If you reveal everything on your own now, you'll become a government witness and would be freed. If you did it by way of polygraph, then my friend…" he smiled threateningly before concluding, "you are bound to be hanged by the noose."

Pheru Ram's throat dried up instantly even as he met the officer's gaze, plaintively.

The officer continued, "You think about it. Things are still in our hands but once it goes up to polygraph, it'll be out of our hands altogether."

Like a collapsed creature, Pheru Ram dropped his head on the table. After a second or two, he raised his head again to meet the officer's eyes and said a little bit resolutely, "Sir, I want to record my confession…"

Less than an hour later, he was sitting in a small studio room in CBI's main office, downtown. He faced a camera that recorded his confessional statement, which was also simultaneously jotted down by an officer on the computer screen and, another one in a register by hand. The grim proceeding was witnessed by a magistrate, who was present in the same room throughout.

At first Pheru Ram read from a couple of lines, which he had written in his own handwriting on a piece of paper. Then he started speaking on his own. He seemed quite composed as he spoke: "I am making this statement in my full consciousness and without any pressure or suggestion of any kind…"

The magistrate and the investigation officer of the CBI exchanged a solemn look as Pheru Ram recapitulated the whole sequence of fetching Saanvri to an old haveli where an old lady lay on the bed pretending to be a patient. Then on Saanvri's turning around in a shocked state, how suddenly she had come face to face with Sulakshana, who had subjected her to a stinging slap that had sent her flying on the floor.

He continued to recall that how Saanvri was completely immobilised by the force of the savage slap. But then she immediately turned around and went for Sulakshana's feet, who advanced at her with bloodshot eyes.

"I beg your mercy hukum, please forgive me." She clung to Sulakshana's feet, wrapping both her arms around them, crying and pleading. "I'll tell you the whole thing, madam. There's no fault of mine at all in this, hukum...Trust me."

Sulakshana grabbed her by hair and slapped her again.

"What would you tell me kameeni*? I'll show you who I am...You'll see what I'll do to you now."*

Saanvri wrapped her arms even more tightly around Sulakshana's feet and pleaded with tears in her eyes, "Hukum, you can give me whatever punishment you choose, just let me go to my house once. My daughter is very ill; let me tend to her for a few minutes."

"First, tell me where the rest of the CDs and photos are?" Sulakshana demanded hoarsely while shaking Saanvri's head violently.

"Everything is at the house. I shall hand over everything. Just let me get home once," she cried out miserably.

"Okay, I'll send you back," Sulakshana said gritting her teeth. "After giving the medicine to your daughter, come straight back here with the CDs and the photographs. My people will wait for you right there to bring you back."

At this Saanvri let go of her feet and said with folded hands amid sobs, "Okay hukum. Very kind of you hukum...Bado-hukum." She touched the earth near Sulakshana's feet with her hand and then touched her forehead with the fingers of the same hand in a gesture of taking the dust of Sulakshana's feet to her forehead to show respect.

Sulakshana shouted aloud, "Pheru, Kamli...Take this woman with you."

Saanvri sent a silent prayer to the gods as she was let out of the main door of the old haveli. It was very dark still and the sole light from a street lamp some distance away made the atmosphere quite gloomy. The rain had stopped but there were small puddles of rainwater here and there. The dirty water stained her saree as she inadvertently stepped on them. Her mind was already engaged in searching for an excuse or a trick that could save her from returning to Sulkshana.

The driver had already been alerted in the SUV. The white vehicle and its headlights that had just been turned on presented an eerie edge to the darkness of the night as Saanvri, Pheru Ram and Kamli walked towards it, appearing ghosts-like due to the sudden illumination and the trails of long shadows behind them. Pheru Ram opened the side door for Saanvri while Kamli slid in from the other side-door to take her position next to her in the front. Pheru Ram then shut the door on Saanvri's side and walked to the rear.

Just as Saanvri had settled herself, a shadow-like person sat up behind her, who was obviously already inside and had been crouching low. He flung a dupatta rolled like a rope around her neck and tightened it with full force. Shocked and surprised, Saanvri struggled to free herself with full might, throwing her arms and legs wildly. She was getting choked and was not even able to squeak a scream. Realising what was planned by her tormentors; her mind was suddenly focussed on one thing—to make a run for her life somehow. One of her flailing arms managed to reach the door and clasping the handle, she pulled it towards her while fighting off Kamli by her other arm as the woman had also started to restrain her with both hands. An unexplained energy propelled her and with a powerful thrust she managed to throw herself out of the door.

Pheru Ram acted with great alacrity. He picked up a baseball bat that was lying on the floor of the SUV for an exigency and returned where Saanvri lay. With a quick sharp hammer-like strike on her head he took care of her. Immediately, like that of a melon being struck open, her skull cracked open and blood spurted out. Pheru Ram struck her once more and then pushed her collapsed body into the vehicle through the open door, unaffected by the blood that had coloured his body and clothes. Kamli swiftly grabbed her arms and pulled her back on the seat, helped by Pheru Ram who quickly shut the door. He then hurried to the back of the vehicle and boarded it to sit on the seat opposite the first assassin. The driver immediately started the car and it rolled off. Due to the motion Saanvri's face slid down, leaving a trail of smudged blood on the surface of the glass. Her eyes were wide open with an expression of shock frozen in them.

Everyone present in the small studio room was speechless, too stunned to react as Pheru Ram concluded his recapitulation. It was not the first time they had heard such a confession, being in the occupation that they were in, but the goriness of the murder left them cold and the fact that the three most important men in Saanvri's life had joined hands to take her to her end.

While the magistrate and the agency staff got down to completing the formalities, the regional head of the CBI picked up the board line connecting to the operator: "Get me the director."

"The director, at this time? Are you sure sir? I don't even know whether he is in Delhi or elsewhere," said a harried night operator.

"He is in Delhi. I have checked it."

"But then he'll be at the residence...sleeping!" The operator sounded hesitant.

"Wake him up...And record the conversation. It is official." His tone was unaccommodating.

"Yes sir," the operator mumbled.

Twenty-Two

A week later Rana's haveli was full of guests again. This being the first Karva Chauth after his daughter Bela's marriage, there was no way that the newlywed could be anywhere else except her *sasural* for the occasion. But her parents-in-law being away in Europe to be with their daughter who was due for delivery, Madhvi had decided to have a full-on celebration at their own place. Elaborate preparations had been made, and guests had turned up in full finery with their families.

Keeping in with tradition, elaborate arrangements had been made for the event. More than one kitchen was operative with celebrity cooks, brought from outside Jodhpur, preparing delicacies from three different regions of Rajasthan. But since most married women were observing the ritual of keeping a strict fast—some even a *nirjal vrat*, fasting without even water till they had spied the moon—the husbands also had to maintain distance from the exotic food, despite the aroma of the mouth-watering varieties playing havoc with their gastronomic senses. But since men folk were allowed to have soft drinks many of them were up to the usual tricks of surreptitiously boosting their sherbet with bottled spirits. For that matter a couple of women were not any behind either in this devious adventure.

There were also arrangements for entertainment by way of cultural programmes performed by folk groups regaling the guests with song and dance numbers, enumerating the valour and sacrifices of Rajasthani royals. As usual a folk dance-drama on the legend of Rani Padmini was prominent among them, for her honour and faithfulness to her husband. It was another matter that most of the time the performers had to contend with a generally inattentive audience, least interested in listening to the musical tales of their cultural heritage.

In a corner of the huge sitting room, seated on the sofas, some women were also observing another ritual, that of listening to the *vrath-katha,* which recounted age-old stories of married women freeing their families of great miseries by diligently observing the strict Karva-Chauth fast, sans water, in the honour of their husbands. The most modern among them, who otherwise smoked and drank unabashedly, had tears in their eyes as they listened to the stories.

Soon, most of the women among the guests followed Madhvi to the terrace of the house. Many men also did the same, even if reluctantly, on being goaded by their wives—a temporary truce in their heavy political discussions—to keep with the ritual.

Madhvi, attired in expensive bridal ghaghra-blouse and gold and diamond jewellery, just as her daughter and many other women, went through the motions of sighting the moon at the edge of the terrace. She stood with the *chhalni*—the steel and wire-mesh sieve in her hand, anxiously searching for the moon, in the clouded sky. Her daughter Bela and nearly a dozen other women were doing the same with their individual sieves.

Luckily the moon obliged quickly, rising majestically from behind the layers of overlapping clouds. Madhvi screamed in excitement, "*Dikh gaya, dikh gaya...*"

A collective scream and sighs followed with proclamations that the moon had been sighted—an auspicious time. With excited screams many women as well as some men exclaimed "*Badhai ho...Badhai ho!*"; "What a wonderful sighting!"; "Chanda-mama is in his full bloom today..."

In no time, several women broke into ritualistic songs. Holding puja thalis with lighted lamps arranged by the maids in their hands, a bevy of women advanced towards their husbands, who sat in chairs some distance behind them.

The men folk stood up as though to heartily greet their wives, led by Madhvi. It was an amusing display of hypocrisy as some women among them had clandestine affairs going on with other men present right there, despite now singing a collective love song in folk style to emphasize their loyalty and chastity towards their husbands. A larger number of men had also been equally skilful in fornicating with other men's wives as well as the maids or minions working in the house.

Rana was exuberant in displaying his love for his wife by taking the lead to reach across to Madhvi. She applied a tilak on his forehead and then fed him a spoonful of kheer from a small bowl on the thali. Rana reciprocated with equivalent zeal by taking another scoop with the same spoon and lovingly putting it in Madhvi's awaiting mouth. She then bent down to touch his feet. Rana placed his hands on Madhvi's shoulders to ease her up and then putting his arm around her, lovingly led her away from the group. Both looked very contented. There was no trace of the tension of the recent weeks as they headed towards their daughter and the son-in-law.

"Good; everything was handled so well," he exhaled with relief.

"It's Natha-ji's kindness bestowed upon us. He only put everything right," she said with folded hands and then took her fingers to touch her bowed forehead gratefully.

Ritual well performed, it was time to resuscitate the humbled spirits.

"Let us get to the bar, what do you say?" Rana beckoned the guests loudly.

"Yes, yes Rana-ji, just what we were about to say," many voices heralded him.

CM Ghanshyam Das shut the flap of the CBI report and sat thinking for a good length of time. His mind recalled what Saanvri had told him in the event of something happening to her. He knew the time for closure had come.

•◆•

In the full-moon night, the waves of layers of sands made the desert look highly captivating. The narrow strip of the sole tarmac road traversing its vast span with its twists and turns and rises and falls, heightened its mysteriousness. The stillness was trampled by the approaching sound of the hooves of an animal. Soon a camel materialised, as if to add intrigue to the enveloping suspense. Two human figures mounted it. One, obviously the minder, sat at the front, close to the neck of the animal, while the other sat on its back, on a small *hauda*-like contraption. Both were indistinguishable because of the large sheets that had been wrapped around them, right up to their noses, almost like cloaks. With the moon being behind them, they appeared more like dark cut-outs rather than humans with features.

Within a couple of minutes, after the camel and its riders had frozen into a stoic stillness, another movement occurred, as if with a pre-set timing. From behind an incline, at the far distance, emerged pairs of headlights from a small caravan of vehicles. It travelled down the descending road, criss-crossing through the dunes, till it came very close and stopped some distance away from the camel.

A couple of human figures got down from the front vehicle, seemingly a police jeep. As they moved a little away from the vehicle, the headlights of other vehicles behind them revealed uniformed men with guns slung across their backs. One of them turned on a torchlight and moved its beam searchingly towards the camel and its occupants. The beam illuminated the face of the person seated at the back, who was Saanvri's mother-in-law, Dhania.

The armed men conferred with someone in one of the cars in the middle of the motorcade before turning around and taking a few steps towards the animal. One of them signalled to the camel-minder with his torch to get down and approach them, while the other kept his rifle trained in his direction. The camel-minder looked at Dhania, who nodded her assent. He then goaded the animal with his stick while making a chuckling sound. The camel growled slightly and squatted down. The camel-minder helped Dhania to alight. She then walked towards the waiting motorcade after throwing a reassuring glance at the minder.

By this time, more armed guards had come out from the jeeps of the caravan. From one of the two identical saloon cars in the middle, a grey haired man, donning a shawl over his kurta-pyjama, was helped out from the rear seat by his security man. It was CM Ghanshyam Das, recognisable in the diffused glow of the car lights. Another aide of the CM also got out with him and stood alongside. The CM swiftly folded his hands as he saw Dhania approaching him. She likewise folded hers in greeting without uttering any word. The aide, who had apparently met her before, also greeted her with folded hands and gestured her to move towards Ghanshyam Das.

After a moment of uncertainty, she reached into the folds of her cloak and withdrew a plastic bag. She pulled out a folder and a few CDs from it for the CM to have a glimpse before handing over the whole bag to him. Ghanshyam Das clasped the bag under his arm and bowed a little with folded hands. Not a single word was exchanged between the two during the entire activity. Dhania also folded her hands again and gestured her greetings to the two. Now after nodding with a smile, he turned around and went back to sit inside the car, just as the aide did. She too turned around and walked back towards the camel.

All the security men and the aides boarded the vehicles of the convoy and with the first one leading the way, one after the other, they turned around on the narrow road and drove away in the same direction they had come from. A pale cloud of dust was all that they left behind, which heightened the mysteriousness of the atmosphere. It sometime revealed and sometime obliterated the view of the rising and falling criss-crossing tail lights as well the frontal beams of the departing vehicles, up and down the slopes of sand dunes.

Dhania was helped by the camel-minder to climb back on the squatted animal. He too took his position and once again goading the camel to rise up; he retraced its steps. The cloud of dust spread wide and thin by then to engulf everything in its translucence. But, it could not hide the sadness in her eyes gradually giving way to brightness of relief.

A couple of days earlier, Alok Pareek, the aide who had accompanied CM Ghanshyam Das, had visited her at her village house after speaking to her on the phone. Everything had been firmed up then, exactly as it was actualised a few minutes earlier. Ghanshyam Das had acted with alacrity.

After ascertaining the veracity of the CDs and other stuff, he wasted no time in intra-party formalities. He made only one call to the right person at the High Command and then simultaneously and entirely on his own, acted as the Chief Executive of the state that he was. He knew that his main adversary was not only on the loose but also exercising an upper hand. He had turned around the case of the CD, which were being shown on news channels as a malicious propaganda engineered by his detractors to upstage him with fake visuals. Direct orders were issued forthwith from his office.

The CM had been informed by the Chief of Police that Yashpal Sarena was participating in an elaborate puja at Tarkeshwar Mahadev temple in the city, in the company of family members and friends. It was preferable that he was arrested quietly from his residence in the evening to avoid unnecessary outcry among his supporters who were bound to be present in huge numbers.

At first Ghanshyam Das was inclined to agree. But as soon as he put down the phone he had second thoughts. Politics was about perception, just as it was also about 'first-mover advantage'. He was aware that for long he had been perceived as a weak CM, more adept at *jugaad* to remain in power rather than with real skill of that of a leader. Time for change had come. He needed to demonstrate his muscle in full public view.

The instructions were unambiguous. He must be apprehended before he takes the first step down from the sanctum-sanctorum. People must call the action outrageous.

•◆•

Police in civil clothes had mingled in the crowd of devotees, in the courtyard amidst the waiting queues and in the sanctum-sanctorum of the main temple. Outside in the perimeter around the temple campus nearly half a dozen police vehicles with armed officers had already taken position.

A bare-chested Yashpal, clad only in dhoti finished the *aarti* and with his wife and family members alongside stepped out into the outer sanctum. Friends and general devotees waiting in good numbers also began taking the *jyoti* offered by him. At the door he turned around and again showed the *jyoti* to the idols inside before handing over the puja thali to an aide. He rang the three bells hanging from the ceiling and bowed once again respectfully. Now as he turned around and moved towards the steps going down to the courtyard, a safari-clad officer levelled up with him.

"Sarena-ji, you have to come with us," the man said courteously.

"What do you mean; I have to come with you?" A little taken aback, Yashpal demanded, "Who are you?"

"We are from CBI, sir," said the man as three more men moved in half a circle around Yashpal.

"What nonsense is this? How can you guys come like that, don't you see Neta-ji is performing puja?" argued one of Yashpal's relatives.

"We have our orders, sir," replied another officer.

"From whom?"

The first man withdrew a court envelope from his pocket and produced a document from it, "Here sir, we have the magisterial orders to take you in custody immediately," he said calmly.

"Whatever for?" Yashpal's relative blasted.

"In connection with the murder of Saanvri Devi, sir."

Everybody present gasped all of a sudden. No one moved from his place for a few seconds.

As Yashpal stole a look around him, he noticed a good numbers of shocked faces of his relatives, friends and followers; there were more numbers of the stern faces of officious looking men who surely were police personnel and who meant business. He acted sensibly and said in a surrendered voice, "Where do we go?"

Please follow us," said the first officer in charge.

Immediately, several men circled around him and he was led out from the compound, leaving a huge number of bewildered devotees in shock.

An hour later, Yashpal was presented in front of the Chief Judicial Magistrate who remanded him to seven days of police custody. News spread like wild fire and all news channels were full of sensational reports about Yashpal's arrest.

Rana had a restless night. He knew that he could not even whisper anything to anybody, much less make a call on cell or the landline. He thought about going to see his lawyer but decided against it, for how would have he explained his connection to Yashpal's arrest. He chose to wait and see what turn the drama took. His dilemma was that he could not breathe about it even to Madhvi who he had kept in the dark about the real conspiracy except stating that the matter had been taken care of. It was only at day break that he caught a wink.

Meanwhile, a posse of vehicles came roaring in as soon as the big gate of the haveli was opened. There were at least half a dozen of them—two jeeps, three ambassador saloons and even a three-wheeler tempo and a motorcycle. Disregarding the shock on the faces of the staff, they spread around in the front yard for a raid.

CBI sleuths in civvies, jumped out. One of them pasted a notice on the wall alongside the entrance to the inner living quarters. The guard at the door was pushed aside after handing him over a copy of the same notice and a loud announcement that it was a CBI raid. They didn't give him an opportunity to make a call on the intercom and just barged in like a tornado. Terrified staff members stood aside to make way for them.

Having barely managed to sleep Rana had come to the gym. He was coming off the cardio-machine when he saw several men make a beeline for him. Before he could say anything, he was surrounded with the announcement that it was a CBI raid in connection with the matter of Saanvri Devi's abduction and murder. Rana offered no resistance and only asked for a few minutes to change and inform his wife.

•◆•

Equipped with high-tech gadgetry, it was the latest among some of the most modern gas stations in the swish Andheri-Kurla complex area of Mumbai. The onslaught of the jets of soapy water and the giant brushes working fiercely, both vertically as well as horizontally, on the car's body gave a sense of false security and freedom to Ramlal, who sat behind the steering wheel. After securing his newly earned booty, he had fled to Rajasthan and had found himself a *benami* apartment in the distant western suburb of Meera Road, where melting into the vast population of outsiders was as easy as losing oneself like an ant in an ant hill. Of course, to flatter himself he had given in to his weakness for new cars by acquiring under a false name a luxury SUV of his own. Every now and then, he also kept up with his fetish for giving the 'new baby' a squeaky clean auto wash at this gas station.

As the brushes withdrew and the car moved forward on the hydraulics through the spray of plain water, what was obscured until now reappeared in full force, taking away with it the sense of escape from the glare of the world. Through the intermittent swings of the wipers, he saw a confusing sight of a group of men waiting for him with ID cards in their hands. His smug smile vanished instantly. Instinctively he knew what was in store.

They dismissed the domestics, including the outside maids working as casual staff quickly, with a fleeting look and an occasional question about his/her nature of work. After an unsuccessful initial search and making no headway at any of her other houses, they laid a discreet siege around the house. They also had decided to thoroughly comb the mansion again after learning about secret tunnels and hidden chambers, capable of hiding a person for days. That was the reason for today's raid.

First, they had decided to quickly relieve most of the serving staff to go home. A woman in her thirties, wearing a conspicuous band of sindoor in the parting of her jet black hair, was irksome with her counter questions, hence they had to be little stern to push her off.

"We told you, didn't we; you don't have to work today. Go home," spoke the officer sternly to the woman who stared back.

"But what about my wages? I was promised that I'll be paid today."

"Come tomorrow," the officer raised his voice.

"I need money," the woman didn't move. At this, a female assistant pushed the woman firmly to the gate, "Sir has told you to come tomorrow. Now, go..." Mumbling curses, the woman left.

The raid was again unsuccessful despite a thorough search of the place, including every little hidden nook and corner.

Later on, as the team began going through their papers again, the picture of one of the servants aroused suspicion. The dark circles under the eyes and some lines apart, the face of the woman they had forced to leave the other day showed remarkable resemblance with the suspect. The only difference was that she sported jet black hair and sindoor in the parting. The hair and the sindoor had done them in. Unwittingly they had let off Sulakshana, who had grey hair.

•◆•

It was a sleazy joint. Khoobchand had just put the glass down on the table after taking a big gulp of his drink when he felt somebody's hands on both his shoulders. He tried to turn around to have a look as to who it was when he was interrupted by three stern looking men in civvies who plonked themselves on the empty chairs around the table. He stole a fearful look around him and found hostile eyes trained at him from other tables in the bar. The man who stood behind him pressed his fingers on Khoobchand's shoulders and said, "Finish your drink…We don't mind. In jail you won't get any."

The man sitting on his right told him in a steely voice that he was being arrested by the CBI for facilitating the abduction of Saanvri with the objective of murdering her.

•◆•

Sulakshana was declared a fugitive 'wanted' for arranging Saanvri's murder. As envisaged, Pheru Ram turned an approver. Many more searches and arrests continued.

•◆•

Subsequent to the screening of Saanvri's brief life story, a live-studio discussion at *Global Nine Network* TV went on for almost half an hour. Alerted by his editor, the anchor invited his guests to sum up their individual reflections in brief.

The lady representing the Women Welfare Organisation was the first to put forth her views: "It mirrors the regressive feudal mindset that believes in the exploitative commodification of women even today."

The bearded professor of social sciences scratched his neck and said: "A modern-day concubine who rose up from being a 'play thing' to 'player' herself and was destroyed in the process."

The old theatre director had a smirk on his face before he mused: "Saanvri—*ek aadi katha*—a timeless story!"